the

VANISHING

ALSO BY WENDY WEBB

The Fate of Mercy Alban

The Tale of Halcyon Crane

the
VANISHING

WENDY WEBB

HYPERION
NEW YORK

Hyperion
Hachette Book Group
237 Park Avenue
New York, NY 10017

www.HachetteBookGroup.com

Printed in the United States of America

RRD-C

First Edition: January 2014
10 9 8 7 6 5 4 3 2 1

Hyperion is a division of Hachette Book Group, Inc.

The publisher is not responsible for websites (or their content) that are not owned by the publisher.

Library of Congress Cataloging-in-Publication Data

Webb, Wendy (Wendy K.)
  The vanishing / Wendy Webb.
      pages cm
    ISBN 978-1-4013-4194-7
  1. Widows—Fiction.   2. Authors—Fiction.   I. Title.
  PS3623.E3926V36 2014
  813'.6—dc23
                                    2013020680

For Steve, my love

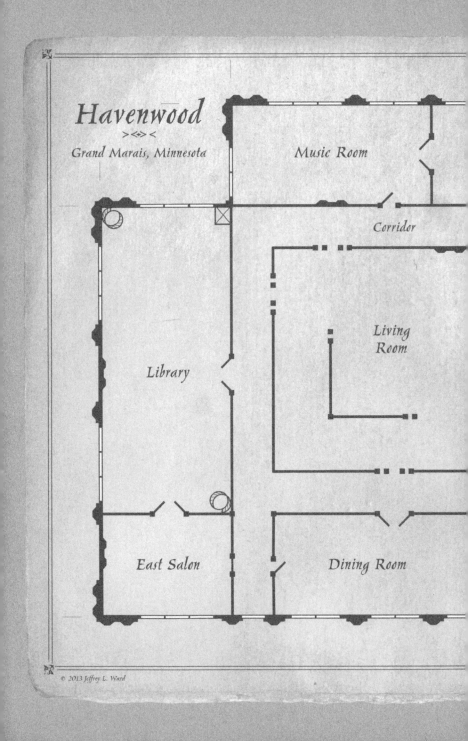

Havenwood
> <◊> <

Grand Marais, Minnesota

Music Room

Corridor

Living
Room

Library

East Salon

Dining Room

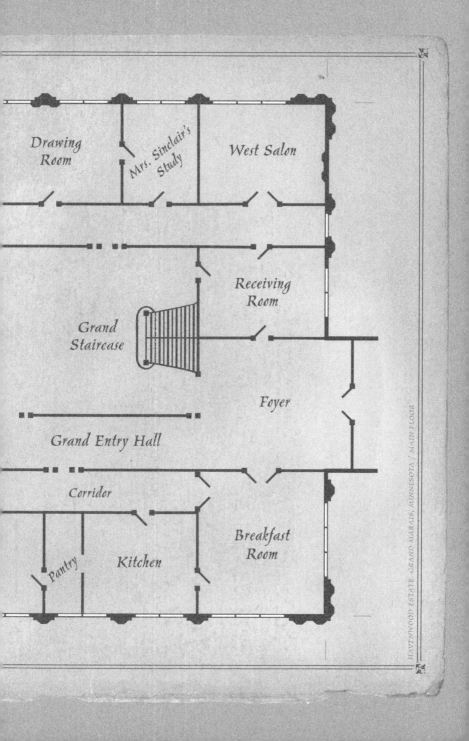

Drawing
Room

Mrs. Sinclair's
Study

West Salon

Receiving
Room

Grand
Staircase

Foyer

Grand Entry Hall

Corridor

Pantry

Kitchen

Breakfast
Room

HAVENWOOD ESTATE · GRAND MARAIS, MINNESOTA · MAIN FLOOR

the
VANISHING

PROLOGUE

Havenwood, December 15, 1875

Something was wrong. Seraphina opened her eyes—the people were still around the table, eyes tightly shut, their hands joined together making an unbroken ring, just as they should be. The candles were flickering, their small, warm glow illuminating the darkened room, just as they should be. But not all was as it should be. Seraphina could feel it. There was a rumbling where a whisper should have been. And then silence, complete and utter silence. There were no spirits. Just a deep, dark void.

She closed her eyes and tried again, knowing she had been at the center of scenes just like this hundreds of times at the request of grieving families, desperate to get in touch with their dearly departed, or simply those who wanted proof of a life beyond this one—the curious, the ones who loved to feel the tingle up their spines when the candles were blown out in a whoosh, when the spirits started speaking.

Some people, when they had seen her perform on the stage or attended one of her séances, would ask Seraphina whether she was actually hearing the voices of the dead or somehow picking up on the wishes of the people around her—the mother desperate to know her child was still somewhere, anywhere but cold and silent in the ground; the widower needing to hear his wife's voice again, gently telling him she would be waiting when his time came; the grown son unable to go on without knowing his mother was finally free of pain and happy. These skeptics wondered if perhaps she had spoken to the people beforehand, asked them about their loved ones, or received the information in another way.

But Seraphina knew what she knew. She heard the voices whispering to her, at first soft in her ear, as though they were wafting on the air from a great distance to reach her. And then she could see them, the dead clinging to the living, hovering nearby, trying to ease their loved ones' pain.

As the people held hands and concentrated, the voices would become louder and louder, the dead swirling around the table in a great jumble, everyone seemingly talking at once, wanting to be heard. *Tell him not to forget about the safety deposit box at the bank! I love you, Lillian! You must tell her! I'm always with you!* Seraphina could hear their words and also feel them, as though the swirling mass of whispers was a tangible thing, sizzling like a lightning strike through her skin.

It always happened that way. But not this time.

The room wasn't the problem—she had conducted séances at Havenwood before, at the request of the house's owner, Andrew McCullough, who was fond of bringing artists and writers and musicians and all manner of cultured souls to his magnificent home in the middle of the wilderness. She had amazed even the great Charles Dickens himself in this very room years before, he no stranger to the spirit world. And still, he had been dumbstruck by what she told him. They all came to see her, whether it was at Havenwood, or in the parlors of some of the finest houses in Paris or Vienna or New York, all of the people aching for a look behind the veil, all of them believing, or hoping to believe.

She did it for them because she could. There were so many charlatans out there in this age of Spiritualism, so many performers, bilking these poor people out of their fortunes and giving them only cheap parlor tricks in return. The levitating tables, the crystal balls, the knocking. As though spirits knocked.

No, Seraphina had always had the gift. And she didn't need a table, candles, a dark room, and people holding hands to use it.

That was just showmanship, entertainment, an experience to give an audience. Her husband had created that part of it for her, and it worked. People really wouldn't believe that she could simply look at them and know the depths of their grief and pain, but the fact was she could. Her gift was always with her. And she knew, with great certainty, that it was the grief of the living that trapped most spirits here on earth, kept them from going to wherever it was that they would ultimately go. The way Seraphina saw it, she was helping both the living and the dead by bringing them together around her séance table—helping the living to let go, which in turn helped the dead move on.

Her gift had never failed her, never once, until now. The silence at Havenwood surrounding the people so desperate to hear from their dead was deafening. She had to do something. She would call the spirits by name.

"John Martin," she said, her voice loud and commanding, naming the husband of the woman sitting next to her, "I call you to join us. Lillian is waiting to talk to you. Celeste Mitchell. Sarah Gale. Mary Longpre. We are waiting to hear from you."

She squeezed the hands of the people sitting next to her, eyeing her host, Andrew McCullough, across the table. His eyes were still closed, his lips slightly moving.

Unwilling to disappoint all of these people, she decided to try something new. Seraphina unclasped her hands and reached into the satchel she always kept by her side, slipping out a lacquered wooden box lined with mirrors that her husband had picked up in the Far East for her. She had never used it in her séances—she had never needed any sort of prop before—but this called for desperate measures. She intended to put a candle in the center of the box to reflect its light off the walls of the room—perhaps that would help set the scene. Perhaps it would call the spirits to her. She knew full well that the people around the table were grieving. She couldn't figure out why she couldn't see, or at least hear, their dead.

As soon as she set the box in the middle of the table, Seraphina began to hear the whispers. Finally.

Open the door. Let me out. I am here.

Were the spirits trapped somehow? Somewhere? Seraphina had never experienced anything like this. She opened the box and set the candle inside, and it illuminated the walls of the room with a thousand tiny dancing flames.

She cleared her throat and spoke again, this time in a tone not entirely familiar to her.

"I, Seraphina, who have called so many others, now call you to join us. I command you to join us!"

But instead of the whispers becoming louder and louder, as they had always done before, she heard that same rumbling she had heard earlier. Far away at first, and then closer, as though it were coming from an unseen animal that was stalking her in the dark, making circles around her before it struck.

She spun her head around—now it was behind her. Now it was in front of her. Now it was to the side.

One of the women across the table screamed in pain and jumped up from her chair. The man sitting next to Seraphina stood and let out a roar. Another woman jumped up and fell to the ground. A third began coughing violently, her face turning scarlet, as though someone was choking her.

"Get your hands off me!" she shouted between gasps.

"What is the meaning of this?" Andrew McCullough cried out. "Seraphina, what is happening here? Do something to stop this!"

Seraphina looked around the room and realized these were not the spirits of the dearly departed. This was something else, something dark and evil and monstrous, something she had never before encountered.

She stood up and raised her arms, shouting, "I cast you out! I cast you out! I command you to leave this place! You are not welcome here!"

But it was too late.

ONE

Havenwood, present day

When I awakened that first morning at Havenwood, for a moment I had no idea where I was. As sleep receded and I drifted back from wherever one goes in dreams, I sensed I wasn't in my own familiar nest of pillows. When my eyes fluttered open and I caught sight of the dark red walls, not the subdued yellow of my bedroom at home, I shot up and looked around, trying to get my bearings.

The bed where I lay, and had presumably spent the night, had an ornately carved wooden headboard and a thick, embroidered comforter. A matching dresser with a pink marble top stood on one wall. My gray sweater was slung over a chair in the corner. A bank of windows was draped with a heavy curtain, and in the fireplace across from the bed, coals were still smoldering from the night before. It all looked vaguely familiar, but distant, as though I had dreamed about this room in another place and time.

I curled back down under the covers when I remembered that these sorts of blackouts were not a new sensation. I'd forgotten conversations, events, even whole days since the scandal and its horrible aftermath took over my life. And, truth be told, even before that.

It began to come back to me, bit by bit, as I knew it would. Images, like a slide show in my mind. Jeremy. A gunshot. The funeral. I squeezed my eyes shut tight, trying to hold back the flood of memories. Wasn't the medication supposed to help with this? That was its purpose, wasn't it? To muddle the mind, to blur the edges of reality just enough to make life endurable despite all manner of horror and heartbreak.

I shook those thoughts out of my head and roused myself, pouring a glass of water from the pitcher on the nightstand before padding across the thick woolen carpet to the windows. I drew back the curtain and felt the warmth of the morning sun shining on my face despite the chill coming from the panes. Outside, I saw the remnants of a manicured garden, now covered by new-fallen snow, and a wide expanse of yard spilling into a forest beyond. The green of the enormous pines contrasted with the whiteness that blanketed everything as far as the eye could see. Cutting through it all, a road followed a river that meandered out of sight. Somehow, it felt like home, even though it was no home I had ever known.

I had been on that road the night before, I knew with sudden clarity. In a car. After the flight! *Ah, yes*, I thought. *I remember.* A wave of excitement washed over me when I remembered whom I'd be meeting, in just a few minutes. I could scarcely believe I was here.

Mr. Sinclair had arrived on my doorstep a few days earlier with an invitation. Now, as I recall that first meeting, shaking his hand for the first time, I remember the feeling of warmth when his skin touched mine, a fiery glow illuminating his eyes with a definite familiarity, though he was a stranger to me. Or maybe my memories are colored by what happened after that day, by everything I know now. Time and experience have a funny way of altering one's recollections of the past.

There was a quick knock at the door. I snapped my head around to see a woman entering the room.

"Oh, ma'am! You're up! I was just coming to wake you for breakfast."

Had I seen her the night before? I wasn't sure. Her round, smiling face, gray hair, and kind blue eyes might have belonged to anyone, and her gray maid's uniform seemed to be something out of Central Casting.

"If you'd like to freshen up before joining Mrs. Sinclair downstairs, towels and everything else you need are in the bath." She pointed to a door I hadn't noticed.

She crossed the room and opened the closet to reveal my clothes, all hanging in neat rows. "Is there anything I can lay out for you?"

I looked from her expectant face to my clothes and back again. "No, I can manage, thank you—" I said, grasping for her name. I couldn't bring it to mind.

"Marion," she said.

"Marion."

She gave me a quick nod. "Right, then. Please be in the breakfast room in thirty minutes. Mrs. Sinclair likes things on a schedule; that's one thing you should know right off."

"The breakfast room?"

"Oh, of course. It was quite late when you arrived last night, and this house can be so confusing for . . . newcomers." She opened the door and gestured out into the hallway. "Follow this corridor around to the left until you reach the grand staircase. Take that down to the first floor. You'll see the living room on your right and the foyer in front of you, with the archway to the dining room on your left. You'll find the breakfast room adjacent to the dining room." She hesitated a moment. "You're on the third floor here in the east wing," she said. "The Sinclairs' suite of rooms is on the second floor in the west wing. I'd advise staying away from those. Mrs. Sinclair likes her privacy when she's in her rooms."

I thanked her, perching on the edge of the bed as she closed the door behind her.

Mr. and Mrs. Sinclair. I struggled, trying to unlock the memory. I knew this game—I was supposed to think of the last thing I remembered to help piece it all together. I played it often enough throughout my life. In a flash, I remembered rummaging through my travel kit on the plane looking for my bottle of pills. Had I taken too much of my medication? Was that the reason my memories of the night before were so fuzzy? I shuddered at the thought of it.

I made my way into the bathroom, where I did indeed find a stack of fluffy towels on the vanity, just as Marion had said, along with my own travel kit. I dug up the pill bottle, then considered pouring its contents down the drain. But instead, I put it right back where it had been. Blackouts might be a troubling side effect, but sometimes forgetting is a blessing. What is it they say about ignorance?

After standing under the stream of hot water washing away the night's sleep, I dried my hair, quickly pulled on jeans and a black turtleneck, and opened the door out into the hallway slowly, wondering what awaited me.

The hallway was so long and dark, I couldn't even see the end of it. *This house must be massive,* I thought, following the corridor as it turned left, then right and right again. As I began to descend the "grand staircase," as Marion had called it, I saw a living room on one side of the stairs and the archway leading into the dining room on the other, just as Marion had described. The rooms in my view were filled with heavy antique furniture, overstuffed chairs and ornate lamps that looked like they had been standing in their places forever. The whole effect reminded me of a museum, or a palace, and it smelled vaguely musty, as though the ghostly memories of other lifetimes hung in the air.

As I walked on, I saw that the ceilings were sky-high, and the walls were lined with paintings in gilded frames, portraits, mostly, of people from another time: women in long dresses, children sitting beside them; men in suits or hunting clothes. The largest portrait, which hung above the mantel of the floor-to-ceiling fireplace in the living room, was of a man wearing a kilt, bagpipe in his hand, a wolflike dog curled at his feet. He was standing in a landscape of rolling hills and heather. Something about this man's eyes entranced me, and I stood there for longer than I should have, lost in imaginings that dissipated in my mind as soon as they formed.

I shook my head. How long had I been standing there? I was expected at breakfast! I couldn't be late on my first day, so I hurried along, my footsteps echoing on the foyer's marble tiles. Where was this so-called breakfast room? I stopped and turned in a circle just in time to see a man—Mr. Sinclair—descending the staircase. His face broke into a wide smile.

"Julia!" he said as he finished the last of the stairs. "How did you sleep? Your room was comfortable, I trust?"

His grin was so welcoming that I couldn't help but smile back.

"My room was lovely," I said, sliding my arm into the crook of his when he offered it. "Thank you, Mr. Sinclair."

"I thought we had dispensed with that 'Mr. Sinclair' rubbish yesterday." He patted my hand.

"Adrian," I said.

He led me through the dining room, down yet another hall, and, finally, through a doorway to the breakfast room, where an elderly woman was sitting at a round table in front of a wall of paned windows. Outside, the creek was babbling along, not yet frozen by the cold temperatures, and the sunlight was bouncing off snow-laden pine trees. A pair of bright red cardinals flew into view and perched on a snowy branch. The whole effect reminded me of a Currier and Ives Christmas card I had received the previous year.

"Mother, this is Julia," Adrian said, motioning toward me. "You were asleep when we arrived last night—the flight was late. And the drive after we landed was quite something, with this new snow. I really must put the Bentley away for the winter. It's time for the Land Rover, I'm afraid."

"Julia, dear," the woman said, folding her hands and beaming at me. "What a pleasure to see you at last."

I took a deep breath before speaking. I could scarcely believe I was in the same room with this woman, let alone conversing with her.

"No, the pleasure is all mine! It's such an honor to meet you. I'm thrilled to be here!"

I took a seat across from her and fumbled with my napkin, not quite sure of what to do or say next.

Adrian poured himself a cup of coffee from the pot on the

sideboard and gestured to me. I nodded, and he poured me a cup as well.

I could see the resemblance between mother and son immediately. Two dots on a timeline, with nearly the same face, one generation apart. They seemed familiar to me somehow, in the way that sometimes happens with complete strangers. Adrian was older than me—late forties, early fifties, perhaps. His dark hair was graying at the temples, and fine lines around his eyes betrayed years of laughter. He wore a dark, tailored suit and a yellow tie, dressed for a workday.

His mother seemed at once utterly ancient and completely youthful. Her deeply lined face, powdery makeup, and rather haphazardly applied lipstick contrasted with her dancing, bright green eyes. Late seventies, early eighties? Older than that? I couldn't tell.

She reached one hand across the table and covered mine with hers. "I'm thrilled as well, Julia, dear," she said. "It will be a wonderful treat to have you with me at Havenwood when Adrian takes his leave today. We have so much to talk about!"

My stomach was doing flips, but I managed a smile as I savored my first sip of coffee. A maid, not the same one who greeted me in my room, clattered through the door carrying a tray, set it down on the sideboard, and began serving a breakfast of eggs, sausage, oatmeal, fruit, and toast. Seeing all of that food made me realize I was famished, and I wondered when I had last eaten anything.

As we took our first bites, Adrian chattered on about the new snow and his hopes that the gardener had turned the roses. Suddenly, the enormity of what I had done seemed to settle in. I realized, as I sat there eating my breakfast with these two relative strangers, that my life, on that morning, was completely different from what it had been the morning before. What my future held, I had no idea. But I knew one thing for sure: I was here at Havenwood to stay.

TWO

*H*ow did I find myself living at Havenwood, a place I hadn't even known existed the day before I arrived there? The answer is it found me. Three months after my husband's funeral, Adrian Sinclair came calling.

Just answering the door had been quite a feat. I had done nothing but drift around the house since I buried Jeremy, not wanting to talk to anyone or go anywhere. And that, I supposed, was a lucky thing, because nobody but reporters wanted to talk to or see me, either.

All of our friends had abandoned us when the allegations came to light, when they realized the full extent of what my husband had done. From the first story in the newspaper hinting at what was to come, they began distancing themselves from us. They stopped calling. Stopped returning my calls. I'm not sure if they thought I was involved in the whole sordid business, but the truth is I was just as much a victim as they were. I was left with nothing— no husband, no money, no friends or family to lean on for support.

It was just a matter of time until my house was gone, too. I was reading the foreclosure notice from the bank when Adrian appeared on my doorstep, standing there in his dark overcoat and hat. I assumed he was another reporter, trying for an interview with the grieving widow of the man who had bilked hundreds of Chicagoans out of their life savings. The Midwestern Bernie

Madoff, the newspapers called my husband. What they called me was no better.

"I have no comment," I said, eyeing the man through the door's glass pane. "I've asked you people to leave me alone. Please."

"I'm not a reporter, Mrs. Bishop," he said to me, smiling slightly. "Nor am I a police officer, an investigator, or a bill collector. I'm not going to issue you a summons or serve you notice of anything. I've come to ask for your help."

This was new. I squinted at him, wondering if he was some sort of religious fanatic. "What kind of help?"

"I have need of your services. And I believe you're in need of ours."

Definitely a religious fanatic, then.

"I'm really not interested," I said. "Please go away."

"I've traveled a very long way to find you, Mrs. Bishop," he said. "Please. Let me say what I've come to say."

"And what is that, exactly?"

"I've come to offer you a job."

I didn't know quite how to respond to that. Apparently the look on my face said it all, because he said: "This is a serious offer that I believe will benefit both of us. Won't you please let me in and we can discuss it?"

With nothing to lose—what could he possibly take from me that wasn't already gone?—I sighed and opened the door.

I led him into the living room and motioned to the sofa. "Something to drink?" I asked as he took off his coat and laid it over the arm of one of the chairs. "Tea? Or something stronger?"

"Tea would be lovely, thank you," he said, and I detected a slight English accent buoying his words. "There's a bite to the wind out there. Winter is on its way."

As he settled onto the sofa, I shuffled into the kitchen and turned on the kettle, glad he hadn't followed me. Dirty dishes were piled in the sink. I hadn't had much energy for housework since Jeremy died—what was the point? I pulled a box of tea bags and two cups from the cabinet, dropped a few of the bags into a pot, filled it with boiling water, and put the whole mess onto a tray.

Back in the living room, I set the tray down on the coffee table in front of the sofa. "I hope you like hibiscus tea," I said, pouring him a cup. "It's all I had."

"That'll do just fine, thank you." He smiled, lifting the cup to his lips.

I sunk into one of the armchairs and crossed my legs, eyeing him. "So. What is this all about?"

He nodded and cleared his throat. "As I said, I'm here to offer you a position."

The earnestness on his face told me he wasn't joking. "Listen," I began, reconsidering the decision to let him inside the house. I pushed myself up from my chair. "Whatever you're selling, I'm not buying. I think this was a mistake and you should go."

"Please, just hear me out," he said. "Give me five minutes. If, after that, you'd still like me to go, I'll simply leave and never bother you again."

I settled back into the chair, studying him warily. "Five minutes."

"My name is Adrian Sinclair." He stopped to take a sip of his tea. "I live with my mother at our country estate. Havenwood."

The sound of that word, "Havenwood," crackled through my mind. I had heard it before. I just couldn't place how, or when.

"It's near the Canadian border not far from Lake Superior's north shore in Minnesota," Mr. Sinclair went on. "My mother is elderly, of course, and in fairly good health, but she does have episodes."

"Episodes?"

He leaned forward and lowered his voice, as if to take me into his confidence. "Times in which she is not entirely lucid."

"I see," I said, but I really didn't. I had no idea what any of this had to do with me.

"I travel on business often, and I'm going away again very

soon," he continued. "Of course, we have several servants, but they're busy tending to the house and grounds, and what my mother needs in my absence is a full-time companion. Someone who can keep an eye on her, especially on the bad days. She has been known to wander. With winter coming on . . ." He looked at me with expectant eyes.

I let what I thought he was saying to me sink in.

"You want me to be her companion, is that it?"

"Yes. Live in, full time."

I snorted. "But that's ridiculous. You don't even know me."

He didn't respond to that. Instead, he just went ahead with his pitch. "The estate is quite lovely, I assure you."

He reached into the briefcase he was carrying, pulled out an iPad, and began scrolling through several photographs. I liked to think I had seen it all—Jeremy and I had traveled to some of the loveliest, most expensive places on earth during the course of our marriage—but at the sight of this estate, my mouth dropped open. It looked like an ancient English castle, someplace where I could imagine kings and queens living.

Havenwood was massive, with turrets and parapets and stained-glass windows and balconies and chimneys. The house was surrounded by several outbuildings and delicately manicured gardens, through which a river flowed. Not far from the house, I noticed a lake—not Lake Superior, but a smaller inland lake. One of the photos showed two kayaks bobbing lazily on its surface, the house standing sentinel in the distance.

I found myself strangely drawn to the photographs and could not look away. "*This* is on Lake Superior's north shore near the Canadian border? It looks like it was built in the 1600s in Europe somewhere."

He smiled an indulgent smile, and I got the feeling he had heard this question many times before. "You're right, it's a replica of a castle that was built around that time. In Scotland. As to how it got here, Havenwood was built by a nobleman who, when charged with running the fur trade in the area in the mid-1800s, missed the opulence he was used to in his native land. Or so the story goes. My family bought it decades ago, when I was just a lad."

"You grew up there?"

"I wouldn't say that, no," he said. "Summer vacations, that sort of thing. I spent much of my youth in English boarding schools, St. Andrews in Scotland after that. It was only after I had graduated from university that I came to live at Havenwood with my mother full time to handle her business affairs."

"And this," I said, still enthralled by the photographs, "*this* is where you want me to live and look after your mother?"

"That is what I've come here to ask of you."

"But why? Why in the world would you ever trust me to move into this place, *your home*, and care for your mother? I don't understand, Mr. Sinclair. You don't know the first thing about me."

"I do know you. I've read the newspapers. I've seen the reports on television."

"That's my point," I said. "Those reports vilified my husband and me. Everyone else, even my own friends and family, believes that I was a part of it."

"I've done a little digging on my own," he said, smoothing his suit jacket. "I know you buried your husband some three months ago. I know he left you with nothing. I know the bank is foreclosing on your home. I know you have nowhere to go and no one to turn to. I know your friends and family have abandoned you. Not to be unkind, but your prospects at the moment are rather bleak."

I sighed heavily and slumped against the back of my chair. He had pretty much summed up my life.

"As for believing you were part of it all, anyone with eyes can see that you weren't," he went on, his voice gentle and low. "You wouldn't be destitute right now, for one thing. You certainly wouldn't be holed up in this house; you'd be on a remote beach somewhere enjoying your ill-gotten millions. So, despite what the police and the courts and public opinion might say, I know you're just as much a victim as anyone else in this case, even more so."

It had been a long time since I had heard words of support from anyone. Now this stranger was saying what even my closest friends couldn't. Or wouldn't. "Thank you," I coughed out. "But even so . . . I'm still not quite getting it. Why don't you simply hire a nurse? Why ask me?"

"Here's where it gets a little bit delicate." He paused a moment before continuing. "I need someone upon whose discretion I can completely rely."

I stifled a laugh. "What makes you think you can rely on mine?"

"Because of your recent circumstances, I gather that you don't have an especially cozy relationship with the press," he said, flipping through the photos on his iPad to a shot of me in bitter confrontation with reporters, and then another, and then another. "In fact, I'd say that it's rather hostile. Correct?"

I shivered when I saw myself on this stranger's computer. It felt intrusive. Yet these photos were public knowledge, they were in the news, and it was only reasonable that he had researched my background. I would have done the same, in his place.

"That's correct."

"So, I can be assured that you, of all people, won't be running to the media about this."

Now it was my turn to smile. "About what? The breaking news that an elderly woman needs a companion?"

"Not about that, no. About my mother's identity."

I put my cup down on the end table. "What about it?"

"My mother is Amaris Sinclair."

The words sent a tingle up my spine and I took a quick breath. "The writer?"

"The same."

Amaris Sinclair's books and short stories were required reading in my high school and college literature classes. They were frightening gothic tales about madness and murder and monstrosities. She was often called the female Edgar Allan Poe. I had devoured her books, one after the other, when I was in school. They had made me want to write similar tales myself, and indeed I had. Amaris Sinclair was the reason I had become a writer, all those years ago, before Jeremy and his machinations took over my life.

"But that's impossible," I said to him, standing up from my chair and backing away from him slowly, calculating in my mind how long it would take me to dash to the door. "Amaris Sinclair is dead."

THREE

*Y*es." Adrian nodded, shifting a bit in his chair. "That's what the world believes. Now you understand my need for discretion."

"But I read about her death," I protested, inching toward the door. "It was some years ago."

"I know."

"But—" I pressed. He held up his hand in response, stopping my words.

"For reasons that I cannot say, my mother chose to drop out of sight a decade ago," he said. A fleeting look of sadness washed over his face and was gone just as quickly. "She has been living in seclusion at the estate ever since."

This stopped me, my hand on the doorknob. "Why would she do that?" I wanted to know. "She was at the height of her success. Why would anyone . . . ?"

"I cannot say why she chose to do it, only that she did."

"She never goes out?"

"Well, it's not like she's a shut-in, if that's what you mean. You have to understand, the estate is quite large. The house and the grounds. Hundreds of acres, maybe more than that. The servants do the shopping in the nearby village and my mother has gone there from time to time—not lately—but the villagers think of her as an eccentric English lady who tends to keep to herself. And quite frankly, the estate encompasses much of the land for miles around it—she owns the town, in other words—so the people there don't ask too many questions, if you get my meaning."

"Amaris Sinclair," I mused. "It would be a real honor to meet her."

His face broke into a grin. "I see I've intrigued you. Imagine the conversations you could have, one writer to another."

I eyed him. "How did you know I was a writer?"

"As I said, I did some digging into your background. By all accounts, you were quite good. One book of fiction, released to moderate success. You mentioned my mother's influence on your acknowledgments page. A pity you gave it up."

I intended to object when he interrupted me yet again. "My mother does not write anymore. Her eyesight is failing, for one thing, and there are a myriad of other issues preventing her from doing so. But her head is filled with stories. And I believe she'd enjoy talking about them with you. You might even get some ideas from her that you could put to use."

He sipped his tea as I waited for him to continue.

"You see, the truth is, my mother doesn't think she needs a companion," he admitted. "I've sold this idea to her on the basis that you're a writer and can learn from her and perhaps even help her. I know she has missed telling stories and I even floated the idea that you and she could collaborate. She's delighted with that prospect. But a simple companion, like a nurse, as you suggested a moment ago? She'd get rid of her the moment I left the house. Indeed she has, in the past. It has been quite vexing. When I came upon your story and investigated your background, you seemed to be the perfect solution to my problem."

I hadn't been the perfect solution to anything in a very long time. Still. This just wasn't adding up.

"You're asking me to believe that you saw me on television, and you thought I, the disgraced wife of the Midwestern Bernie Madoff, might be a good companion to your elderly, obviously wealthy mother? Most people would think: fox, meet henhouse."

He smiled. "The Sinclairs aren't most people," he said.

"I'm starting to see that."

We held each other's gaze for a moment, and then he spoke. "Yes, we saw you on the news. And no, I didn't immediately think of you as a companion. But the more time went on, and especially after your husband's death, we began to see you as a victim of all of this. I wondered if, and how, I could help. When I saw that you had mentioned my mother's influence in your novel, that just sealed the deal. It seemed like it was meant to be."

I nodded, considering. It was starting to make a strange kind of sense.

"Let me close the deal with one more reason you should take me up on this offer," he pressed.

"What's that?"

"It's an opportunity for you to vanish, just as my mother did."

The words crept up my spine and took hold. Vanishing, dropping out of sight—the very idea of it seemed utterly peaceful after the chaos that my life had become.

"Think about it, Julia," he said, his face serious now. "You need saving. Your legal troubles didn't stop when that gunshot ended your husband's life; in fact, they just began. As an officer in his company, you are going to be held accountable for all the money he defrauded investors out of. People's life savings, Julia. The police are compiling their case against you right now, and there are private lawsuits snaking through the civil court system with your name on them."

"But I don't have a dime to my name!" I protested. "There's nothing left after the police froze our assets. What are they going to take?"

"Future earnings, for one thing," he said, shaking his head slightly. "And that's not all. There could be some serious jail time. Not to mention hundreds of angry victims, any one of whom might turn violent. Surely your attorney . . ."

But his words trailed off when he saw my expression. I ran a

hand through my hair and sighed. My attorney had stopped returning my calls long before Jeremy's funeral. He knew full well I
couldn't pay for his services.

Adrian was exactly right: legal trouble was hanging over my
head, poised to crush what was left of my life. And I'd had to
change my phone number twice since Jeremy's death because of
the threatening calls I'd been getting from angry victims. I was
paranoid to leave my house—I couldn't remember the last time I
had. And I could indeed be facing jail time. All of it had been eating me up for months.

"This is your way out," he said, his voice dropping to a whisper. "Nobody saw me come here. Nobody else in the world knows
that we know each other. Nobody will come looking for you at
the estate. Nobody in the village will have any idea who you are.
Havenwood is a world away from Chicago. This is your chance,
Julia, to leave your nightmare behind."

"I'm not sure . . . ," I began, but let the words drop off as the
possibility of a new life danced in my head.

"You can choose to stay at the estate indefinitely, or, when
some time has passed and things cool down, say, a year from now,
you can start somewhere else with a new identity," Adrian said. "I
can make that happen for you."

My mind was swimming. This man was a stranger to me. How
could I possibly consider what he was offering? And yet . . . The
bank was going to take my house in a matter of weeks, and then
where would I go? To a homeless shelter? To jail?

"Come with me, right now," he said, his eyes gleaming. "Pack
an overnight bag and decide what else, if anything, you'd like to
take from this house. When we're gone, my people will pack up
the rest of your things and follow behind us."

Could this really be happening? Was this my way out?

I let myself dream for a moment, but then reality crept in. I
shook my head. "No," I said slowly. "This is crazy. I don't even
know you. I can't possibly . . ."

He stood and picked up his overcoat. "Please, Julia, take the night to consider my invitation. I'll be back at ten o'clock tomorrow morning. If you decide to take me up on my offer, I'll be delighted to take you to Havenwood with me and make all of this"—he gestured to the dining room table, which was full of bills, foreclosure notices, and other legal documents I hadn't had the courage to open—"go away."

And then he was gone, leaving my house even more disturbingly empty than it had been before he had arrived.

FOUR

I picked up the phone and dialed an old friend, Kathy O'Neill. She hadn't spoken to me in months. She and her husband had lost everything because of Jeremy—every last cent of their retirement account was gone. But we had known each other for aeons and I thought that perhaps she . . .

But all I got was her voice mail. I tried another of my friends, then another. I should have known better. Nobody answered the phone, as if they knew it was me calling despite my having changed my number. I was foolish to think that somehow, magically, something had changed and I could return to some semblance of the life I had had before. I realized that, with or without Adrian's offer, my life was completely different from what it had been before the scandal. My only choice was what type of "different" it would be.

I wandered through my house that night, eyeing the bills and other legal documents on my dining room table, struck once again by the complete and utter disbelief that Jeremy could have done this to all of our friends and so many more, and to me. I mulled over the two options that lay ahead. Do I stay and face the aftermath of everything Jeremy had done? Or do I vanish?

I marched down to Jeremy's prized wine cellar and opened one of the bottles, poured myself a large glass, and lifted it skyward. "Here's to vanishing," I whispered into the damp air.

I downed the wine in my glass and wondered how quickly ten A.M. could possibly come.

I was all packed and ready to go, but the gnarling in the pit of my stomach had me wondering if Adrian Sinclair was really going to show up to take me away, or if he had been a figment of my wild imagination.

I looked around the room, considering what else I wanted to take with me, but found there was very little. Most of my photographs from the past several years were on my computer, which the police had confiscated after the scandal broke. But what about the furniture? The silver? The crystal? The jewelry Jeremy had bought for me? I didn't care about it in the least. Better to make a clean break from the past. Let the police have a garage sale with all of my things and give the proceeds to Jeremy's victims. I didn't want anything that might have been paid for from somebody else's retirement account. The very thought of it made my stomach turn.

As I sat waiting for Mr. Sinclair, my gaze settled on a framed photo of Jeremy and me, all smiles, on a vacation we had taken to Aspen the previous year. What a lie it was. If only the laughing, happy Julia in that photo could have seen what her life would crumble into in just a few months' time. Maybe she could have done something to stop it.

There was a knock at the door. I flew to it and let Adrian into the house, seeing him for what he was—a godsend. This was happening. I was really going to escape from the nightmare I had been living. The weight of the world slipped from my shoulders and crashed to the ground.

"I won't be a moment," I said to him, racing toward my waiting suitcase.

"That's all?" he said, eyeing my carry-on bag. "Remember, you won't be coming back here. My people are standing by to move anything else you'd like to take with you."

I pointed up the stairs. "I've got a couple of trunks with clothes in them," I explained. "They're in my bedroom. I'm not sure how long I'll be staying at the estate, so I packed clothes for all seasons. But as far as anything else"—I looked around the living room and flailed an arm—"let the bank take it all."

Adrian and I locked eyes, and I took a deep breath. "I guess this is it," I said.

He smiled. "I'm very glad you're coming with me, Julia. You won't regret this. It's the start of a whole new life for you."

I grabbed my cell phone from the table where it had been sitting, but before I could slip it into my purse, Adrian reached out and encircled my hand with his.

"You're going to have to leave this behind, I'm afraid," he said. "But—"

"Rule number one of vanishing: don't take anything that can be traced. If you made one call, or even turned the phone on, the police would be at our doorstep within minutes. You should leave your credit cards here as well."

I hadn't thought of any of that, but what he was saying made sense. I fished my wallet out of my purse and plucked the cards from their slots, dropping them on the table one by one. They were useless to me anyway—the police had frozen all of our accounts. Then came my insurance cards, loyalty cards I had picked up over the years for various places that I shopped, my Social Security card, even my library card. I placed my checkbook on the table as well, and dropped my driver's license on top of the pile.

"Good-bye, Julia Bishop," I said, looking at the various pieces of plastic that identified me.

When we were sitting in the back of Adrian's black sedan, several miles away from my house, I turned to him.

"You literally saved my life," I said, my eyes brimming with tears. "Why? Why would you do such a thing for a complete stranger?"

He reached over and brushed away one of the tears, which had escaped despite my best efforts to contain it. The gesture was so tender and gentle, kinder than anyone had been to me in what seemed to be forever.

"As I told you, dear Julia, your plight touched me," he said, his voice soft and low. "You needed saving; I needed a companion for my mother. It was as simple as that."

The memories become vague and watery after that. I remember snippets of the rest of the day—getting out of the car at a small airport, boarding a private plane and settling deep into a seat that seemed to be made of the most opulent, velvety leather.

"Sleep, Julia, dear," I remember Adrian saying, before everything went black.

FIVE

*A*drian and I walked together through the house after breakfast that first morning at Havenwood. Mrs. Sinclair had taken her leave of us, retreating to her rooms for some quiet meditation and reflection, as apparently was her morning routine, and Adrian had offered to show me around the estate.

"I'm leaving today," Adrian said, leading me into the drawing room, which was filled with heavy, ornate furniture but was somehow welcoming all the same. "Feel free to explore, go wherever you like. This is your home now, please remember that."

"Thank you," I said, a flicker of unease taking root in my stomach as I thought about wandering through room after room in this house on my own after Mr. Sinclair had gone. I wondered what secrets this ancient place contained and whether I'd want to stumble across them alone.

"My mother has her schedule, revolving around meals," he went on, disrupting my train of thought. "Breakfast is at seven thirty, followed by a morning of quiet time. She meditates or reads. Some days she'll paint, or just sit in the gardens. Lunch is at noon. After that she'll be raring to go. She likes to walk, outside when weather permits, or inside, like we're doing now, on inclement days. Usually she'll want to go to the stables to see the horses, which she loves. And you should know that the dogs will be in and out of the house, at their whim."

I nodded.

"She enjoys 'tea,' which actually means a cocktail or two—she thinks I don't know about that—at four thirty or so," Adrian continued, chuckling slightly. "She usually takes dinner in her room, but it depends on the day. Sometimes she likes everyone to dress for dinner in the formal dining room. I'd like you to plan to be with her at breakfast—you'll get a read of her mood and state of mind then—and from lunch until after teatime."

"Got it," I said, trying to keep everything straight in my head. "Breakfast, quiet time, lunch, afternoon activities, a cocktail or two."

"That's it. You'll settle into the routine quickly enough and find that you have plenty of free time. If you choose to do so, you may venture into the village. It caters mainly to summer tourists, but even at this time of year there are some lovely shops still open, along with good restaurants and a bookstore you'll enjoy."

"It sounds charming," I said.

"We never talked about compensation—" Adrian began, but I cut him off.

"Just being here is compensation enough! I didn't expect to be paid on top of it."

He shook his head. "I wouldn't hear of it. You're doing me a great service. I am depositing a sum into an anonymous account, which we will transfer into your name when the time comes—and when you decide what your new name will be."

I exhaled. "I don't know what to say. 'Thank you' doesn't seem to quite cover it."

"No thanks needed." He smiled. "It's I who should be thanking you.

"Oh, one more thing," he continued, turning to me and looking into my eyes. "The estate is the epitome of civilized living, but remember, we aren't in the English countryside here. We're on the edge of the Boundary Waters Canoe Area Wilderness, which is exactly as its name implies. Millions of acres of unspoiled, untouched wilderness. When you leave the estate, you might meet the residents of said wilderness—black bears, moose, wolves, lynx, and even the occasional mountain lion."

The look on my face must have amused him. "Don't worry," he said with a chuckle, "you'll be quite safe. But like everyone who lives in this area, you need to respect where you are and know the rules of the road, so to speak."

"I'm from the city, Mr. Sinclair," I said. "I'm really not what you'd call an outdoorsy kind of person. What, exactly, are the rules of the road here?"

He patted my hand. "Anytime you venture out alone, tell someone where you're going and when you'll likely be back. If you'd feel safer, carry pepper spray—there are cans of it in the stables— and a walking stick. Or better yet, take the dogs. Are you comfortable around dogs?"

I wasn't quite sure about that. "I guess so."

"Good," he said, apparently not hearing my trepidation. "We have three giant Alaskan malamutes that are extraordinarily well trained. My mother's pride and joy. There is nothing in this forest—not a bear, not a wolf, not a mountain lion, and especially not a person—that will come near you when you're surrounded by those dogs."

I smiled at him. "I wish I'd had them with me in Chicago these past months."

"They're especially aggressive toward members of the media," he said, raising his eyebrows.

An ancient clock, somewhere in another room, chimed the hour.

"Look at the time," Adrian said, glancing at his watch. "I must dash."

"So soon?" Before the words even had escaped my lips, I could feel the heat rising to my face. Of course he was leaving. That was the whole point of me being here.

"I'll be back soon enough. And by the time I return, I'm sure that you and my mother will have become fast friends, and you'll be even more at ease around the estate than I am."

"I hope so," I said.

He sunk a hand into his jacket pocket and pulled out a business card, which he handed to me. "My private number," he said. "Don't hesitate to call if you need me."

He began to walk back the way we had come, but he stopped and turned around.

"There's a library in the east wing," he said. "It's one of the largest private collections of books in the country. I'm sure you'll find it fascinating, so I've had the staff open it up for you." He pointed down the hallway. "Go through those double doors and you'll find it at the end of the corridor."

And then he walked on, his footsteps echoing on the floor long after he had faded from view.

SIX

$\mathcal{I}$ made my way down the dim corridor. There didn't seem to be a light switch anywhere as far as I could discern, but sunshine from the floor-to-ceiling window at the end of the hallway was doing its best to illuminate the full span of it, which to my estimation was more than a city block in length. I looked around and marveled, once again, at the sheer enormity of this house. As I drew closer to that window, the area became brighter and brighter, and I was grateful to leave the gloom behind.

The hall was flanked by several archways, through which I could see splendid sitting rooms and salons, all with thick Oriental rugs on the floors and enormous paintings on the walls. Before I knew it, I was moving from one to another as though I was in an art gallery, which, I supposed, I was. I didn't see any works by the great masters—no Picassos, Monets, or van Goghs—but I wouldn't have been surprised to find them in such a grand home. Instead, there were portraits of, I assumed, the people who had lived at Havenwood over the years and the events that had taken place in the house and on the grounds: a hunting party on horseback with Havenwood looming in the background, a group of musicians entertaining a crowd in the very room where the painting hung, a formal party with men in black tie and women in glittering gowns, children playing in the snow with enormous dogs that looked like wolves. I realized that whoever had built this house used artwork to chronicle life here.

As I walked, the gnarling I felt earlier in the pit of my stomach began to grow into a strange sense of déjà vu. *I know this,* I thought, stopping in front of a massive, dark wood armoire with stained-glass inlays of rich greens and blues on its doors and intricate carvings of boars' heads and wolves on its sides. It looked like something that might have been plucked from a Grimms fairy tale set in the deepest, darkest Black Forest. *I've seen this before.* But that was impossible. I had no idea Havenwood even existed two days prior. I had certainly never been here. But I couldn't shake the feeling. It wasn't just the armoire, but the house itself seemed all at once foreign and familiar, as though I had read about it . . . *Ah, yes.* At this, a smile crept to my lips. Of course I had read about it. Mrs. Sinclair often set her tales in enormous old homes just like this one. Perhaps exactly like this one. That was why certain things seemed so familiar. She had probably put certain aspects of Havenwood into her stories. Satisfied with this explanation, I walked on, the déjà vu drifting along behind me as I went.

The library doors stood open at the end of the corridor, and a flickering light from inside the room was casting shadows on the opposite wall. Although the effect was warm and welcoming, a strange feeling of dread spread through my veins as I approached the room's entrance. This was more than simple déjà vu. I stopped a few feet away and simply could not go on. Goose bumps arose on my arms, and a chill whispered up my spine. *This is silly,* I told myself, longing to see all of those books awaiting me in the library. But something, deep down in the depths of my being, would not let me take even one step closer.

And that was when I heard it, soft and low, almost as soft as a whisper.

"Sing a song of sixpence / A pocket full of rye." It was a small voice, the voice of a child.

I whirled around in a circle. "Who's there?" I called out, my voice cracking and thin. "Mrs. Sinclair? Marion?"

"Four and twenty blackbirds . . ."

I froze, my heart pounding. The voice seemed to be coming from far away and long ago, as though it were buoyed on the wind from another time, or trapped somehow within these very walls.

"Baked in a pie . . ."

And then laughter, the tinkling, musical laughter of a young girl.

This isn't a child, I thought. *A living child, anyway.* I had no idea what was singing at the other end of the hallway, but I wasn't about to stick around to find out. I backed away, slowly at first, and then turned and hurried down the hallway, hoping to catch Mr. Sinclair before he left. But of course he had gone long ago. I knew that Mrs. Sinclair and Marion, along with other household staff, must be around somewhere, but I had no idea where. All at once, I wished to be back on the streets of Chicago. Even angry reporters would've been welcome company just then.

I took several deep breaths, trying to quiet my racing heart, and realized I had made my way back to the formal living room. I ran a hand through my hair and gazed up at the portrait above the fireplace of the man in the kilt. His face seemed so familiar somehow. I could see the laugh lines around his eyes, the kindness. I could almost hear his voice whispering in my ear, the drone of bagpipes floating in the air around me. All at once I knew this was the man who built Havenwood.

"What was that back there?" I asked him, wishing he could give me an answer.

I eyed my watch. With a couple of hours to go until lunchtime, I hurried up the stairs and, after several wrong turns, found my way back to my room. Once I was finally safe inside, I shut the door behind me, sunk into the armchair next to the window, and propped my feet on the ottoman. Covering my legs with an afghan that had been draped over the back of the chair, I turned my face to the window and stared out at the snow, imagining the original owner of the house and his children playing there, the painting come to life. Suddenly I wondered if it was one of their

voices I heard, a tiny moment in time somehow caught and re-
played.

A while later, there was a knock at the door. Marion poked her
head into the room.

"Lunch, ma'am. Please come with me."

I followed her back out into the hallway, down the stairs,
across the massive foyer, and into a part of the house I hadn't yet
seen. We walked from room to opulent room until we reached a
closed set of ornately carved double wooden doors.

"Mrs. Sinclair wishes to take lunch today in the west salon," she
informed me, opening the doors to reveal a high-ceilinged room
with an entire wall of paned windows on one side and a grand fireplace on the other. The wood floors gleamed.

Whereas many of the rooms that I had seen at Havenwood
were formal and imposing, this one had a more casual feel. A long
window seat, strewn with colorful pillows and afghans, ran from
end to end in front of the windows, and two couches, upholstered
with a deep tapestry print, faced each other in front of the fireplace, flanked by wing chairs with ottomans. Four tables with ac-
companying chairs stood in the corners of the room, almost as
if this were set up as a library or place of study. One of them, a
round table nearest the wall of windows, was set for two.

"Mrs. Sinclair will join you in just a moment," Marion said before she turned and made her way back down the hall.

I settled onto one of the couches, sinking down into its soft
cushions, and as I did so, a slight coldness brushed past me. A whisper of a breeze. I glanced toward the windows, but none of them
was opened. Why would they be on a winter day? I crossed my
arms in front of my chest and reasoned that, in a house this size,
breezes must waft down halls and through corridors and around
pillars all the time.

"Julia!" It was Mrs. Sinclair, entering the room with her arms wide, as though she were alighting after floating here on that very breeze. "You haven't gotten lost yet in this maze of a house, I trust?"

She had changed clothes since breakfast. Now she was wearing a green velour jogging suit, accented by several long strands of silver beads around her neck. Silver bracelets jangled on one wrist, and on one finger, an enormous diamond ring, so big it seemed to weigh her down. Her hair, colored bright red, was cropped short and tousled, bangs framing her face.

She seemed somehow much younger now than she had just hours earlier. This was the Amaris Sinclair I remembered from book jacket photographs and talk show appearances.

I got to my feet and smiled. "Hello, Mrs. Sinclair," I said, moving across the room toward her. "Did you have a pleasant morning?"

"Oh yes, oh my yes," she said, pulling out one of the chairs at the set table and gesturing toward the other. "Are you a fan of yoga, my dear?"

I sat down across from her and placed a napkin on my lap. "I've done it a few times at my gym in Chicago. It's more difficult than it looks!"

"Indeed," she said, taking a sip from her water glass, her green eyes shining. "I highly recommend it as one ages. It keeps these old muscles on their toes."

Marion returned, pushing a silver cart.

"Ah, Marion. What do you have for us today? Not scallops, I hope." She winked at me, a slight smile curling up at the corners of her mouth.

"After fifty years, if I would be serving you a scallop, you'd know to call the paramedics for I'd be out of my mind," Marion huffed, sliding open the roll top on the tray to reveal two earthenware crocks, a basket of bread, and a pitcher of water. "It's French onion soup today."

She set the bowls of soup in front of us, golden-brown cheese still bubbling across the rims, and the basket of crusty French bread and butter in the middle of the table. The sweet aroma of caramelized onions swirled between us. It smelled heavenly.

"Well now, dear," Mrs. Sinclair began, raising a spoonful to her lips and blowing on it slightly, "let us set about the business of getting to know each other, shall we?"

"I'd like that very much."

"Tell me all about yourself, Julia. I love nothing better than to hear the story of someone's life. It's so much more interesting than fiction."

"Well, I don't know about that, at least where my life is concerned," I said, taking a spoonful of the caramelly soup. "My story is fairly ordinary." I winced as I thought about Jeremy.

"Oh, I doubt that," she said, and looked at me with expectation in her eyes. "As in any good story, let's start at the beginning. Where were you born?"

"In Minneapolis," I said. Long-forgotten memories flooded back as I told Amaris Sinclair about growing up in a split-level house three doors down from a creek that ran through the suburban neighborhood where I lived until I left for college. I told her of playing outside during the endless summers of childhood with a gaggle of friends who had long since faded from view, of catching crayfish in the creek and listening to the frogs sing at night. It seemed so old-fashioned and simple in comparison to the way my life had evolved.

"Lovely! And your parents? What did they do?"

"My mom was a secretary and my dad was in sales," I said, the words catching at the back of my throat as my parents' faces floated through my mind.

"They're both gone now, I understand." She reached across the table and covered my hand with hers.

"Yes," I said, dabbing at my eyes with my napkin. "It's been more than fifteen years already. Mom was killed in a car accident on the way to work, and Dad died just after her funeral. Everyone said it was a broken heart."

She squeezed my hand. "That thing people say about time healing all wounds? Rubbish. Complete and utter rubbish."

This brought a smile to my lips. "You learn to live with it, but the pain never goes away."

"You had finished college by that time, yes?"

I nodded. "I was in Europe—a graduation gift from my parents. I rushed home and . . ." I sighed, not really knowing how to continue.

"That's when you wrote your novel," she prompted.

"I didn't know what else to do." I gave a halfhearted shrug.

She cleared her throat. "Now that Adrian has gone, we might as well be honest with each other," she said. "I know he has hired you as a companion for me. It's a little game we play. He hires them; I drive them off. Since we mentioned your novel, I thought I'd simply let you know that he is trying to do this under the guise that you are a writer in need of mentoring. I suspect this isn't quite the case. Am I correct?"

Her candor caught me off guard. Was I about to be ejected from this house like so many other "companions" before me? I grasped for the right words.

"Both are true," I said, thinking quickly. "Adrian—Mr. Sinclair—wants to make sure you are well cared for during his absences. After knowing you for just a few hours, I can see you don't need a companion. But I can also see a son who wants to do all he can for his mother."

Mrs. Sinclair smiled. "Adrian is a good boy."

"I've been a fan of yours for years, and frankly, that's the main reason I accepted his offer," I continued. I didn't bring up anything about my recent life and my desire to drop out of sight. I didn't know how much she knew about that, and I figured the less, the better.

"Thank you, my dear."

She took another spoonful of soup and a silence fell between us. I waited until she spoke again.

"You see, Julia, just as my son had ulterior motives for bringing you here, I must confess to harboring ulterior motives of my own for agreeing to the situation, and agreeing willingly." Her green eyes danced.

A trickle of fear crept up my spine. Her comment seemed to tint my current state of affairs in very dark hues. It occurred to me that I was sitting across the table from a famous horror novelist—a woman whose character I really didn't know at all.

The look on my face must've betrayed what I was thinking, because Amaris Sinclair giggled, eyeing me as she took a sip of her drink. "It's nothing nefarious, I assure you. Don't worry, my dear. I probably shouldn't have brought it up at this time. It's just that something in your background made it especially attractive for me to welcome you here."

She gazed at me, her eyes wide with expectation. I wasn't quite sure what to make of that, until a thought entered my mind then, chilling me from the inside out. "You're not—you weren't one of my husband's investors . . . ?"

I thought I detected a look of sadness wash over her face that dissolved into a sigh. "Oh, goodness, no," she said, breaking off a piece of bread and dipping it into her soup. "It's nothing to do with that."

So she did know about it. I squirmed in my chair. "I want you to know, Mrs. Sinclair—" I began, but she waved her hand in the air to stop me.

"You owe me no explanation, Julia. Adrian told me all about the particulars of your husband's less-than-savory business affairs, and how public opinion is against you. Unfairly, he thinks. And so do I. He explained to me that this house would be living up to its name with you here. It will indeed be a haven in the woods for you just as it has been for me, and so many others, I have no doubt."

I exhaled a breath I hadn't realized I had been holding. "My life for the past year has truly been a nightmare."

"Nightmares." She smiled at me, rather sadly I thought. "Now, I know all about those. Many of my books were inspired by nightmares I had in this very home. It is good to awaken, isn't it?"

I thought about the dark nature of Amaris Sinclair's novels and shuddered, but at the same time a tingle sizzled through me.

"So you wrote here, in the house?"

"At this very table, my dear," she said, running her hands across its wooden surface. "Just me, my typewriter, and the various monsters and mishaps that were swirling around me begging to be put onto the page. Those were the days!"

"I've read all of your books. And the short stories."

Her face lit up. "Do you have a particular favorite among them?"

"*Seraphina*," I said, referring to her book about a psychic medium who got more than she bargained for when she contacted the spirit world during a séance in a house, I just then realized, that was a great deal like Havenwood. "I read it so many times when I was growing up, I think I knew every word by heart."

She stared at me then, her spoon suspended midway from her bowl to her mouth. It was as though her eyes were grasping at mine, trying to see into my brain. My skin began to prickle, and I felt like a mongoose in the thrall of a cobra.

"Of course you did, my dear," she said finally.

Her gaze was directed at me, but her eyes seemed to be looking at something else, not beyond me, but through me. As though I weren't there. Was this one of the "episodes" Adrian had warned me about?

"Mrs. Sinclair?" I reached across the table and grasped her hand, which still held her spoon aloft. This seemed to startle her, bringing her back from wherever she had gone. She shook her head and blinked several times.

"I'm sorry, my dear," she said. "The mere mention of my books seems to have sent my thoughts hurtling back into the past. It was such a wonderful time, you see. I loved it all, the writing, the book tours, meeting my readers." She sighed audibly. "Glorious, so glorious."

"Mrs. Sinclair, forgive me for asking, but why did you give it all up?" I asked her. "The world thinks you died."

"Oh, I know what the world thinks," she said, finishing the last of her soup. "But the real reason I gave it up? That's a conversation for another time, my dear." She turned her gaze to the window and seemed to be looking at something I couldn't see. "No, today the sky is too blue and bright for a tale as dark as that one."

SEVEN

$\mathcal{I}$ stood stock-still as three giant dogs bounded toward me. Mrs. Sinclair had suggested we take a stroll around the grounds, so we bundled up and headed out into the chilly air. In the pasture, I saw the dogs Adrian had told me about—three giant Alaskan malamutes, chasing one another and yowling. He had told me they were large, but I was unprepared for exactly how large. They saw Mrs. Sinclair and raced toward us, and I braced for impact.

Before I knew it, I was on my back in the snow, a giant red-and-white dog on top of me, licking my face. I held my breath, not quite sure what to do. One bite from this dog's mighty jaws would break a bone, I had no doubt.

"Molly!" Mrs. Sinclair barked. "That's enough now!" She snapped her fingers at the dog. "Get off, Molly, for goodness' sake."

The dog hopped into the snow next to me and wagged her tail furiously as I scrambled to my feet, brushing the snow off my backside. My knees were knocking.

"It's not every day you get a greeting like that," I said, trying to sound steadier than I felt.

"The old girl has taken to you, Julia!" Mrs. Sinclair informed me. "I knew she would. Reach out your hand and let her sniff it."

I did as I was told, and Molly moved her great head toward me, nuzzling her snout against my palm. I scratched behind her ears; her fur was as soft as cashmere.

The other two dogs, both gray and white with bright yellow eyes, circled us, looking like two gigantic wolves on the hunt.

"You mustn't be afraid, my dear." Mrs. Sinclair smiled at me. "You live at Havenwood now. You are a member of their pack." She turned an adoring gaze back to the dogs. "Tundra is the alpha," she said, gesturing at the largest of the three. "And Molly is just positively an angel."

She reached down and gave Tundra's back a good scratch.

"Think of them as your bodyguards, Julia. They take that responsibility very seriously."

We took a few steps and the dogs fell into line, the largest of the three walking ahead of us and one on either side of Mrs. Sinclair and me. They did seem like bodyguards, I thought, as we walked along, me relaxing more and more with each step. Lions and tigers and bears had nothing on those three.

Soon we came to the creek that I saw from the breakfast room, which meandered its way to Lake Superior, and Mrs. Sinclair pointed out a path that led to the village, some three miles away.

"It's a lovely ride on horseback," she said. "Nelly is quite gentle and slow, just right for someone new to riding. Would you like to do that one of these days?"

I could almost see myself there, in the distance, trotting through the landscape on a horse. "It sounds wonderful," I said.

"It's decided, then," she said. "We shall have a riding party. But it will have to be another day." She sighed deeply. "Now, my dear, let's make our way back to the house, shall we?"

I took her arm and she leaned on me as we walked through the snow, the dogs leading the way.

Back inside, the dogs loped off to parts unknown as we peeled off our jackets and hats.

"I believe I'll have a nap now, Julia," Mrs. Sinclair said, her usually bright eyes suddenly filled with what seemed to be sadness.

"Are you all right, Mrs. Sinclair?" I asked, moving toward her. "May I help you upstairs?"

"Thank you, my dear, but no," she said. "I'm just a bit tired, but I can make it on my own."

She then took her leave of me, and I watched as she walked slowly up the grand staircase, seeming to age with every step.

I hurried after her. "Are you sure I can't help?"

She touched my cheek with one papery hand. "This old gal still has a bit of kick in her." She smiled at me. "Please, darling, feel free to make yourself comfortable. Explore the house. Snoop! You never know where secrets might be lurking!"

I got the distinct impression she didn't want me to help her to her rooms—why, I had no idea—so I respected her wishes but stood where I was on the stairs to make sure she reached the second floor with no trouble. As she disappeared into the dark hallway, I turned and walked back down to the foyer alone.

After what had happened that morning, I didn't want to venture too far afield into the house. I found myself in the living room once again, with the massive portrait of the man in the kilt. I had been drawn to this painting, so I decided to sit down and spend some time with the man who already seemed like an old friend. The room was rather dark—all of that wood paneling seemed to capture whatever sunlight was coming through the windows—so I flipped on a table lamp and gazed upward.

"I see you have found Mr. McCullough." It was Mrs. Sinclair with Marion behind her holding a tray with two cups and a pot of tea. Mrs. Sinclair settled onto the sofa next to me while Marion lit a fire that had already been laid in the fireplace.

"I thought you were having a rest!" I said, surprised to see her again so quickly.

"It didn't feel right, leaving you on your own on your first day," she said, patting my hand. "We can both rest here."

Marion served the tea and left us. We sipped in silence for a while, both gazing at the painting.

"Most visitors to Havenwood are curious about its origins, Julia," Mrs. Sinclair said, as the flames began to crackle and dance.

"The man who built this house, Andrew McCullough, the handsome fellow right up there, was quite the colorful character. Would you like to hear about him?"

I smiled broadly. Adrian had told me his mother wanted to talk about stories with another writer—this must be just the kind of thing he meant. I couldn't believe it. I was about to hear a tale spun by the great Amaris Sinclair.

"I'd love to!" I said.

"It's not a sweet and gentle tale, however," she said, narrowing her eyes. "Not all of it, anyway. I'll just warn you of that. Are you sure you're up to hearing it?"

I nodded, eager to learn more about the man in the painting.

Amaris Sinclair folded her hands in her lap, stared into the dancing flames, and began to speak:

"The year was 1850, and unlike life on the East Coast of this country, things here in the wilds of Minnesota near the Canadian border were anything but civilized, at least by the standards of a young and rather spoiled Scottish nobleman sent here to run his family's fur-trapping business. Despite a few settlements here and there, this was the wilderness, darling, pure and simple."

She paused to take a sip of her tea, so I asked a question. "You said he was a young man? I imagine coming here would have been quite an adventure back in those days. Probably not something that an older gentleman would have undertaken."

"You imagine correctly. As the eldest son of an aristocratic family, Andrew stood to inherit his family's considerable wealth and position. But his father simply couldn't bear for that to happen, not to the man that young Andrew was at the time." Mrs. Sinclair's eyes sparkled. "He was what we might call a wild child. Gambling, drink, women—if there was a vice possible to have, Andrew succumbed to it. By all accounts, he was a spoiled, self-centered, entitled playboy with no sense of direction and no sense of responsibility, either. I'm sure you know the type."

I wondered if she was referring to my husband, and at the

thought of him, my stomach curdled. "It sounds like he needed to man up a bit," I offered.

"Indeed," she said, raising her eyebrows and taking another sip of her tea. "Andrew's mother, Marcelline, was French Canadian, the daughter of a prominent fur trader in Montreal. Her father had given her a line of his business, the fur trade along the Canadian border with Minnesota, as a dowry when she married Andrew's father, Hugh. And when the wild Andrew turned twenty, Hugh charged him with a task: he was to run the fur business and make it successful, before he would be eligible to inherit the family fortune, lock, stock, and barrel. Hugh thought the experience would make a man of his son. He had no idea."

Mrs. Sinclair chuckled and looked into my eyes, as though we were sharing a joke. "Andrew came to this land, sailing from Scotland to the East Coast, up the St. Lawrence River to the Great Lakes, and finally making landfall in Duluth. From there he went on horseback, and what he found, my dear, was like nothing he could even imagine in his wildest dreams. Or nightmares."

My arms tingled. I wondered how dark and twisted this tale might become. She had warned me, after all.

"Unlike what was happening in other parts of the state at that time, the native tribes in this area were friendly and welcoming," she continued. "Andrew settled into a modest cabin north of Duluth and began, as his father had instructed, to learn the business with the goal of one day taking it over."

"Obviously, he achieved that goal," I said, gesturing to the opulence around me.

Mrs. Sinclair smiled. "Don't get ahead of yourself, my dear. You haven't heard the full story yet."

I snuggled deeper into the sofa and curled my legs under me.

"It's my opinion, Julia, that the voyage itself and the rustic, and one might say harsh, living conditions began to work their magic on young Andrew. One might think this spoiled, rich young man would have rebelled against his circumstances, but in fact the opposite occurred. I suppose he had a good deal of time to think on the voyage over here. Or perhaps he was awestruck by the beauty of this land, which was wild and untamed and like nothing he had ever seen. Whatever the case, by all accounts Andrew was a fast learner who embraced his new life. In no time he mastered the business and accounting side of things and was itching to get out into the field, so to speak. Soon he asked the business's manager to go on a trapping run with the Voyageurs."

"Voyageurs?" I had heard the term before, but I wasn't quite sure what it meant.

"These were the men, many of them French Canadians like Andrew's mother, who got into canoes and paddled up and down the lakes in the region. They worked the traps, bringing in the pelts that drove the business," she explained. "They were savvy about the surroundings and very friendly with the native people, who shared secret knowledge about the land and the rivers and the lakes. Andrew wanted to know what they knew, and after several months of asking, he was finally allowed to go on a trapping run with them. It was an experience that changed Andrew's life."

I was silent, sipping my tea and waiting for Mrs. Sinclair to go on.

"After days of paddling in the massive canoes with eleven other men, portaging from lake to lake, sleeping under a canopy of stars each night, and seeing all manner of wildlife along the way, they reached what is now known as Gunflint Lake, not far from where Havenwood is today. There, they were invited to join the natives for a meal. The Voyageurs brought fish they had caught earlier in the day; the natives had venison and wild rice. After they had eaten, they sat around the campfire and began to tell young Andrew a tale. It was a warning about a monstrous being that roamed these woods."

I wrinkled my nose. "Not Bigfoot . . . ?" I hoped this wasn't where the story was going. I didn't believe that old legend. Science would have discovered the creature by now if it existed.

She shook her head. "Nothing as benign as that, I'm afraid. They told him the legend of the Windigo."

She visibly shuddered as she said the name. I knew I should know what this was; I had heard the name of this creature before. My mind reached back into the dusty recesses where it stored all of its not-often-used information but couldn't grasp it.

"The Windigo, darling, is a Native American legend. It is said that there is a beast that roams this area that is, well, for lack of a better term, Julia, a cannibal. It is a monstrous thing that had once been human. But now it feeds on human flesh."

I shivered. "I have heard about this," I said, the long-forgotten ghost stories told around campfires when I was a child seeping back into my brain. "So, Andrew learned about the Windigo from the natives?"

"More than learned." There was a dark sheen in her eyes. "As the story goes, Andrew became obsessed with the beast and aimed to catch it and kill it. He had grown to love this land and wanted to rid it of this evil."

"So he thought the Windigo was real? But it's just a legend."

"Where do legends come from, Julia?"

I held her gaze. Surely she didn't mean to suggest this old fairy tale was true, that a monstrous cannibal was roaming these woods.

"In any case," she said quickly, "real or not, Andrew set out to find it." She took a sip of her tea and stared into the fire. "That was a mistake."

"A mistake? What happened?"

Mrs. Sinclair turned to me and smiled. "We're not quite sure. After a month or so alone in the wilderness, he returned to his business's base, and then came the news that his parents had died in a stagecoach accident. The family fortune was now his. But instead of returning to his beloved Scotland, as everyone thought he would do, he built a replica of his family home right here. At incredible expense, I might add."

"So, he loved it here enough to stay."

"That's one way to look at it. He certainly had success here, and by all accounts became a good man. After several years, he fell in love with a local girl and got married, and they had children. And once the house was completed, he began holding salons for the arts—he brought in musicians and artists and writers from not only the East Coast of the United States but from all around the world."

"I sense there's a 'but' coming right about now."

Mrs. Sinclair nodded. "Exactly right, my dear. He never left. Never again did he venture beyond the estate."

"He never went back to Scotland, even for a visit? Why?"

"That's the interesting question, isn't it?"

I sensed she was trying to tell me something, but I couldn't quite grasp it. "Was he compelled to stay?"

"Or prevented from leaving . . . by someone or something. There is more magic, both good and evil, in the woods beyond this house than you could imagine in your wildest dreams."

"Or nightmares," I said, shuddering.

"As the story goes—and this is just pure speculation, now, nobody really knows for sure—Andrew did indeed encounter the Windigo one lonely night in the woods. He saw the creature—tall, thin as a skeleton, sunken eyes, with an insatiable hunger for human flesh, the remains of its victims strewn around it. Andrew froze in terror as it turned its horrible gaze toward him. He surely would've been killed but for a Native American shaman who had also been hunting the Windigo to rid his people of its menace. He used dark magic to kill the beast, saving Andrew's life in the process."

As she took a sip of her tea, I noticed her eyes were twinkling with delight. She set her cup on the end table and continued. "It was a magical gift, but a price came with it, as is most often the case. Andrew McCullough could indeed live on, but only where he was. Here." She opened her arms wide. "And that is how he came to own this property. That is why he reconstructed his beloved family home here, brick by brick. That is why he never left. He chose the name of the house for that very reason. This was Andrew's haven in the woods. If he ventured one foot beyond the estate, he would fall dead. If he stayed, he would live on, charged with protecting the estate and all who live here from the same menace that almost took his life."

A shiver ran up my spine, thinking of a creature as horrible as the Windigo on the estate.

"So what happened to Andrew in the end? He married and had children, you said, right?"

She nodded. "He did indeed. But what ultimately happened to Andrew is a bit murkier than that." She leaned in toward me and lowered her voice. "Around the time of his fiftieth birthday, he walked into the woods and was never seen again. Some say he still roams through the forest to this day, playing his beloved bagpipe, keeping the Windigo at bay. You can hear the music of the pipes buoyed by the wind on the deepest, darkest nights of the year."

I shivered but was delighted all the same. *That*, I thought, *is how a master of the craft spins a ghost story.*

"And now, my dear, I'm going to make my way up to my rooms," Mrs. Sinclair said, pushing herself up from the sofa. "We usually have cocktails before dinner, but I think we'll skip it tonight if you don't mind. I'm a bit tired."

"Not at all," I said, rising with her. "I enjoyed the story."

She put a hand on my cheek. "I knew you would, darling. One can't possibly be a part of Havenwood without knowing its founder."

She made her way upstairs, and I settled back onto the sofa in front of the fire. I gazed up at Andrew McCullough—the very sound of his name sizzled through me—and wondered what had really happened to him. Windigo indeed.

"Miss Julia?" I was so lost in thought that the sound of my own name made me jump.

"Oh!" I said. "I didn't hear you come in."

She smiled. "I'm just letting you know that Mrs. Sinclair will be dining in her suite this evening," she said. "Might you like your dinner upstairs as well?"

Dinner? I had no idea it was so late. I glanced out the window and the fading glow of twilight told me I had been sitting there longer than I thought.

"Sure," I said, pushing myself up. "That'll be fine."

"Very good," she said, turning to go. "I'll have one of the girls bring it up at six thirty, along with a bottle of wine and a few books for you to read. The evenings can get a bit long at Haven-wood if we don't have a formal dinner."

"Thank you, Marion." I smiled at her, pleased that I remembered her name.

After finishing the dinner of roast beef, vegetables, and crusty bread, I poured a glass of wine and tried to open one of the books Marion had sent up. But I found that my imagination swirling around everything that had happened to me that day was much more entertaining. I closed the book and set it in my lap, and spent the rest of the evening looking out my window into the dark woods, strangely lit by the moon and stars on the new-fallen snow, wondering about poor Andrew McCullough out there, somewhere. I squinted into the falling darkness, hoping a monster didn't lurk just out of sight.

As I was turning off my bedside lamp, I could've sworn I heard the strains of bagpipe music in the distance. But I knew it was just my imagination playing tricks on me, and certainly not an ancient, immortal Scotsman patrolling the grounds.

A small, faraway voice awakened me in the middle of the night.

"Sing a song of sixpence / A pocket full of rye . . ." And then it dissipated into the air, as though it hadn't been there at all.

I sat up and flipped on my bedside lamp, looking around the room, my heart pounding hard and fast in my chest. It was the same singsongy voice I had heard earlier. I slipped out of my bed and peeked underneath it. Nothing was there. I turned on the overhead light and approached the closet door, throwing it open—nothing but my clothes, hanging in neat rows. The bathroom was empty as well. This was silly, I told myself. I had probably just dreamed it. Trying to calm myself, I poured a glass of water, but my hands were shaking terribly as I lifted it to my lips.

I turned off the light and slipped back down under the covers, but now I was fully awake, a heightened sense of terror overtaking me. I couldn't explain it—I knew it was probably just a dream—but I lay there feeling more frightened by this tiny voice than I ever had been of anything. I pulled the covers over my head and shivered, deep in my core.

I don't know how long I lay there frozen still, not wanting to move a muscle, but at one point, I tried to do my own personal version of counting sheep—piecing together the events of the previous day that might have been blurred as a result of my medication. Only then did it occur to me—I hadn't taken any. The only thing I forgot yesterday was to take the pills that made me forget everything else.

I slipped out of bed and into the bathroom, fishing around in my travel kit for the pill bottle. I couldn't pop one right then—I was supposed to take them with food. Instead, I set the bottle on the vanity so I wouldn't forget to take one just before I went down for breakfast.

As I crawled back into bed, something hit me. I had been told there could be side effects from stopping this medication too abruptly. I took stock of how I was feeling after just one day off the pills—no shaking, no withdrawal symptoms of any kind that I could discern other than a slight headache. I tried to remember what the side effects were supposed to be . . . Sleep disruptions? Well, it was the middle of the night and I was wide-awake. What else? Depression? Hallucinations? That word hung in the air as though I had said it aloud. "Hallucinations." Was that all this sing-songy voice was? Something I was making up in my own head? That had to be it.

Satisfied with that explanation, I felt the tension in my body begin to melt away. I lay there focusing on how comfortable the bed was and how safe and warm it felt to be nestled there under the blankets. Before I knew it, I was opening my eyes to a new day.

I stretched and yawned, marveling at how different life seemed from what it had been just two days before. No angry victims stalking me, no bill collectors, no banks threatening to foreclose, no former friends giving me the ultimate cold shoulder. Instead, I was in a magnificent old house with a fascinating, if a little odd, lady and servants to attend to my every need. How did I ever get so lucky?

I glanced at the clock. Six fifteen. I had lots of time before break-fast, so I thought I'd shower and head downstairs early. Maybe I could find a copy of the morning newspaper.

It wasn't until I was out of the shower and toweling off that I noticed the pill bottle. It was floating in the toilet, its contents spilled and at the bottom of the bowl. I stood there staring at it for a while, not quite believing what I was seeing. I remembered put-ting it on the vanity in the middle of the night, but did I open it? I must have. I fished the bottle out of the water and flushed, watching the pills go down the drain, thinking there surely must be a phar-macy in town where I could get a refill.

Only then did it occur to me: I couldn't do that. How does a woman who has vanished get a prescription filled? One call to my doctor's office and my opportunity to leave my past behind would be ruined. I shook my head and told myself Adrian could handle it for me somehow when he returned. That was the best I could do. I'd simply have to go without my medication until then. I'd al-ready gone twenty-four hours without it, slightly the worse for wear, but nothing I couldn't handle. For now, maybe coffee could ease my headache.

I dressed and headed downstairs. After a few wrong turns, I found my way to the kitchen and poked my head around the swinging door. Marion and two other young women I hadn't met were buzzing around the stove. The aroma of coffee filled the air, and one of the women was pouring batter into muffin cups while the other was cracking eggs into a bowl.

"Hello? I don't mean to bother you," I began, still not quite sure of the etiquette of dealing with maids.

"Yes, Miss Julia," Marion said. "What can we do for you?"

"I was hoping for a copy of the newspaper and some coffee?"

"Of course. Go on into the breakfast room and I'll bring them to you."

I sensed the slightest hint of irritation in Marion's voice. I was varying the routine, it seemed. I wondered how frowned upon that sort of thing was. But in any case, a few moments later I was sitting with the morning paper and a steaming cup of coffee, reading the day's news, so it couldn't have been too big a breach in protocol.

As I turned the page from the local headlines to the national news, a photograph caught my eye. And then the headline above it made my blood run cold.

"Bishop House Burns to the Ground. Arson Suspected."

My house? I held my breath and scanned the story:

Last night, Chicago firefighters were called to the Lincoln Park home of Jeremy Bishop, a.k.a. the Midwestern Bernie Madoff. Neighbors reported the house had gone up in flames around 2 A.M. The house was engulfed by the time they arrived. Firefighters are calling it a total loss.

Bishop died of a self-inflicted gunshot wound three months ago, but his wife was believed to have been in the home.

I dropped the paper as though it, too, were on fire and stared at the page on the table. Something about the photo had caught my eye and wouldn't let go. I bent down and squinted to get a better look and . . . could it be? I gasped aloud when I realized what I was seeing. In the crowd on the sidewalk in front of the smoldering wreck that had been my home, a familiar face. Adrian's.

I pushed my chair back from the table and stood up, turning to the window, my heart beating so loudly that I was sure the cardinals perched on the pine tree outside could hear it. A flurry of conflicting thoughts were running through my mind, not one of them gelling into anything that I could use to make sense of what I had just learned. My house had burned to the ground and Adrian had been standing outside of it. I had no idea what I was supposed to do with that information. I felt like I had just slipped into a nightmare. Or one of Mrs. Sinclair's stories.

Was it really him? I wasn't sure, but it certainly looked like him. Could he possibly have . . . I couldn't even finish the thought. Surely he didn't. He couldn't have been the arsonist.

Although . . . He did promise to make me disappear from my old life. Had he taken it one step further?

I crumpled the newspaper and threw it into the garbage just as Marion appeared with breakfast on a tray.

"Mrs. Sinclair will be joining you in just a moment." She furrowed her brow at me. "Are you all right, Miss Julia? You look rather pale."

"I'm fine!" I said, a little too loudly, and reached for my coffee cup. I set it down quickly when I saw how badly my hand was shaking.

"Has it gone cold?" Marion asked, still staring at me with a quizzical look in her eyes.

"Yes" was all I could manage to say.

She set the dishes on the sideboard, and picked up the coffee pot and poured some of the steaming liquid into a new cup. "Here you are," she said, handing it to me and taking my old cup away. "Lukewarm coffee is just ghastly, isn't it?"

"Ghastly." I nodded, holding the new cup to my lips.

She pushed the door open to head back into the kitchen but stopped before going through it and turned to me. "Please let me know if you need anything, Miss Julia," she said, a concerned look on her face. "Anything." And then she was gone.

I had the urge to get up and run away, to somewhere, anywhere that I knew was safe. But where was I to go? So I just slumped back into my chair at the table and sat there, stunned. The house I shared with Jeremy, a pile of ashes, just like the state of our marriage itself.

Was Adrian responsible? Did he set that fire to erase all traces of my old life, so I could vanish into thin air just as his mother had? I shook my head, as if trying to shake that particular thought out of it. I couldn't bear to think Adrian would've done something so dangerous on my behalf. But if he wasn't the one who set the fire, who did?

I tried to comfort myself by repeating what I had been thinking just moments before—how lucky I was to be living in a whole new world. What did it matter to me, really, if my house had burned to the ground? I had no plans to go back there. I had left my life in Chicago willingly, gratefully. The person who lived in that house didn't exist anymore—why should I be upset that the house didn't exist, either?

But I knew I was grasping at straws. I had indeed chosen to take Adrian up on his offer for me to disappear, but I didn't bargain on this. My whole body tightened as I wondered exactly what offer I had accepted.

EIGHT

I'm not quite sure how I got through breakfast with Mrs. Sinclair that morning. She was chattering away about something or other, and I was nodding and responding to what she was saying, but I wasn't there with her, not really. All I could see in front of my eyes were flames, and I needed answers about who set that fire.

After we finished our meal and Mrs. Sinclair retreated for her morning quiet time, I rushed back up to my room and began fumbling through my things. Where had I put Adrian's business card? I finally found it in the top drawer of the dresser—I hadn't remembered putting it there, but whatever—and dug into my purse for my cell phone. I stopped cold when I remembered I had left it, along with every piece of identification I had, at my house, which was now gone. And so was I. Julia Bishop was well and truly dead.

I sunk into the chair by the window and stared out at the snow. What was I supposed to do now? I needed a plan, but my mind simply couldn't formulate one.

I really didn't know anything about Mrs. Sinclair and Adrian other than the fact that she was a famous novelist, and he was . . . what? Her son. That was about it. They could be a pair of psychopaths for all I knew. And here I was, living in their home. I couldn't believe how monumentally foolish I had been to give up everything, my entire identity, and come here. I briefly thought of gathering my things and slipping away before anyone realized I was gone.

But as I gazed out into the wilderness beyond the house, I knew

I couldn't do that. I had no idea how to get to town. One wrong
turn and I'd be lost in the woods with goodness knows what kinds
of animals at my heels, just as Adrian had warned. No, like it or
not, I had to stay where I was.

I turned Adrian's card over and over in my hands. I needed to
talk with him, not just about the fire, but about my prescription as
well. Maybe he had a personal doctor on staff—wealthy people
had that, didn't they?

I looked around my room and only then did I realize there was
no phone. I supposed that wasn't so odd. Old houses like these
didn't exactly come with telephone jacks in every room. But there
was probably a phone on my floor, I reasoned, so I pushed myself
out of the chair to go on a hunt for one.

I poked my head out the door and peered up and down the
hall. The grand staircase was to the left. I shut the door behind me
and set off in the other direction, where I hadn't yet been.

The hallway was dark despite the light of day, and I walked by
closed door after closed door. Guest rooms? Most likely. I turned
this way and that and finally spied one door that was ajar. I pushed
it open gingerly and found that it was just what I needed: a small
study with a desk in the middle of the room and a couple of armchairs facing it. I was delighted to see a telephone—an old-fashioned
model with a heavy black handset and a rotary dial—sitting on the
desk. I pulled the door shut behind me and sat down.

I picked up the receiver and realized I had no idea what I was
going to say to Adrian. "Did you burn my house down?" isn't exactly an easy line of conversation to initiate. But I wanted to get to
the bottom of it, so I took a deep breath and dialed the number on
his business card.

*This is Adrian Sinclair. I'm sorry I'm not here to take your call right
now . . .*

I should have known. Of course he wouldn't answer. I left a
rather rambling and disjointed message after the beep.

"Adrian? It's Julia. Julia Bishop. Your mother is fine. It's nothing about her. I don't want to worry you. I'm just calling to check in with you and talk over a couple of things." I sighed. "I'm not sure when you're coming back to Havenwood, so please call me if you can. I saw the news about the fire."

I hung up the phone and wished I could take it all back. If Adrian was involved with it somehow, would he want me to know? Or would he think I was so removed from the world here at Havenwood that this news might have eluded me?

Either way, it didn't matter. I had made the call. What was done was done.

Slipping out of the study, I jumped back when I saw Marion standing just outside the door.

"Marion!" I said, a little too quickly. "You gave me a fright."

"Miss Julia," she said, a tight smile on her face. "Is there anything I can do for you?"

The knot tightening in my stomach told me I probably shouldn't be there. I got the distinct feeling she had followed me somehow—but why?

"Oh!" I said. "I was just making a phone call. I noticed there was no phone in my room and—"

Her eyes narrowed and she shook her head slightly. "I'll be happy to take care of that for you, Miss Julia, should you ever have need of using the phone again. Mr. Sinclair doesn't like unauthorized calls going out of Havenwood."

I furrowed my brow at her.

"I'm sure you understand," she said, reaching out and pulling the door shut with finality before she disappeared into the dark hallway.

She'd take care of that for me? I fumed to myself as I stomped back toward my room. I couldn't make a phone call now? Where did she get off? What was this, a prison?

And then it hit me: not a prison, but an isle of exile. He didn't want unauthorized calls going out of Havenwood because they could be traced back here. For all he knew, I would try to call friends or relatives or even a lawyer, who could then verify my whereabouts by tracing the call. It was for my own protection, and that of Mrs. Sinclair.

*C*ome, my dear," Mrs. Sinclair said, pushing herself up from the table after we had finished our lunch. "Let us take a walk through this labyrinth of a house. Adrian suspected you might especially enjoy the library. Why don't we spend a few hours there among the musty shelves?"

My stomach flipped as I remembered the singsongy voice that had swirled through the air the day before when I tried to go into the library, but I pushed those memories out of my mind as best as I could. Hallucinations. That was all they were. I had always loved libraries. Why should this one be any exception?

We chatted about the dogs and the horses while we made our way through rooms and hallways, from the west salon all the way to the opposite end of the house. Adrian was right—a person really could get a lot of exercise just walking the halls.

When we arrived and Mrs. Sinclair opened the doors leading into the grand library, I gasped aloud. What had I been so apprehensive about? The moment I laid eyes on that room, any trepidation I had been feeling melted into sheer awe. Three stories tall, it was like nothing I had ever seen in a private home.

I craned my neck to look all the way to the ceiling, three floors up. The walls on each floor were lined with bookshelves. In the center of the main floor, leather couches and armchairs were grouped here and there, flanked by tables with soft green lamps.

It looked familiar somehow, as though it had been used in a movie that I had seen long ago. It very well could have been, I thought.

"Unbelievable," I mused, noticing the spiral staircases with their gleaming gold handrails, one on each end of the room, twirling from the main level to the second and on up to the third. "This is bigger than the public library in my neighborhood when I was growing up."

"Thousands upon thousands of books," Mrs. Sinclair said, holding her arms wide. "When I first saw it as a young girl, I thought it was the eighth wonder of the world. I knew right then I would own this house—and this library—one day."

I gave her a sidelong glance. "Adrian said you bought Havenwood when he was a boy. You were here before that? As a child?"

"Oh my, yes," she said, sliding her hand along the leather back of one of the sofas before sinking down into it. "I am related to the McCulloughs. Somewhere along the line, Havenwood was passed down to a cousin of mine whom I never particularly liked"—she wrinkled her nose—"and when I heard he was having trouble keeping it up, I swooped in. Thank goodness I had the means to do so. My parents first brought me here for a visit when I was no more than ten years old, and I've been in love with this house ever since."

A picture swam through my mind: a little girl with auburn pigtails and dancing green eyes, her mouth agape as she stood in the very spot where I was standing. "I can see you here as a girl, awestruck by this library," I said.

"I imagine you can, my dear." She raised her eyebrows and smiled. "I imagine you can."

I turned in a slow circle to take it all in, my eyes straining to see all the way to the third floor. "This is just amazing. So, most of these books were here before you bought the house?"

"They were indeed. I've added a few hundred to the collection, but many of these were the property of the first Andrew McCullough. He was a voracious reader and seeker of knowledge. And a great patron of the arts who loved the written word."

"It would take years to go through them all," I mused.

"Lifetimes," she said. "It is a true library, a literal storehouse of knowledge. There are centuries-old maps of the world, drawn by ancient mariners. Victorian textbooks. Encyclopedias from every age. Druid writings. Celtic tales." She gestured to the second floor. "Up there you'll find our collection of Bibles. We have a Gutenberg—the first book printed on a printing press. We have an original King James."

I wondered what other manner of literary treasures I could find languishing on these old shelves. "Wow," I said, now knowing what I would be doing with much of my free time on the cold and snowy winter days ahead. "I feel like I've been given the keys to the lost library of Alexandria."

"Not quite." She chuckled, pushing herself up to her feet. "But it's a close second. It can be a bit overwhelming, coming into this library for the first time and trying to decide where to start looking for the endlessly interesting bits and pieces you'll find in here. So I've got a suggestion."

She took my arm and led me across the room to a shelf with lead glass doors. As she carefully opened them, the ancient hinges creaked their disapproval.

"First editions, many of them signed," she said. "Andrew Mc-Cullough collected signed first editions of books, and he regularly invited famous authors of the day to visit Havenwood—some even used it as a writing retreat. All he asked was for a copy of the authors' works. His son and grandson continued the practice, as did I when I bought the house. So there is quite a collection of literature here."

One quick glance at the spines on the shelves caused my heart to skip a beat and nearly stop. Conan Doyle, Steinbeck, London, Hemingway, Fitzgerald, Tolkien, Salinger, Capote. Gabriel García Márquez. C. S. Lewis. Madeleine L'Engle. And more. So many more.

"All of these writers were here?" I squeaked.

"Many of them, yes."

"Can I touch the books?" I asked. "I mean, do I need gloves or . . . ?"

"Goodness, no. These are meant to be enjoyed." She gave my arm a quick squeeze and winked at me. "I'll leave you to look. I'm going up there." She pointed toward the third level. "I feel like doing some snooping in the Elizabethan section."

"Do you need a hand?" I asked, eyeing the circular staircase.

"Elevator's in the back." She smiled. "I don't climb those infernal things anymore."

After she had disappeared toward the back of the room, I don't know how long I stood there, staring at the priceless treasures on the shelf in front of me, afraid to touch any of them. I couldn't remember even seeing one first edition classic, let alone an entire shelf of them.

I ran my finger along their spines, one by one. *The Great Gatsby. The Sun Also Rises. Gone with the Wind. The Lion, the Witch and the Wardrobe.* On and on. It was a collection of the greatest works of literature in the past two centuries. I was wary to pull any of them out of their places, not wanting to disturb their slumber.

But then a slim volume caught my eye and I could not resist. *A Christmas Carol*, one of my favorite stories of all time. I read it every year in December and watched countless movie versions of the tale, and even went to see the annual stage play version at Minneapolis's famed Guthrie Theater more times than I could count. I pulled the leather-bound book from the shelf with shaking hands, as though I had come upon the Holy Grail itself.

I held my breath as I carefully opened the cover to the first page.

With awe and delight during this spirit-filled season,
Charles Dickens
December 1867, Havenwood

I blinked several times and squinted at the page, not quite sure what I was seeing. I seemed to recall that Dickens had visited the United States twice during his lifetime, but how could he possibly have come all the way to the wilds of Havenwood? And more important, why?

And then the name on the inscription called out to me, as clearly as if someone had uttered it. *Seraphina.*

NINE

*M*rs. Sinclair!" I called out, shattering the quiet that had settled in around me. "Mrs. Sinclair!"

"What is it, dear?" she sang back to me, leaning slightly over the third-level balcony, bifocals dangling on a chain around her neck.

"Wait until you see what I've found!" I called up to her, slipping the volume into my pocket and hurrying up the spiral stairs.

"What sort of treasure have you unearthed, Julia?" She was clearly amused at my enthusiasm.

I held the book out to her as I tried to catch my breath. "Charles Dickens," I huffed, bending low at the waist and taking a deep breath in and letting it out again. "Dickens! He was here at Havenwood!"

She took the copy of *A Christmas Carol* and turned it over and over in her hands. "Ah, yes," she said, nodding her head. "I shouldn't be surprised that the first book you were drawn to, of the thousands upon thousands here, was this one."

She smiled at me, rather sadly I thought.

"It's inscribed to somebody named Seraphina. It was—" I intended to tell her it was signed by Dickens himself during Christmastime in 1867, but the look in her eyes told me she already knew what I was going to say. Of course she did. This was her library, after all, and had been for decades. Of course she had already seen this treasure.

"Mrs. Sinclair?" I began slowly. "Was the Seraphina you wrote about in your novel a real person who was here at Havenwood?"

Amaris Sinclair exhaled and held my gaze. "Well," she said finally. "This has certainly happened quite a bit more rapidly than I thought it would. It's only your second day here."

My stomach tightened. Was she about to ask me to leave? "Have I done something wrong?"

"Oh, my goodness, no." She slipped the book into the pocket of her jogging suit and took my hands in hers. "On the contrary. This is why I've asked you here, my dear."

She looked deeply into my eyes—almost in a trance, as she had been the day before at lunch.

"I don't understand, Mrs. Sinclair."

She opened her mouth to speak, but then seemed to think better of it. She shook her head and turned toward the elevator. "Come. Let us put Mr. Scrooge and Mr. Marley back into their place on the first editions shelf."

I was feeling a bit like a naughty schoolgirl, caught doing something she shouldn't, so I did damage control as the elevator creaked its way down to the first floor. "If you'd rather I didn't touch the books or take them from their shelves—"

"Don't be silly! Only the items under glass—the Gutenberg Bible, ancient scrolls, that type of thing—need to stay where they are. But the rest are here for your pleasure. And if I know anything about you, Julia, darling, you will be in this library more often than not."

As we exited the elevator, I looked around at the stacks, imagining what other wonders they contained. "I think you're right," I admitted with a sly smile.

As Mrs. Sinclair was slipping the book back into its place on the shelf, Marion appeared in the doorway.

"Sorry to disturb, ma'am," she said, smoothing her apron.

"Not at all, Marion. What is it?"

"It's Mr. Sinclair. He's on the telephone."

That was quick, I thought. I moved to follow Marion out of the room, thinking he had returned my call. But Mrs. Sinclair spoke up, her face alight with twinkling eyes. "Ooh!" she cooed. "My boy!" She turned to me and said conspiratorially: "He's been gone for only a day and already I miss him."

"It's for Mrs. Sinclair?" I said, my words falling on top of one another with a thud. "I thought maybe . . ."

But Marion's face told me all I needed to know.

"Excuse me while I take this," Mrs. Sinclair said.

"Of course," I said, but she was already off with Marion, leaving me alone.

After she had gone, I wasn't sure if I should poke around the shelves anymore on my own or not. So I meandered through the library's first floor, past shelf upon shelf, the tables, and a reading area that was clustered around a fireplace, until I found a set of double doors, much like the ones we went through to get to the west salon.

"This must be the east salon," I said to myself, remembering an architectural drawing of the house that I had spied my first day here. I wondered if this room was as warm and welcoming as its mirror image on the other side of the house where Mrs. Sinclair and I took our lunch these past two days.

I stood at the doors for longer than I normally would have, that same feeling of dread circling around me. It was stronger here, almost emanating from the doors themselves.

"Hallucinations," I said aloud, remembering my unease at entering the library, which turned out to be full of wonderful surprises. Maybe this room would be the same. "It's just an old house."

I pulled open the massive doors, which creaked with what seemed to be their anger at being disturbed. After the opulence in the library, I was unprepared for the sight that awaited me.

Sheets were draped over the furniture. The windows were

shuttered closed. A layer of dust blanketed the fireplace's mantel. And the floors, which gleamed in other parts of the house, were dull and dark with age.

One round table sat in the center of the room, its chairs haphazardly pushed back as though their occupants left in a hurry. Plates sat where diners had left them, remnants of their meals long since devoured by industrious mice. Silverware was strewn here and there, and delicate wineglasses—some broken, some still standing at attention beside their plates—completed the strange tableau.

A complicated pattern of cobwebs adorned the walls and upper corners of the room, the woven masterpieces of generations of spiders undisturbed by humans. A bird's nest was perched on the great chandelier that hung from the ceiling, and the soft skittering of mice whispered along the parquet floorboards. A rug in the center of the room had been chewed and shredded—squirrels? raccoons?—and it appeared that something had built a nest in the long-cold fireplace. Dust floated in the air, and I heard the scratchy strains of music. A vision began to formulate to go with the tune: men in tuxedos, women in glittering gowns, laughter, celebration, dancing.

It was such a stark contrast to the rest of the house that it caused me to take a quick breath in. Clearly, this room had been shut up and unused for years, and once that realization took hold, that same sense of dread began to wrap itself around me, with something added to it—guilt. Crushing guilt and sadness. I realized I did not want to know what had happened here that had caused people to leave in a hurry. I just wanted to follow them out.

I started to back out of the room and pull the doors closed, when something caught my eye.

An enormous painting hung above the fireplace mantel. In the gloom, I couldn't get a good look at it, but I was drawn to it somehow.

Forgetting my haste to leave, I crossed the room to the windows and pulled open the dusty shutters, and as I did so, a shock of sunlight illuminated the darkness. I pulled open another set of shutters and another until the room was well lit. Then I turned to the painting, and my knees nearly gave out because of what I saw.

People in Victorian dress were seated at a round table—the very one in the center of the room before me. They were holding hands. Candles burned and a fire was lit in the fireplace.

It might have simply been a depiction of an evening's post-dinner entertainment, if not for the specters. Swirling around the people at the table were ghostly images: a woman whose mouth was open in a scream, three children dressed in white gowns with wicked looks on their faces, a dog with bared teeth and red eyes. An elderly couple hovered beside one of the men at the table, each with a hand on his shoulder. A man floated in the corner holding his own severed head.

A woman stood in the midst of it all. She was wearing a long, light-colored dress with a high collar and a sash at the waist. Her dark hair was piled on top of her head in a loose bun. Her arms were raised, and she seemed to be commanding the scene.

I was compelled to move closer and closer until the image seemed to engulf me, and then I saw what it was about the painting that mesmerized me so.

The woman's face. It looked exactly like mine.

TEN

I don't know how long I stood there, openmouthed, staring at my own face in the painting. Any thoughts of quickly exiting what seemed to be a forbidden, if certainly unused, room vanished. All I could do was stand and stare at the image of this woman who seemed both familiar and strange. It was me, and yet decidedly not me.

As I looked closer, the people in the painting seemed to stir. It was almost as if they began to breathe, slowly coming to life until they were no longer flat pictures on a canvas, but living beings around me. At the time, I was not sure if they entered my world, or if I was drawn into theirs, or if the whole thing was nothing more than my imagination. But whatever it was and however it happened, I found myself in the midst of the séance depicted in the painting—a place I had no wish to be.

The specters swirled around me, their ghostly moans ringing in my ears. The three children moved closer, whispering to one another. The screaming woman turned and said: "Hear me." The man's severed head began to grin.

For a moment I was frozen in terror, but then I found my feet. I backed out of the room, slamming the doors behind me in the hopes of containing whatever had been unleashed there.

I pounded through the library, out its double doors, and into the hallway, which was empty and dark. My footsteps echoed on the marble floor as I hurried along, desperate to find Mrs. Sinclair,

Marion, or anyone. I had no idea where in this massive house she had taken the call from Adrian—her own private suite of rooms, for all I knew—and I became more and more frantic as I went from room to empty room.

Finally I found her, in the study just off the kitchen. She was seated in an armchair near the fireplace, a pot of tea on the end table next to her.

"Mrs. Sinclair! There you are!" I was breathing heavily from all my rushing.

"Yes, dear," she said, greeting me from behind her teacup. "I just finished talking with Adrian when Marion brought me some tea. Join me?"

I slumped into the chair opposite hers and stared at the fire, which was dancing and darting and crackling merrily. The room was so warm and welcoming, such a contrast to where I had just been, that I leaned my head against the high back of the chair and exhaled.

"Is something wrong, Julia?" Mrs. Sinclair leaned toward me and extended her hand. "You seem rather disturbed."

How was I to begin? I wanted to ask her about the painting of the woman who looked exactly like me, but I wasn't sure I was even supposed to have been in that shuttered-up room. I wanted to tell her what I had seen—but then I remembered the side effect of stopping my medication. Was it all just a hallucination?

I took a deep breath before speaking, giving myself time to gather my thoughts.

"I'm fine," I finally said, and sighed, deciding to keep whatever had happened in that room to myself, at least for now. It might well have been a hallucination, for all I knew. And as for the painting, I must've been imagining the resemblance. She was just a woman with similar coloring and a similarly shaped face to mine; that was all. It was just a coincidence. What other explanation could there be?

Mrs. Sinclair smiled an indulgent smile. "I know, dear. I know.

In this old house, it can seem like ghosts are around every corner
when one is alone."

"Is Havenwood haunted, Mrs. Sinclair?"

She leaned forward in her chair and raised her eyebrows. "It's
positively chock-full of spirits, Julia," she said with a slight smile.

I wasn't sure what to make of that. "Are you serious? Because it
seems like you're teasing me."

A more solemn expression replaced her grin and she looked
into my eyes. "Do you believe in the spirit world, my dear?"

I turned my gaze to the fire for a moment before responding.
"I'm not sure."

"Have you had any strange experiences since arriving here at
Havenwood?"

"What sort of strange experiences?" The words caught in my
throat.

"Anything that might be construed as seeing something that's
not entirely . . . alive." Her eyes were filled with concern and seemed
expectant, somehow.

I didn't answer her. How could I? I wasn't about to admit that I
had seen a painting gurgle to life, or heard a child singing, when
I knew full well they were probably hallucinations brought on by
abruptly stopping my medication. I didn't want her thinking I was
crazy. So I just sat there, not knowing quite what to say next.

Fortunately, she spoke, breaking the silence between us. "Let
me tell you a little story," she began, lifting her teacup to her lips,
but then stopped before sipping. "Shall I call Marion? Would you
like some tea?"

I shook my head. "I'm fine. Thank you."

"Well, then," she said, clearing her throat and staring into the
fire. "This is a story about the time in my life when I was a young
novelist. Before Adrian was born, so that gives you an idea about
how long ago this was."

She took a sip of her tea and I settled back into my chair, calmed by the sound of her voice and the thought that I was going to hear another of Amaris Sinclair's stories.

"I had just published my first novel."

"The Haunting of Hattie Doyle?"

"That's the one, my dear. As you know, it's the story of a woman who moves with her family into a haunted house, but nobody can see or hear the ghosts except her . . ."

"And then the ghosts turn their attentions to her husband." I finished her thought. "Are you going to tell me it was real?"

"Just the opposite." She smiled. "When I wrote that story, darling, I was a young woman with very little life experience. I conjured it up in my own head, without any sort of facts or reality entering into it. I knew nothing about ghosts, just that they made for good storytelling."

I nodded. "They did make for good storytelling. That book reached the bestseller list."

"Exactly," she said. "It made me an overnight sensation. The story I want to tell you happened on the book tour for that novel. My publisher sent me nationwide."

I smiled, imagining the young Mrs. Sinclair meeting and greeting her readers. "It must have been thrilling."

"Oh, it was," she said, waving a hand in the air. "All of my dreams came true. But something unexpected happened as well."

I looked at her. "What was it?"

"Every time I did a reading or a signing, people would tell me about their experiences with ghosts," she said. "That was what the discussion turned into. Not just once, not just twice, but every time, at every bookstore or library I visited. People would share these experiences with me. One woman told me how her dead mother's perfume would waft through the air on special family occasions. Another told me how, when she was unpacking boxes in her new house, her children saw a photo of her grandfather who had died several years before they were born and whose photo they had never seen. 'Oh, that's Grandpa,' one of them said. 'He comes to play with us in our room. Will he come to the new house, too?' I've heard thousands of stories like this, Julia."

I nodded, but I wasn't sure what she was getting at.

"The point is, I started writing ghost novels before I believed. Now I do."

"Because of what people had told you about their experiences?"

She shook her head. "Not just that. I had one of my own."

My eyes widened. "What happened?"

"It was on that first book tour," she said, settling back into her chair and gazing into the fire. "I was under contract to finish my second book, but I had delayed working on it because I was so busy doing readings at bookstores and libraries and enjoying every minute of it. Remember, this was my first time on the road as a novelist, and meeting people other than my family who had read and loved my work was intoxicating and even addicting. It was as though I wanted to squeeze every ounce of joy out of that first tour before I turned my focus to my next book, and that meant the next book was going to be late to my publisher. It had me a little worried, frankly, thinking I should buckle down and get to work already."

She took a sip of tea before continuing. "At one particular reading, I told the audience of my predicament," she said. "Later, when I was signing books for all the people who had come to hear me speak, a woman of about my age approached me. She looked strangely familiar, but I couldn't quite place her. She said to me: 'Don't worry about focusing on this book tour instead of writing your next book. It's the right thing to do. Your next book will take care of itself. Enjoy every moment of your first book tour that you can. Later, you'll be glad you did.' And then she just stood there, smiling at me." Mrs. Sinclair's face lit up as she said this. "She didn't have a book for me to sign. She just left, but not before she turned around and said: 'We're all so proud of you.'"

"Who was it?" I asked her.

"My grandmother."

I squinted at her. "I thought you said she was about your age."

"That's right," she said. "The woman in the bookstore was about my age. But it was my grandmother, I'm sure of it. Months later, I was looking through some old family photos with my mother, and we came upon one of her. She had died before I was born."

"And you're sure you weren't mistaken?"

"She lived, died, and is buried in the very town where I did that reading," Mrs. Sinclair said. "I didn't know that before I met her."

I raised my eyebrows. "Whoa."

"Whoa, indeed. My point is, Julia, there is more to this world than meets the eye. That story isn't any different from any of the others that I've heard from readers for forty-odd years. This is what happens to people. These are people's ghost stories. It's a universal experience. And that means spirits are among us."

"Even here at Havenwood?"

"Especially at Havenwood, darling," she said, rising from her chair and opening her arms wide. "How many years of history have happened within these walls? Births, deaths, betrayals, scandals, marriages, love, hate, even the odd murder or two. Don't be surprised to encounter the odd spirit wafting down the hallways here, Julia. Be surprised when you don't. That means something a bit more sinister is at work."

My stomach cramped. "Sinister?"

She extended a hand to me, which I took, and she pulled me out of my chair.

"That's enough talk of dark things for one day," she said. "I promised to introduce you to the horses. It's time to bundle up, Julia, dear!"

I didn't know quite what to make of this woman, who at once could talk of ghosts roaming the halls of Havenwood and allude to something more dangerous than that, and in the next moment become as giddy as a schoolgirl at the idea of seeing her horses.

As I looked into her dancing green eyes, bright with anticipation of the afternoon to come, I could see the face of Mrs. Sinclair as a much younger woman, the lines around her eyes gone, the droop of her jowls lifted, her skin glowing. And then it faded, the wrinkles returning, the sallowness of her skin taking hold once again.

I stood there squeezing her hands, looking into her now-aged face, and I smiled. This strange and even eccentric lady was beginning to get under my skin. I wanted answers, not just about the horrific fire and Adrian's involvement in it, but about what it meant for me, here, now, at Havenwood. I wanted to know what sorts of specters lurked in these hallways, and why Mrs. Sinclair kept alluding to something darker. I wanted to get another look at that painting—did the woman really resemble me, or was I imagining things in the heat of a terrifying moment? Most of all, I wanted to know what I had really gotten myself into by coming to this house in the first place.

But I wouldn't get any of those answers, not on that day. It was time to find a parka and boots and follow Mrs. Sinclair out to the stables. That was my job. I had promised Adrian I'd look after his mother in his absence, and I intended to keep that promise, and then some. If it were my mother, I'd expect no less. So, if she wanted to go to the stables, we were going to the stables.

As I hurried up to my room to change, I told myself that the mysteries wafting through the hallways at Havenwood would have to wait for another day. I didn't know then that our afternoon in the snow would swirl up even more.

ELEVEN

*T*wenty minutes later, I was waiting for Mrs. Sinclair at the back door leading out of the kitchen toward the greenhouses and stables beyond. I had changed into a pair of jeans, a heavy sweater, and my sturdiest boots. Over that, I put the cozy red parka and mittens I had found in the closet in the foyer earlier in the day.

She burst into the room in full western riding gear—chaps, boots, leather duster, cowboy hat, and all, over a thick woolen sweater and pants. I stifled a grin.

"Oh, come on, darling." She laughed at me. "You didn't think I'd show up with a riding crop and helmet, did you?"

I shook my head and let the grin loose. "You are full of surprises, Mrs. Sinclair."

She pinched my arm as she walked past me. "I wouldn't have it any other way. Now, my dear, it's on to the horses!"

We skimmed through the dusting of new snow down the pathway to the stables. Inside a fenced pasture, I saw a man of about my age tightening a saddle on one of two horses, both a deep shade of auburn with black manes and tails. Something about the scene stopped me in my tracks. As I stood there watching this man, that same sense of déjà vu I had felt earlier wrapped itself around me again. I had seen him before. Stood here before. And yet I knew that was impossible. I was beginning to think I was right about having seen a movie that was filmed at Havenwood—that would explain everything.

"Hello, my boy!" Mrs. Sinclair called out to him. Upon seeing us, he dropped the bridle he was holding. I couldn't see his eyes because he was wearing sunglasses, but somehow I knew he was staring at me. I could feel the force of it on my skin, an intensity that made me shiver.

He shook his head, as if to dismiss whatever he was thinking. He turned to Mrs. Sinclair. "What, may I ask, are you doing?"

This stopped her short. "Whatever do you mean?"

"You're dressed for riding!" he said, putting his hands on his hips.

"How observant of you," Mrs. Sinclair cooed, sliding up to him. "When I mentioned riding to you this morning, you didn't think it would just be you and Julia, did you?"

"I bloody well did," he said, a Scottish accent making music of his words. "Adrian gave me strict orders to keep you off these horses. He said—"

"My son is not here, unless you know something I don't." She smiled, taking the reins of the larger horse. "Hello, my lamb." She nuzzled her face against the horse's great head. "You were planning to ride Sebastian, I take it?"

The man threw up his hands and turned to me. "Is this your doing? You should know full well she's not supposed to be out here."

I didn't quite know what to say. But his sheer frustration in the face of Mrs. Sinclair's amused calm was tickling at my funny bone. She winked at me, a devilish look in her eyes, and I stifled a grin. Mrs. Sinclair laughed out loud.

"Oh, now it's funny, is it?"

Mrs. Sinclair cleared her throat. "Julia, this is Drew. He's our vet, stable hand, and all-around worrywart, who, unfortunately, is making a very poor first impression. I assure you he can be quite charming. At times."

He rubbed his hand clean on his parka and extended it to me. "Welcome to Havenwood."

Even through my mitten I could feel a spark when his hand

touched mine. I drew it away quickly. Before I got a chance to say anything, he turned back to Mrs. Sinclair. "You know that if you insist on going out riding, I'm going with you."

Mrs. Sinclair glanced mischievously me. "I wouldn't have it any other way, my darling. Saddle up Nelly for Julia. I'll take Sebastian today."

Drew disappeared into the stables. Mrs. Sinclair easily swung up into the saddle and I waited for Nelly, hoping she'd give me a more gentle reception than her vet had.

"All right," Drew said to me, emerging from the stable leading a horse. "Do you remember the last time you rode?"

I shrugged, eyeing Nelly. "It's been a long time."

"Not to worry." He smiled at me. "Nelly is as gentle as a kitten, and I'll be right by your side."

He helped me get a foot in one of the stirrups—there was that spark again—and gave me a shove upward. I swung my leg around Nelly's back and sat down as delicately as I could, holding the reins with both hands.

"That's the way!" Mrs. Sinclair sang out to me, as her three enormous dogs bounded out of the stables. "Look, Julia, we'll have an escort party through the woods to town! We won't have to worry about wolves with these girls by our side!" She cackled loudly then, and clucked for her horse to start moving. "On, Sebastian!"

"Now all we have to worry about is keeping up with Barbara Stanwyck there," Drew said under his breath with a chuckle, nodding his head in the direction of Mrs. Sinclair. "Not too fast!" he called out to her as we began to follow along.

I snorted. She did sort of look like Barbara Stanwyck.

"I'm sorry about this," I said to him, trying to keep my balance in the saddle as my horse sidled up beside his. "I didn't know she's not supposed to be riding."

"Adrian would prefer she didn't," he said. "But if you know anything about Amaris Sinclair, you know she's not one who takes direction easily."

I chuckled. "I've only been here for a couple of days, but I have figured that out."

"He's worried she'll fall and hurt herself or worse," Drew said, his eyes on Mrs. Sinclair. "But look at her. Sheer joy. And she's an expert, better than you and me combined. She loves these horses but I can't remember the last time she rode."

With Mrs. Sinclair in the lead and Drew next to me, we fell into an easy rhythm as the horses walked along the river, which was not yet frozen over by the cold temperatures though the trees were dotted with snow. I took in the landscape around me. This was the wilderness, no doubt about it. Not a car or house or telephone pole as far as the eye could see. Only enormous, age-old pine trees, rolling hills, and clean, crisp air. There was an ancientness that was hard for me to define. The trees themselves seemed to be holding secrets within their ramrod-straight trunks, their pine needles swaying gently in the breeze. It seemed as though they were signing a message to us as we passed.

I could see why Andrew McCullough had wanted to build Havenwood on this land.

We crested a ridge and I saw a lake before us—not Lake Superior, which was still some distance away, but an inland lake. Its surface held a thin layer of ice that glinted in the bright sunshine, and its rugged, rocky shoreline was covered with more enormous pine trees. I held my breath as a massive moose appeared from within the forest, broke the ice with its hoof, and lowered its great head, enormous rack and all, to take a drink.

Drew pulled his horse to a stop next to mine. "Ever seen that before?" he whispered, lifting his sunglasses to get a better look.

I just shook my head, watching until the moose had drunk its fill and disappeared back into the pines.

I looked at Drew, my heart beating hard and fast in my chest, and knew my eyes were as wide as saucers. He smiled with the pride that comes from showing the wonders of one's home to a newcomer.

"We have a lot of them up here," he said, clucking for his horse, and mine, to resume walking. "Not as many as in years past, but we still do see them, especially in the winter. It's a great treat, isn't it?"

"This is what it must've looked like here, hundreds of years ago," I mused, knowing I was seeing the land just the way Andrew McCullough had. "Civilization hasn't yet crept in, with its paved roads and telephone poles. This is how the native peoples saw it, back before . . ." I suddenly felt a bit ashamed when I thought of the end of that sentence. Before my ancestors came and destroyed life as the natives knew it.

Drew nodded. "You're exactly right. Not everybody picks up on that. This view hasn't changed much in hundreds of years. It's just as rugged and beautiful and harsh as it was back then."

We rode in silence for a while, listening to the wind whisper to us through the pine needles. I had never heard such a thing before. The world around me was utterly devoid of the sound of civilization—no planes flying overhead, no car noise from any nearby street, no radios blaring, no voices. Just the soft hoofbeats of the horses' feet crunching through the snow, and the whispering pines. It was a wispy, almost human sound that seemed to convey welcome and wisdom and warning.

My body swayed in time with Nelly's gentle gait. I couldn't pinpoint the last time I had ridden a horse and had been nervous about attempting it, but it was almost as though my body remembered what my mind couldn't grasp. The movement felt as natural and calming as breathing in and out.

As we rode, Drew kept turning toward me, as though he wanted to say something.

"What?" I said finally.

"What do you mean, what?"

"You keep looking at me," I said. "I was just wondering why."

He opened his mouth to say something and then closed it again, seemingly fumbling for words. "I was just monitoring how you're doing on Nelly," he eventually said.

I knew that wasn't it, or all of it. But I wasn't going to push it. Everyone at Havenwood seemed to have their quirks, and I supposed this man was no exception. We rode along in silence for a while, until Mrs. Sinclair turned and called out to us. "I'm just going on ahead a few paces, dear ones!"

"Now, listen, lassie," Drew began, but she circled around us and cut him off.

"I'm not the one in this riding party who needs your watchful eye, I'm afraid," she said, winking at me.

"It has been a long time since I last rode, but I think I'm getting the hang of it," I said, holding tight to the horn on the saddle. "I'll be fine."

Her eyes danced. "I know you will, my dear. Nelly won't go faster than a whisper and you seem to have taken to her quite well. The problem is poor Sebastian wants to stretch his legs."

"Why do I have the feeling you set this whole thing up?" Drew said, taking off his sunglasses and squinting at her.

"*Moi?*" She laughed. "Never! I'll take the dogs with me and meet you at the edge of town. Who knows, maybe we'll go wild and get a cappuccino. Or a glass of wine!"

"But—" Drew protested.

"Nonsense. I've got the dogs. If we come upon anything that frightens Sebastian, the girls will take care of it. Right, girls?"

She didn't wait for a response. She was off at a trot, the dogs leading the way. It was quite a sight, Mrs. Sinclair in her cowboy getup, surrounded by a posse of giant malamutes.

I turned to Drew and grinned. "You can't make this stuff up."

He chuckled. "Oh, Julia, just you wait."

"You don't have to babysit me back here, you know," I said, clutching the reins and trying to look more confident than I felt. "If you're worried about her—"

He held up a hand to cut me off. "It's a game we play, she and I," he said, smirking. "I protest, she goes right on ahead and does whatever it is she wants. We both know she will. But I've got to make a good show of it."

As I watched Mrs. Sinclair loping off into the distance, I was beginning to see what he meant.

"Besides, she's a better horsewoman than she is a driver, I'll tell you that."

"A driver?" I asked.

"You do not want to be anywhere in the vicinity when that woman decides she's going to get behind the wheel of a car. Trust me on that."

We lapsed into silence again, broken every once in a while by Drew giving me gentle instruction and pointers. The horses made their way up and down a steep embankment, and we found ourselves in a field of rolling hills. I could see Lake Superior glittering in the distance and a town perched on its edge.

"This is the golf course," Drew said.

This surprised me. "You've got a golf course here?"

"We're not all wilderness, all the time here, lassie. We have refinements. Besides, a Scotsman founded this town. Of course it's going to have a golf course."

I laughed. "Cappuccino, a golf course—what's next, a yoga studio?"

"Wednesday afternoons in the high school gym."

"Okay, so my expectations are duly squashed." I chuckled. "I understood that we were in the middle of nowhere."

" 'Nowhere' is a relative term," he said. "By Chicago standards, it's nowhere. But for me, it's got everything I need."

So, he had been informed I was from Chicago, too. I wondered what else Adrian had told him about me. "And what do you need, apart from cappuccinos, yoga, and golf?"

"In addition to all of this"—he gestured widely at the landscape— "which for me is nearly everything, there are a couple of fantastic restaurants serving local fare that I love, my favorite watering hole in the entire universe, a movie theater with a full bar attached, a grocery store with gourmet selections, and very nice people who are friendly but don't ask too many questions. Some might call what we have a small existence. I call it perfect."

I gazed toward town. "It sounds lovely," I said, meaning it.

Our horses quickened their pace and soon we saw Mrs. Sinclair waiting for us on the crest of the next hill, dogs lying around Sebastian's feet.

"There's the old girl now," he said, his face breaking into a wide grin. "Thank goodness."

I gave him a long look. "She's really lucky to have you," I said. "You care so much about her."

"Of course I do."

"So, where did she find you? I'd ask if you were a local, but your accent betrays you. I don't know of too many northern Minnesotans with Scottish accents. Canadian, yes, but yours, no. What brought you here?"

"I came with the place," he said, looking straight ahead. "I'm Andrew McCullough."

TWELVE

I nearly fell off Nelly when he said that. What could he possibly mean? Before I could ask him to explain himself, Mrs. Sinclair charged toward us on Sebastian at a full-on run. "Goodness me, you two are slowpokes," she said, her horse circling us as she spoke. She was in complete control of the animal and obviously an expert horsewoman.

"Listen, children, I've had an idea. It's the middle of the month and I haven't heard from Tom." She looked at me and explained, "He's my land manager. He handles collecting all the rents in town. We own the town, Julia. I'm not sure if you are aware of that."

I nodded. "Adrian said something about it, yes."

"Anyhoo, I thought, since we're headed toward town, I'd just stop by and pay him a visit. See what's up, so to speak."

Drew's mouth hung open for a moment before he said, "You're going to pay him a visit."

"Yes! Whyever not?"

"No reason," he said slowly, eyeing her. "In town, though? Are you sure you don't want me to ask him to drop by the house?"

"No! We're right here, and I thought I'd save him a trip, and . . ." She looked at Drew and threw her head back and laughed at his expression, which was a mixture of bemusement and downright horror. "Oh, for goodness' sake, boy. Don't get all worked up. My wanting to go into town is not evidence of the apocalypse. We've only got three horses here, not four!" She let out another great laugh. "I'm just going to pay a little visit to an office in town to transact some business."

With that, she was off. "I'll meet you at the Laughing Otter in an hour!" she called over her shoulder. "We'll have cocktails!"

"The Otter is it, now?" Drew said, shaking his head and giving me a look. "For cocktails? I don't quite know what to make of this."

"I'm guessing she doesn't go into town much?" I said, watching her disappear over the horizon, dogs at the horse's heels.

"Very rarely. Almost never. I can't remember the last time." He scowled in the direction of town before calling out: "You're meant to be lying low! You're dead, remember?"

This made me chuckle. Dead, indeed. He turned to me. "Do you think you can make it to town alone?"

I eyed the distance. It wasn't far and on relatively flat ground. "Of course!" I said, not knowing quite where my confidence was coming from. "Nelly and I are old friends by now." I patted the horse's neck and hoped she felt the same.

"I'm after her, then," he said, picking up his pace. "Meet me at the Otter. It's on the main street. Can't miss it." And then he was off, too.

It wasn't until he was out of sight that I began to wonder what I was supposed to do with Nelly when I got to the bar. Or when I got to town, for that matter. I had never ridden a horse through city streets. How would she react to the cars?

But when I got there, I saw it was really no problem at all. Only a couple of cars were parked on the street, and I didn't see any people, either. Adrian had been right: this place really did seem to wind down when summer tourist season was over.

The long main street curved with the Lake Superior shoreline. All the buildings on it faced the lake, and there were several cross streets of just a few blocks in length. None of the buildings was more than two stories tall. I rode on Nelly past a department store, a drugstore, a bookstore, and a smattering of shops. I saw the movie theater on the next block, several small restaurants, and a wilderness outfitter. The courthouse stood on the hill a few blocks away, next to a building I presumed to be the library.

Simple, as Drew said, but delightful all the same. There wasn't a strip mall or a fast-food restaurant in sight. I hadn't been in too many small towns like this, where the main street was still the hub of activity. It was like a slice of life from another time.

I found Drew waiting for me in front of a building with a wall of windows overlooking the lake. The colorfully painted sign of a very happy-looking otter told me this was the place. I jumped down from my saddle as Drew took the reins and tied them to a hitching post on a side street, where three other horses stood, along with a young boy of about fifteen years of age.

"Give them some water, will you, Ben?" Drew asked him, slipping a few bills into the boy's palm. "We'll be about an hour or so."

I stumbled a bit as I followed Drew inside—my legs felt wobbly from hanging on for dear life on the ride—and found the Laughing Otter to be a Northwoodsy place with tongue-in-groove pine-paneled walls decked out with bright paintings of whimsical-looking woodland creatures. Wooden booths with fabric seats in a bright mosaic pattern lined the wall with floor-to-ceiling windows facing the lake. The opposite wall was dominated by a long, wooden bar with rows of interesting microbrews on tap. Several tables stood in between.

Drew unzipped his parka, pulled off his glasses and hat, and took a seat in one of the booths facing the window. As I slid in across from him, a tall man with long blond hair pulled back into a ponytail appeared with a beer in hand.

"The usual for you, I'm assuming," he said, setting the beer down in front of Drew with a smile.

"Scottish ale," Drew said, and took a long sip. "There's nothing finer."

"Unless it's an icy shot of aquavit." The server turned to me and raised his eyebrows. "What can I get you?"

"I'll have a chardonnay, please," I said.

Sitting across from Drew, I got my first good look at him. Curly auburn hair with just a hint of gray dancing throughout it. Bright blue eyes. An easy smile. Something about his face was familiar and yet distant at the same time. And then, as the realization of where I had seen him before washed over me, my entire body began to shake.

"You *are* Andrew McCullough," I said, remembering the painting above the fireplace—those same blue eyes, that same jawline. Put a kilt on him, and he'd be the same man.

He held my gaze, and in that moment, the room seemed to fall away. I no longer saw the paneling or the whimsical artwork; I no longer heard the chatter of other patrons. I only saw a man who had lived forever, a living curse.

Then the server came back to the table with my glass of wine and broke whatever spell had overtaken me. I felt completely foolish for saying what I said, and for even thinking it, as Drew exchanged jokes with the server. Immortal, indeed.

"So," I said tentatively. "You look pretty good for a guy who died more than a century ago."

"It's the cold northern air." His eyes twinkled at me over the rim of his glass.

"So, you're a descendant, I take it?"

He looked at me, silent for a bit longer than it would take most people to respond to a question like that. "Fourth generation," he finally said, twirling his glass on its end. "Havenwood is part of my family's history, and I had heard stories about it my whole life. A proper manor house, just like ours, built in the middle of the American wilderness by a rather eccentric ancestor making his fortune here but longing for home. My grandmother had told me the tale so often, it seemed more like a legend than reality."

"You never visited as a child?"

He shook his head. "No, my family—my grandfather's brother—sold it to Mrs. Sinclair before I was born, but she extended an invitation to us to visit whenever we liked. When I was old enough, I took her up on it. I just had to come and see the place for myself."

"And you stayed." I smiled.

"And I stayed." He smiled back at me. "Havenwood has a way of getting under your skin."

"And so you take care of the horses?" I wanted him to tell me more; I was so enjoying listening to the music of his words and the softness of his voice.

"And the dogs," he said, taking another sip of his beer. "About a week after I arrived, one of the horses went lame. The vet in town wasn't available and Mrs. Sinclair was frantic, so I took a look. I had spent a lot of time as a lad in our own stables at home, learning from our stable hand, who was miraculous with animals. Had a real gift. But Mrs. Sinclair had some clown from the village looking after the horses, and I could see right away that he was useless. The stable was a mess, for one thing." He wrinkled his nose at the memory of it. "I spent an afternoon cleaning and organizing, brushing the horses and filling their water troughs. Mrs. Sinclair was very keen on having me stay on after she saw what I had done."

"She offered you a job?"

"She did indeed. I knew my mother wouldn't be too thrilled about the McCullough heir being a stable hand, but somehow that didn't matter to me. I had already fallen in love with the place, and working with the horses was so natural, it felt like breathing. It was like Mrs. Sinclair had found my true calling, here, so far away from my home."

"If it's working with the horses that you love," I said, "why not just do that back home in Scotland? Why stay here?"

"Oh, it's not only the horses," he said, downing the last of his beer. "I'm invested in Havenwood. This place goes to me when she passes on."

I coughed on my sip of wine. "You? Not Adrian?"

"It was more like a long-term rental arrangement than an out-and-out sale. If Amaris Sinclair owned it for a while, fine. But it had to revert to family after she died. That's something the first Andrew McCullough made very clear."

I blinked a few times and looked at him. "What do you mean, family?"

"Family," he repeated. "The McCulloughs."

"But she is family," I said. "She told me so."

"Oh, did she now?" Drew said, amused.

"She did! She told me she was first here as a little girl, and a cousin owned it. When he came into financial difficulties, she was a successful novelist and able to buy it to help him out. She said she's always loved Havenwood."

"Well, I suppose that's true." He smiled. "Her mother's sister married one of my great-uncles, or some such thing. She's on an outer limb of the family tree, you might say. Not related to us by blood, in any case."

"So Havenwood will be yours one day," I said. "Forgive me for asking, but how does Adrian feel about that?"

At the mention of Adrian's name, a vision of flames shot before my eyes and extinguished just as quickly. I toyed with the idea of bringing up the fire to Drew, but thought better of it. If I was supposed to be starting a new life as another person, I might as well begin with him, I reasoned. I had no desire to tell him who I really was, even if he might have some insight to share about the fire. No, I'd keep quiet about that for now.

The server appeared with another round of drinks and Drew took a sip as he considered this.

"I've never asked him. He's always known about it, so he's under no illusions. When she does pass away—and I pray it's a good many years from now—I don't think anything much will change at Havenwood, other than it'll be emptier without her. I'll go on as I have been, Adrian will go on as he has been, Marion and the rest of the staff will go on as they have been. Nothing much ever really changes there."

Something about the way he said that sent a chill up my spine. Lightening the mood, I said, "So you're not going to kick everyone out and turn it into a nudist colony, then?"

He laughed. "That hadn't crossed my mind. But now that you mention it . . ."

"Of course, that would extend to the town as well"—I looked around the bar—"but somehow, I don't think these folks would mind."

"I've got big plans for the town, once it's mine." He smiled. "I'm planning to change the name to Drewville, where there will be free drinks for ladies on Wednesday nights, no beets sold anywhere in the city limits, and cell phone use in public will result in immediate death."

"I think you should outlaw rude people as well. And the truly nasty ones should be exiled."

"We'd make a fine pair of rulers, you and I." He chuckled. "We can joke about it, but it's really not like that, you know. It's more of a rental situation, in the name of the estate. Havenwood, for all intents and purposes, is the town's landlord."

"All the merchants pay rent to Havenwood?" I asked. "What about the homeowners?"

"Merchants, yes, homeowners, no," he explained. "Mrs. Sinclair terminated that contract a long time ago at great personal expense. She didn't want any homeowner beholden to her. Gave them their land. The merchants, that's another matter. They're doing business, a great deal of business during tourist season, and they can well afford to pay the rent she charges."

I took a sip of the oaky wine and lowered my voice further. "Does anybody know who she is? I mean, Adrian told me she dropped out of sight and . . ." I paused for a minute. "The whole world thinks she's dead."

He nodded. "Indeed. If any people here know who she is, they don't say. I think it's part of the arrangement she has with the town—they don't ask, she doesn't tell. But the thing is, Julia, she never shows her face here. Well, let me think," he backpedaled a bit. "Not never. But rarely. I've seen her in town rarely. And now she's running off to Tom's office like it was nothing. And in that getup, yet!"

"As though that won't call attention to her." I tried to stifle a giggle.

He grinned. "What do you think old Tom will do when she shows up in his office, dressed like that? Call the paramedics?"

"For her or for him?"

We laughed together about that for a bit, and I marveled at how easy it was to talk to this man. It was like we had known each other forever.

"Do you know why she did it?" I asked.

"Did what? Dressed like Barbara Stanwyck and paraded through town like a lunatic?"

"No. Dropped out of sight in the first place. Stopped writing. Let the world think she was dead."

A cloud passed over Drew's face and he folded his hands on the table. "That's something you're going to have to ask her."

"I did. She changed the subject."

"How about those Vikings?"

"Very funny," I said. "Do you know and just won't, or can't, tell me?"

He shook his head. "Whatever it was happened a long time ago. Because of it, she said she'd never take pen to paper again."

I sighed and shook my head. "It's truly bizarre."

He nodded. "One of a myriad of bizarre things swirling around Havenwood."

*D*rew and I were still on our second round of drinks when Mrs. Sinclair breezed through the door. At the sight of her, all heads turned, all conversation stopped. She didn't seem to notice as she slipped into the booth alongside Drew and pinched his cheek.

"Hello, poodles!" she said, beaming at us. "You should have seen Tom's face when I materialized in his office! You'd think he had seen a ghost!"

Drew caught my eye and grinned before quickly looking away. "I'll bet. Did you have to call the paramedics for him, then? I didn't hear any sirens."

"Oh, you." She dismissed his joke with a wave of her hand as the server appeared at the table, slightly unnerved by the sight of her.

"Can I get you something, ma'am?"

"Oh, my goodness, yes," Mrs. Sinclair said. "But what? Do you have any mulled wine?"

Drew couldn't suppress a snort. "Did you just step out of a Victorian English Christmas, then? Mulled wine?"

Mrs. Sinclair scowled at him. "I thought it would be nice on such a cold day."

The server tried to suppress a grin. "No mulled wine, I'm afraid. But we do have wine."

"That sounds wonderful." Mrs. Sinclair smiled broadly at him. "I'll have what Julia is having."

When he had gone, she looked around the bar. "What an adorable place!" she said. "I'll have to come here more often!"

"Who are you?" Drew asked her. "And what have you done with Amaris Sinclair?"

"You're quite the comedian today, Mr. McCullough." She squinted at him. "But the fact is I do feel as though I have a new lease on life lately. Julia brought a fresh perspective with her when she came to us."

Drew looked at me and furrowed his brow, and then looked back at her. "Whatever you say," he said, and lifted his glass. "To new leases."

THIRTEEN

$\mathcal{B}$ack at the house, I had just enough time to clean up before dinner, the first formal one since I had arrived.

Marion had instructed me to be in the drawing room by six thirty. Mrs. Sinclair and I would have drinks by the fire before adjourning into the dining room for dinner at seven. And I was to *dress* for dinner tonight, Marion had sniffed, eyeing my jeans and turtleneck.

As I was showering and getting ready, I thought of what a delightful distraction the day had been, especially after my rather unsettling night and my discovery of the east salon. Riding on horseback through the pristine wilderness with the cold air nipping at my cheeks, seeing the town, and chatting with the great Amaris Sinclair. It all worked together to lighten my mood and lift my spirits, and made me forget about the fire and my troubling "side effects" for a while.

All of it got me thinking. Maybe I would start to write again. After all, I'd have hours of free time during the days when I wasn't with Mrs. Sinclair. I didn't have my computer, of course, and didn't have much hope of finding one here—I hadn't noticed anything more modern than an old rotary telephone at Havenwood—but there had to be pen and paper around the house somewhere. Or maybe a typewriter! I could start by simply jotting down notes and ideas, and see where they led.

And then a thought hit me. Just hours earlier, I had been wondering about my own safety here at Havenwood, coloring Adrian and even Mrs. Sinclair in very dark hues. And here I was now, busily planning how I'd spend my days at Havenwood for the foreseeable future. I realized that the fact of my house in Chicago burning to the ground seemed very small and far away. Like it existed in another world and didn't matter in the least.

All I knew was that I was getting ready for a formal dinner in the grandest home I had ever seen. This was my world now.

I slipped into an ankle-length jersey knit dress in deep purple that I had bought the year before, grateful that I had thought to bring it, and found a pair of black flats in my suitcase. I wound a colorful scarf around my neck, put on a dash of lipstick, and took a last look in the mirror. I wasn't exactly the lady of the manor—the dress was much too casual—but it would have to do.

I made it to the drawing room, which I found just off the formal living room, without taking too many wrong turns and discovered a blazing fire in the fireplace, candles flickering everywhere, and Drew sitting in a leather armchair by the fire. He stood when I entered the room.

"Hello." I smiled, rather surprised to see him. I didn't know he was going to be joining us, but apparently that was part of the plan.

"Don't you look lovely," he said.

I could feel myself blushing, and was grateful for the darkness in the room. "You clean up quite nicely as well!" I said, eyeing his dark suit and tie. "But what kind of Scotsman are you? No kilt?"

"I save that for Sundays and holidays." He smiled and I noticed how his combed-back hair was curling around the collar of his shirt. As he moved to the bar to pour us both some drinks, I was thinking about how handsome he was. But then I shook my head and put it out of my mind. My husband had been gone only a few months. Whether our marriage had been a sham or not, I had no business finding this man, or any man, attractive. Not now. Not yet.

"What's your pleasure?" he asked me, bringing another blush to my cheeks. "We've got just about anything."

I moved closer to the bar and saw several crystal decanters and mixers of all kinds. "Wow, they certainly like their liquor, don't they?"

"It's a tradition, like everything else here at Havenwood. Drinks before dinner, wine with dinner, cognac or Scotch after dinner. That's just how it's always been done. Livers be damned. Gin and tonic for you?"

"Make it a weak one," I said, grateful to see him pouring much more tonic than gin. "I'm not used to drinking this much."

"Luckily, you don't have to drive home." He grinned and handed the drink to me.

"That is lucky. But finding my way back up to my room after a few of these might be a little challenging, though."

I followed him back to the armchairs by the fire and we both sunk into them.

"So, it's formal dinner here most every night, then, unless Mrs. Sinclair doesn't feel up to it?" I asked, remembering the lonely dinner in my room the night before.

He shook his head. "Oh no. Once or twice a week at most. And some Sunday afternoons. But Sunday isn't formal, the way this is. It's more of an all-afternoon affair of movies and games in the entertainment wing and constant nibbling throughout the day."

"It sounds like fun," I said, wondering where the entertainment wing might be.

"Marion will let you know when we're expected and when we're not," he explained. "It's at Mrs. Sinclair's whim. Whatever she feels like doing."

"Hello, darlings!" It was the lady herself, floating into the room dressed in a green-and-indigo gown embroidered with a pattern of peacock feathers. "I see you've already got your drinks. Splendid!"

Drew and I both stood up—I wasn't sure of the protocol, so I followed his lead—and he made his way back over to the bar. "Dubonnet cocktail for you?"

"That sounds lovely, dear. With a lemon, if you don't mind."

When she had her cocktail in hand, she raised her glass. "To Julia," she said. "We are so delighted that you have come to our wonderland."

As I took a sip of my drink, I mused about her choice of words, wondering just how much like Alice I really was.

Over a dinner of beef Wellington, red potatoes, and a crisp salad—I had scarcely eaten anything more than a Lean Cuisine for dinner in months, and the food awakened taste buds that I forgot I had—we talked of the day's events.

"I thought you did remarkably well on Nelly today, Julia," Mrs. Sinclair said, raising her eyebrows. "I see the makings of a horsewoman in you."

I took a bite of the beef's flaky crust and considered this. "You know, I really had fun," I said finally. "There's just something about being on a horse that feels, I don't know, natural."

Mrs. Sinclair and Drew exchanged sly smiles. "I knew you'd love it, once you tried it," she said. She nodded her head to Drew.

"The Otter was nice," I said.

"That's the first time I've been in the place!" Mrs. Sinclair said, beaming. "I'll have to go back again. It was quite a treat."

Drew caught my eye and furrowed his brow, shaking his head slightly. "You are certainly full of surprises, Amaris Sinclair," he said.

"I wouldn't have it any other way," she said, winking at me.

Conversation turned to other things, then—the dogs, whether it was going to snow again this week, when Adrian was returning home—until we heard the clatter of a pan dropping in the kitchen, just beyond the dining room's doors.

"Who's there?" It was Marion's voice, high and shrill. "What do you want?"

Drew was out of his chair like a shot, with Mrs. Sinclair and me close behind. He burst through the dining room doors, through the butler's pantry, and into the kitchen, where we found Marion standing at the open back door, looking out into the darkness, holding a rolling pin high above her head.

"What's happened, Marion?" Drew asked her, gently taking the rolling pin from her hand.

"A face!" she said, breathless. "I was getting the pudding out of the oven when I looked over to the window—I don't know why I did that, but I did—and saw a face. I think it was a man. Outside."

"Good Lord," Mrs. Sinclair said. "Are you sure?"

"I'm sure," Marion affirmed. "I'm not seeing things. Not yet, anyway."

Drew turned on the outside light, illuminating the snow around the house. He and I looked out the door together, and sure enough, there were footprints just under the kitchen window.

"Bloody hell," he said under his breath. "What's this now?"

I turned to Marion. "Is there a flashlight here in the kitchen?"

She crossed the room to a cupboard, opened it, and produced one, handing it to me. I turned it on and shined it out the door, following the footsteps from the kitchen window out to the forest beyond. A quick check of the pristine snow in either direction told me whoever it was hadn't gone any other way, before or after Marion had confronted him. The tracks went from the forest, to the kitchen window, and back again the way he had come.

"Well, he's gone now," I said, my stomach clenching into a tight knot. Was it one of Jeremy's victims, someone who had followed me here? I didn't even want to think of that possibility. My old life seemed so long ago and far away, and the thought of someone tracking me all the way to Havenwood gave me a chill.

"I'm going to see if I can catch him," Drew said, closing the door. "He can't have gotten far."

"Do you think that's wise?" Mrs. Sinclair said, her hand touching her throat. "He might be armed. Or worse."

I didn't know what "or worse" meant, but thought best not to ask.

She turned around in a circle. "Where are the dogs?"

"In the stable with the horses," Drew said. "I gave them all their dinner before changing for our own."

"I think it's clear they should come into the house. Immediately. Drew, will you fetch them? And if they go off into the woods—"

"I'll go after them, don't worry."

He didn't bother to put on a coat; instead he simply walked out of the kitchen door and disappeared into the dark night.

Mrs. Sinclair turned to me and exhaled. "Now that that's handled, Julia, let's take our dessert and nightcap in the drawing room. Marion?"

"I'll be right behind you, ma'am."

I wondered if I should help Drew track whoever it was that had been looking into our windows, but the finality of Mrs. Sinclair's statement led me to do as I was told. I followed her into the drawing room, looking out the window over my shoulder all the while.

Later, after Mrs. Sinclair and I had finished our bread pudding, Drew came back inside, flushed with the cold, dogs at his heels. He sunk into a chair next to the fire as the dogs took a few laps around the room before curling up on the Oriental rug beside him.

"They followed the scent into the woods," he said. "I didn't think we should go farther, not in the dark."

"Goodness, no." Mrs. Sinclair sighed. "Not in those woods." She rose from her chair and crossed the room to the bar, where she poured two cognacs. "Nightcaps?"

She handed one to me and one to Drew. "It's unsettling, darlings, but undoubtedly, this is somebody who saw me in the village today and was curious. We get that here from time to time."

Drew caught my eye and shook his head, so slightly it was almost imperceptible. I got the distinct feeling they *didn't* get this from time to time.

"And now, it's about time for this old bat to retire." She smiled at us. "We've had quite a day, children. I enjoyed it more than you know."

I stood up and took her hands into mine. "It was a wonderful day, Mrs. Sinclair," I said. "Thank you. I had more fun today than I've had in months. I can't remember the last time I laughed."

"That was the idea, Julia, darling." She kissed me on the cheek, turned, and joined Marion, who was standing in the doorway. "Home, James," she said, extending her arm. Marion took it, and the two of them walked out of the room and into the darkness of the hallway.

Drew and I sat in silence for a few moments before he spoke.

"I didn't want to say it to Mrs. Sinclair, but the footprints looked like they were headed back toward the village," Drew said.

"Somebody followed us from town, then?"

"It looks that way, yes."

"Why would he do that?" I asked him.

"I have no idea," he said.

We both settled back down into the armchairs by the fire, talking about everything and nothing. We drank our cognacs, and then things began to get a little hazy around the edges. I do remember feeling quite drunk all of a sudden, and realizing I had better get back upstairs sooner rather than later.

The room began to spin. "Oh," I said, putting a hand to my forehead. It was odd: a couple of cognacs usually didn't have that dramatic of an effect on me, but this time they did. "I think I should call it a night."

I pushed myself out of my chair and stood next to it for a moment, getting my bearings.

"Are you okay?" Drew asked.

"I'm fine. All I need is some water, a couple of aspirin, and my bed."

I walked a few hesitant steps and then turned around, putting a hand on the archway into the hall for support. "Thank you for a lovely day," I said to him, slurring my words ever so slightly. "I loved Nelly, I loved the town, I loved the whole thing."

"Sleep well, Julia." He smiled. "We're all very glad you're here with us."

Walking through the dark hallways of the house, illuminated here and there with the soft glow of a wall sconce, I began to feel as though I were in a strange and magical labyrinth. Rooms seemed to fold in on one another, circling back around so that they were in front of me once again. Every hallway I went down seemed to lead to the same place, leaving me back where I had started.

And then I heard something. I stopped walking to listen closer. Music? It was so soft and faint, it sounded like it was coming from another world. I followed the sound down the hallway. It seemed to be coming from a certain room with an arched entrance, so I poked my head inside. I saw a harpsichord in one corner and a cello propped next to a chair in the other. Between them, yet another enormous fireplace. I took a few hesitant steps inside and looked around.

Portraits of musicians with their instruments hung on the walls. Over the fireplace, I saw a large painting depicting an evening of chamber music—wealthy people congregating after dinner, drinks in hand, dressed in their fineries. A woman sat at a harpsichord, a man at her side with a cello. I gasped when I realized it was a painting of an event in the very room where I stood. This was the music room.

As I stared at the painting, it was almost as if the image on the canvas transformed from oils and brushstrokes into flesh and blood, and I could see the scene in the painting come to life, there in the room around me, the people wispy and transparent, like holograms. Or ghosts.

I could hear the crinkling of the fabrics as the ladies, dressed in taffeta and silks, floated past me. Their laughter and chatter filled the air, first distant and low, and then louder. I heard the clinking of wineglasses as someone made a toast to the musicians. And then a hush fell as the audience took their seats and the first strains of music wafted through the air.

I stood there, caught up in the moment, when suddenly, all heads turned—toward me! I saw their faces, eyes wide, mouths agape at the sight of me. I heard gasps as the image of their party faded back into the painting, as quickly as it had come.

I backed out of the room and started down the hallway, slowly at first, shaking my head, trying to make sense of what had just happened. Then a chill ran through me and I picked up speed. Was it the alcohol, or my lack of medication producing these strange sights? Or was it something else? Whatever it was, I made a mental note to ask Adrian about refilling my prescription.

I finally found my way to the grand staircase—how, I don't know—and ascended slowly, holding on to the handrail for support as reality seemed to spin around me.

As I made my way up, stair by stair, the portraits hanging on the walls seemed to flicker and sway with life, whispering to me as I went. I could hear them, louder and louder, hissing and moaning all around me. I hurried my pace and was nearly at the top of the stairs, when I tripped on the hem of my dress, hitting the ground with a thud. I heard laughter and jeers, voices taunting me, and I curled into a ball, there on the floor, hands over my ears, trying to make it all go away.

That was when I felt a pair of strong hands grasping my arms. "You're all right," he said. "I'm here now, don't worry."

At first I didn't know who it was, but in the darkness, I could make out Drew's face. I let him pull me up, and leaned against the wall. We stood there for a while, looking at each other in that dark hallway.

"My God," he whispered. "You're so beautiful." And then his arms were around my waist and his lips were on mine, kissing me with such force that I thought he was going to engulf me. I put my hands around his neck and pulled him even closer into me, closing my eyes.

"Andrew," I whispered into his ear.

But then I felt the most horrible emptiness and I realized I was alone. I opened my eyes and looked up and down the hallway—nobody was there. Where had he gone?

I took a deep breath in. Had it even happened? There's no way he would have simply left me lying there. Had I passed out and been asleep on the stairway? Had I dreamed the whole thing? I wondered how much time had passed. I didn't feel drunk any longer, or even dizzy. Had I been lying there for hours?

I hurried to my room and shut the door behind me, grateful for the fire that Marion had laid in my fireplace and for the pitcher of water she had left on my nightstand. I poured a glass and drank it down quickly. My gaze settled on my windows and I thought of whoever might be lurking out there in the woods. I drew the curtains closed to block out the night, shivering to my core.

After washing my face and peeling off my dress, I slipped under the covers and watched the fire crackling in the fireplace, all the mysteries of Havenwood dancing in my mind.

FOURTEEN

$\mathcal{M}$y dreams that night were strange and jumbled, a funhouse of distorted images. Jeremy. Me, falling asleep in my dorm room in college, surrounded by a roomful of friends whom I had long since lost touch with. The dog of my childhood, running in the backyard of the house where I grew up.

I was awakened by the sound of a telephone ringing. I sat up and shook my head, the dreams still at the edge of my consciousness. Was that a phone I heard? I listened closer. Yes, it was, coming from another room, perhaps next door.

I gazed around. The fire had died down, the last embers glowing. I poured a glass of water and took a drink before slipping out of bed and moving across the room to the windows. I pushed the curtain aside and looked out. The night was still deeply dark. No hint of man-made light whatsoever. I watched as northern lights blazed across the sky.

And there was that phone again. I wondered why Marion wasn't answering it. Well, I sighed, it had nothing to do with me. I hadn't gotten a phone call in the months prior to coming to Haven-wood, and certainly nobody would be calling me now. I climbed back into bed, drew the covers around me, and closed my eyes. I had a few more hours to go before morning and desperately wanted to sleep.

But the ringing just wouldn't stop. I rolled this way and that, trying to muffle the sound, to no avail. I didn't have a phone in my room—where was this noise coming from? And then I remembered the study down the hall where I had tried to call Adrian. The old-fashioned black phone with the heavy handset. That had to be it. It didn't seem possible I'd hear it ring all the way down the hall in my room, but sounds do tend to carry in old houses, especially at night when everything else is silent. That was what I told myself, anyway.

I threw the covers aside and grabbed my robe. The only way I'd get back to sleep was to find that phone and answer it, or at least take it off the receiver to stop that infernal racket.

I opened my door and walked down the dark hallway, turning this way and that before reaching the wing where the study was located. Sure enough, the door to the study was ajar, and I could see light coming from the room. I marched toward it, wondering who on earth was calling at this hour and letting the phone ring and ring and ring. I intended to give whomever it was a lecture about disturbing an entire household in the middle of the night.

I reached the study and pushed open the door. I didn't see a lamp or a ceiling light, and yet the phone, and the desk it was sitting on, was bathed in a soft glow. No matter, I thought. It was just one more strange thing happening at Havenwood. I was starting to get used to it. I stared at the phone, which was still ringing, but a knot in the pit of my stomach was telling me that I shouldn't answer that call. Who on earth could it be, in the middle of the night? I almost turned and left the room, I almost went back to my bed, but then I thought: What if it's Adrian? So I picked up the heavy black handset and put it to my ear.

"Hello?" I said.

"Julia? Is that you?"

I recognized the voice. But it couldn't be. It just couldn't. What sort of magic was this? I wanted to drop the phone and run from the room, but I was frozen in place, unable to move, unable to take the handset away from my ear.

"Julia!" the voice repeated. "Are you there?"

"Jeremy?" I croaked out.

"Yes, it's me. Listen, I don't have much time."

"But how?" I said. "Did you—are you . . . ?"

This was my husband . . . who was supposedly dead. My first thought was he must have faked his own death to escape prosecution. Obviously he had, the crafty devil. How had he done it? And how had he found me? Had he somehow followed me here to Havenwood?

But then a more disturbing thought occurred to me. Had he put Adrian up to the whole thing, the arson included? It was all too convenient—we were both "dead," as far as the rest of the world knew. Did he now think we were going to run away together with his ill-gotten millions?

"Were you the man outside the kitchen window tonight? Have you come here for me, Jeremy?"

But as I said the words, I knew he wasn't, and hadn't. A chill enveloped me as I remembered the scene in our basement just a few months before. I was the one who had found his body. His blood had been spattered all over the room. The top of his head was gone. Jeremy was dead; there was no question about it.

"No, I wasn't there tonight."

"Jeremy . . . ?"

"Don't freak out, Julia," he said, his voice urgent and stern. "I can tell you're freaking out. You need to focus. I told you, I don't have much time. You need to listen to me. Are you listening, Julia?"

"I'm listening," I whispered, my voice shredded by the terror that was overtaking my body.

"Get out of there."

"What?"

"I'm calling to warn you, Julia, and believe me, this is not allowed."

"Why did you do it, Jeremy?"

I heard him sigh. "None of that matters right now. What matters is your safety. And you're not safe there, Julia. You have no idea what you've gotten yourself into, but believe me, you need to get out of there. You are in danger. They had no right to bring you there. No right at all."

I couldn't process what he was saying.

"How can you be talking to me?" I said, shaking my head. "You're dead."

"As it turns out, that's not as final as it seems," he said. "But now I have to go. I don't know if I can contact you again."

I opened my eyes with a start. My pillow was wet with perspiration and the sheets were tangled around my legs. I took a few deep breaths to get my bearings and looked around the room, where I saw light peeking from the edges of my curtains.

I disengaged myself from my sheets and sat up to pour myself a glass of water with shaking hands. It was just a bad dream.

FIFTEEN

*B*ut why should I dream such a thing? Perhaps the jarring news of the fire, combined with finding the painting of the woman who resembled me, combined with my strange experiences and the sheer volume of alcohol I had drunk the night before . . . surely it all worked together to create this oddly detailed dream. A product of my overactive imagination.

But as I stood in the shower, I couldn't wash away the feeling that it was something else. A myriad of questions with no answers swirled through my mind. The dream felt so familiar, so true to life. Was it truly a warning? I shuddered to think of it.

Was I in danger here? I thought of the footprints in the snow outside the kitchen door the night before, and felt a tendril of dread slither around my insides. Maybe that was what the dream was warning me about.

I intended to ask Mrs. Sinclair about all of it at breakfast, but I didn't get a chance to do so, not that morning. As I was about to enter the breakfast room, Marion let me know that Mrs. Sinclair was up in bed with a migraine. I didn't doubt it, considering the amount of alcohol she had consumed the day before. My own head felt more than a little fuzzy and I was looking quite forward to my first cup of coffee. And maybe I could get a peek at the morning paper as well for an update about my house fire.

I pushed open the door to the breakfast room and was surprised to find Adrian at the table drinking a cup of coffee of his own. I wouldn't need the newspaper to give me an update after all.

"Good morning, my dear," he said, smiling. "You must tell me everything about your first days here at Havenwood. I want to hear it all. How did it go with my mother?"

"I saw the newspaper report about the fire."

"Ah, yes," he said, as Marion came into the room carrying a tray. We were both quiet as she served us each an omelet—spinach, goat cheese, and onion, along with broiled tomatoes and a basketful of warm croissants, just out of the oven. *If I am in danger here at Havenwood, at least they are feeding me well,* I thought.

"Well?" I pressed, my voice still low. "I saw your picture, Adrian. You were there when my house burned down."

He shook his head. "A fortuitous development, to be sure," he said, taking a bite of his omelet and chewing thoughtfully.

"What does that mean? Fortuitous development. I hate to ask you this but I *have* to ask it. Did you set that fire?"

"What if I had?"

I nearly choked on my croissant. "Well—" I coughed, not knowing quite how to respond to that. What *if* he had? I had no desire to return to the place, and as he had said to me the day we met, this was my opportunity to drop out of sight. My house burning down was the perfect escape.

I just looked at him.

"The answer is no, I didn't set the fire," he said, taking another bite of his omelet. "But as I said, it is fortuitous for you."

Adrian reached across the table and took my hand in his. "You look terrified, Julia. No, I didn't burn down your house. But yes, I do have some . . . pull, shall we say, with the media and certain factions in Chicago. That's why I went to the scene when I heard about the fire. I recognized it as an opportunity. The press will report, and the world will believe, you died in that fire. It's best not to ask how."

A pang of sadness coursed through me as I thought of all of my friends who would now be grieving for me. But then I realized I had been dead to them for months. They might feel a little bad for how they had treated me, but would anybody *really* grieve my passing? Maybe they'd believe both Jeremy and I got what we deserved. It made my stomach seize up.

Adrian took a sip of his coffee. "Isn't this omelet delicious? I've eaten in the finest restaurants all over the world and nothing compares to Marion's cooking here at Havenwood."

I knew he was trying to change the subject, but I just couldn't let it go. "But if someone deliberately set it—"

"Julia, it's best not to get too worked up about this. Please, just let me handle it."

I sat back in my chair and realized I was shaking on the inside. I took a sip of coffee and buttered my croissant with trembling hands, trying to breathe deeply. "Okay. I'm not worked up."

But I was. It seemed like my sight was closing in on me, that the edges of the world were turning black. I shook my head, wondering what kind of strange world I had gotten myself into by coming to Havenwood. I thought of Jeremy's warning.

Adrian went on. "Before you paint me the villain, Julia, you need to realize something."

"What's that?"

Now it was his turn to lower his voice. He leaned in toward me before he spoke. "Someone deliberately set that fire. I don't want to alarm you, but I think that means only one thing."

"What's that?"

"Vengeance. Somebody was trying to kill you."

My mind was swimming. If what he was saying was true, and if Adrian hadn't appeared on my doorstep that day—just days ago!—I might very well have died in that fire.

Last night's footprints in the snow flashed in front of my eyes and I began to get a very sick feeling in the pit of my stomach.

"Adrian," I began, "do you believe it's possible that the person who set the fire in my house could have tracked me here to Havenwood?"

"Certainly not," he said. "I'm not in the habit of leaving a trail of bread crumbs for someone to follow. I have a man on it, in Chicago, looking for the arsonist. He'll get to the bottom of it. But you must believe, Julia, you're perfectly safe here."

"I'm not so sure about that," I told him. "There's something you need to know. Last night after dinner, Marion was in the kitchen and saw someone standing outside the window, looking in."

At this, Adrian put down his fork. "Who was it?"

"I don't know," I said. "We heard screaming and ran into the kitchen just in time to see Marion brandishing a rolling pin and yelling at whoever it was out the kitchen door."

Adrian tried to suppress a chuckle. "A rolling pin?"

"She was fierce enough with that thing to scare whoever it was away." I smiled. "Drew followed his footprints into the forest."

At the mention of Drew's name, my stomach began to churn, thinking of my dream, or vision, or whatever it was on the stairs, the night before. I tried to shake the thought of it from my mind. And then it hit me. That was why I dreamed of Jeremy. Guilt. I had felt a strange attraction to a man I barely knew within months of my husband's death, and I manifested said husband in my dreams to let me know how wrong that was. I made a silent pledge to keep my distance from Drew.

"He didn't find anyone?" Adrian asked, pulling me back into the room from where my thoughts were taking me.

"No one," I said.

Adrian considered this as he finished his omelet. "It might be wise for him to take the dogs and track those footprints in the light of day." He took a sip of coffee. "I'll wager that's what he's planning to do. Sometimes we get curious onlookers here at Havenwood. People from the village, tourists, anyone who has heard about this house and wants to see it for themselves."

"We were in the village yesterday," I told him. "Your mother, too."

"Mother?" His eyes grew wide. "She went into town?"

"She did," I admitted, careful not to let on the manner in which she got there. "She needed to see her rental manager. Tom, I believe, is his name? Drew and I went along and met her at the Laughing Otter afterward for a drink."

Adrian smiled broadly and shook his head. "I can't believe it. You're here just a few days and you're already coaxing Mother out of her shell. I knew you were right for this job, Julia. You belong here at Havenwood."

"We had a wonderful day," I said. I couldn't help but smile at the thought of it.

"Well, that's it, then. Mother went into town, someone thought they recognized her and was curious enough to follow you all here."

"That could be what was," I said, but I wasn't so sure.

"I can see exactly what you're thinking," Adrian said, rubbing his chin and holding my gaze. "I'm thinking the same thing."

"Trip to town or not, you're thinking the timing is pretty suspicious—my house burning down and now this."

"Indeed," he said, resting his napkin on his plate and pushing his chair away from the table. "I have several calls to make. I want an update on this situation from my people in Chicago. Would you be so kind as to seek out Drew and ask him to take the dogs and track those footprints in the meantime? He's likely in the stables."

So much for keeping my distance. "Won't your mother need me this morning?"

He shook his head. "I'm going up to check on her now. She's got a 'migraine,' which means she's tired out and wants some solitude. And no wonder, you had quite the day yesterday. A trip to town, an unannounced visitor."

"And a bit of alcohol last night, I'm afraid," I confessed.

He laughed. "That's the way of formal dinners at Havenwood. Did she have her Dubonnet cocktail?"

"Several."

"Right, then. You go find Drew, I'll bring a bottle of aspirin to Mother and give her a lecture about the evils of alcohol, and then I'll be busy in my office the rest of the day. Consider yourself off the clock, so to speak, until dinner. I'm sure the old gal will have perked up by then."

"The drawing room at six thirty?"

"You already know the drill. Excellent, Julia, excellent!" He extended his arm to me and we left the breakfast room together. We parted ways at the grand staircase.

"Please don't let this worry you," he said to me. "No harm will come to you at Havenwood, of that you have my promise."

I shook my head. "I'm more worried I'm bringing harm to all of you," I said. "If it really is the arsonist . . ."

"Nonsense. We will catch whoever it was at the window last night. And he will tell us what we need to know. It's as simple as that."

"You sound very sure."

He grinned. "The dogs will track whoever it was. And when they find him, well, there's just something about being surrounded by three growling giant malamutes that makes a man feel like talking."

I got the distinct feeling he'd had experience with that before.

He started making his way up the stairs when I remembered something.

"Oh!" I said. "I nearly forgot. Do you have a doctor on staff?"

He turned and trotted down the few steps he had ascended. "Are you not feeling well?"

"No, it's nothing like that. Not really. It's just—" I didn't quite know how to say what I had to say. "It's just that I'm out of the medication that I've been taking for some time now, and it occurs to me that I can't just ring up the pharmacy for a refill."

"Of course," he said, drawing out his words. "I can ask my personal physician about it, but I'm not sure he'll be willing to write a prescription for someone who isn't his patient. He could come here to Havenwood to see you, of course, but I happen to know he's in the Caribbean now. Minnesota winters don't agree with him. Is it crucial to your health? Blood pressure pills, for instance?"

I shook my head. "No, it's . . ." My words trailed off as I tried to remember exactly what the pills were for. I had been taking them for so long, it was just a habit. "They stabilize my mood. Antidepression pills, I guess you'd call them."

He frowned at me. "Is it something you truly need? Doctors tend to overprescribe, in my experience."

"I'm not sure," I admitted. "I've been off them for a couple of days now."

"Any ill effects?"

I wasn't about to tell him about the strange experiences I'd been having. The last thing he'd want was a companion for his mother who was seeing things. "Not anything too bad so far," I said weakly. "Headaches, mostly."

He patted my arm. "Good. You monitor the situation and I'll make an inquiry about getting you a refill. But maybe you don't need them at all."

Adrian jogged back up the stairs while I went in search of the parka and boots I had worn the day before. I'd need them if I was going to follow those tracks into the woods.

SIXTEEN

I crunched my way through the snow toward the stable, my breath hanging in the air like mist. It was colder than it had been the day before, and I could feel the icy tingle of chill on my cheeks.

My stomach did a quick flip when I saw Drew in the field with a horse. He saw me, waved, and began walking toward me.

"And how are we this fine morning?" he said, grinning.

"We are a touch the worse for wear," I conceded. "No cognac after dinner tonight, definitely."

"Tonight again, we're to have a formal dinner? That's unusual, two nights in a row. You've brought change with you, Julia, so you have."

"Adrian's back," I told him.

He nodded. "Ah, that's the reason for it, then."

We stood there for a moment, neither of us saying anything. Finally, he broke away and glanced back toward the stable. "I've got spiced tea brewing. May I offer you some?"

I thought of my dream about Jeremy the night before, and I knew I shouldn't go into that stable with him. Everything in me was telling me to turn and go back to the house. But instead I heard myself saying: "That would be lovely."

We walked together toward the stable and Drew pulled open the wooden door, revealing a structure that was not so much a horse barn as it was an annex of the house itself, just as opulent, in its own rustic way. Six empty stalls lined one side of the stable;

each, I noticed, was paneled with dark, gleaming wood and lined with sweet-smelling hay. The stalls had running water, shutters that could be opened to the outdoors, and large troughs. Bridles, saddles, and other horse accoutrements adorned the walls and sat on shelves.

"May I take your jacket?" Drew asked as he peeled off his hat, gloves, and parka, revealing a cream-colored fisherman's knit sweater and the broadest shoulders I had seen in a long time. Didn't I notice them the night before? I unzipped my parka and handed it to him, and he hung both jackets on wrought-iron hooks.

On the other wall, I noticed two bigger stalls. One contained an ornate black carriage that might have been transported there from the 1800s—it was like something I imagined Sherlock Holmes's wealthiest clients traveling in, an enclosed vehicle with windows and a door, and a spot for the driver to sit up on the top. In the other stall sat a magnificent sleigh, also black, also ornately carved with red accents. I imagined myself sitting on its red leather seat, covered by a thick blanket, dashing through the snow.

"Where are the rest of horses?" I asked Drew as we walked down the length of the stable. "I only saw Sebastian out there with you."

"In the fields. They love it outside, even in this chilly weather. True northern horses, they are."

At the opposite end of the building, I saw a stone fireplace, where a small fire crackled. A leather sofa strewn with woolen pillows woven in reds, oranges, and blacks stood in front of the fireplace. Armchairs and ottomans flanked the sofa, with crocheted afghans lying here and there. I noticed a teakettle hanging on a steel rod over the fire. I could have curled up in one of those armchairs and never left.

But, as wonderful as it was, it felt wrong, somehow. This was a stable, and it should be run-down . . . shouldn't it? Somewhere deep in my mind, I saw fading wood and dilapidated stalls, dust covering hanging farm implements. I could even smell the decay. And then the image dissipated, as quickly as it had come.

Drew smiled, pouring tea into two mugs and offering one to me. "It's humble, but it's home."

I took a sip of the cinnamony tea and it warmed me, through and through. "You live out here? I thought you were in the main house."

"I am. But sometimes I prefer staying out here. There's just something about it that appeals to me."

"Just you and the horses?" I smiled at him.

"And the dogs," he said, his eyes traveling to the far side of the room, where I saw three massive dog beds and blankets, various toys and bones, and three sets of ceramic dishes. One of the dogs, the red one, curled up on her bed, wrapping her tail around her nose and settling in. But she was not at rest. Her brown eyes were trained on me.

"Would you like a tour?" he offered. "I've newly renovated it, and I'm quite proud of the way it turned out."

I followed him through the door, completely unprepared for the sight that awaited me there. I can only describe it as Northwoods chic. We entered into a living room that shared a wall with the main stable, and I saw the fireplace served both rooms. A mirror image of sofas and armchairs surrounded this side of the fireplace, along with a flat-screen television hanging on one wall. Photos and brightly colored, whimsical paintings of animals that inhabited this part of the country—bears, moose, loons, otters, and others—were hung here and there.

Drew led me down a short hallway. "Kitchen," he said, and I poked my head in to see an Aga stove humming along, stainless steel pots and pans hanging above it, and an old, scrubbed table, which I could immediately tell was worn by years of meals with family and friends.

"Den," said Drew, pointing to an archway, through which I

spied bookshelves, a ceiling lined with heavy wooden beams, and more leather furniture accented with thick woolen pillows in those same reds, oranges, and blacks.

"Guest room," he chirped, opening a door and revealing a heavy, dark bedroom set, obviously antique, the dresser lined with a pinkish marble top. A red-and-white floral bedspread lay over the bed, along with several pillows in various hues.

"It's so lovely," I murmured, staring at the bedroom set and wondering how many hundreds of years old it was.

"Guest bath is here," he said, opening another door, where I saw a claw-foot tub, a glass shower, and light pinewood paneling on the walls.

"And the master suite," he said, revealing a huge room with a king-sized bed, its headboard and footboard made out of logs, and a woolen blanket, striped with red, yellow, and green, draped over it. A fireplace, where coals still smoldered, was flanked by the now-ubiquitous leather armchairs and ottomans and another flat-screen television. Sunshine streamed through a wall of windows, where I saw the river burbling past, along with several horses in a distant field. Across the room there was another door, which was ajar. I presumed this was the master bath.

"Let's take our tea and sit by the fire, shall we?" he said, leading me back down the hallway toward the living room, where I settled into one of the armchairs.

"You said you renovated these rooms recently?" I asked him, looking around at the fresh paint and gleaming tongue-in-groove wood paneling. "I ask because, well, the main house is so ancient and this all seems rather new."

He nodded, sipping his tea. "I did indeed. Just this past year. It had always had rooms—the stable hands of the past lived in here—but they were very run-down."

"I remember," I said, the words escaping my lips before I even knew what I was saying.

Drew stared at me. "You remember?"

I shook my head. "I don't have any idea why I said that," I told him. "What I meant was I can imagine. This isn't how a stable should look."

The look on his face dropped, just a bit. And for a moment I got the distinct impression that whatever I had said had disappointed or confused him. He stood to pour himself another cup of tea, and when he turned back around toward me, the smile was back on his face.

"Now, I spend a lot of time out here," he went on, as though I hadn't said anything. "It's the strangest thing, but I began to feel the presence of my ancestors very strongly in the main house." He shuddered and turned his gaze to the fire. "It was as though the house itself . . . the portraits . . ." I could tell he was caught up in the memory of it. He shook his head and turned toward me.

"But that's silly. You must think I'm completely daft."

"Not a bit," I said, thinking he, too, might have had a rather otherworldly experience in the house. I wondered whether to bring up what had happened to me, but I decided against it. "The house has a way of spooking you, doesn't it?"

"Sometimes it does. So many memories hanging in the air."

"I can see what drew you to come here, though, and I can see why you stayed. And frankly, although the house is breathtakingly beautiful, there's also a coldness to it, a formality. This place you've created here is comfortable and warm and cozy."

He smiled. "And it's more in keeping with its surroundings, isn't it, with the Northwoods decor. I wanted this place to reflect the local culture, not rebel against it, as the main house has done."

"Exactly," I said, sipping my tea and noticing for the first time a portrait above the fireplace. I stood up to look at it more closely. Andrew McCullough, dressed in a kilt, with a woman and two small children, and dogs that looked to be malamutes curled up by their feet.

"Your great-great-grandfather?" I asked him.

"Yes," he said, coughing slightly. "And his family."

I detected a tone of melancholy in his voice, and wondered if he was thinking about a family of his own. All of a sudden I realized I didn't know if he had ever been married, or had any children for that matter. There was much about Drew that was still a mystery.

"And what about you, Julia?" he said, interrupting my thoughts and changing the subject. "What brought you to Havenwood? I know you're meant to be a companion to Mrs. S., but why did you decide to give up your life to come here?"

I had been dreading those questions. I wasn't interested in telling Drew my history, even though he had been relatively honest with me about his. So I chose my words carefully.

"My husband died a few months ago," I began.

"Oh, Julia, I'm so sorry."

I shook my head. "Thank you. Anyway, I was sort of at loose ends. He died, the bills were piling up, I discovered"—I hesitated—"discrepancies in our finances. I basically went from having everything to nothing in the blink of an eye."

He leaned over and put a hand on mine. I felt an itch in the back of my throat and hoped I wasn't about to start weeping. That was all I would need.

"And that's when Adrian showed up at my doorstep. I don't know how he found me, but he did. He made the offer for me to come to Havenwood, and with nothing to lose, I accepted. I was here the next day."

"And now?"

"Now? When I first got here, it was overwhelming, to tell you the truth. I'd seen pictures of the estate but I didn't imagine it to be so—"

"Daunting?"

"Exactly." I nodded, then shuddered. "Mrs. Sinclair has her schedule—her quiet time in the morning and all of that—and initially I wasn't quite sure what to do with myself during that time." I cast an eye out the window toward the house, which stood loom-

ing like a specter across the snowy lawn. I didn't see any signs of
life.

"But then I got to know Mrs. Sinclair a bit better. And you," I
added shyly. "Yesterday was so much fun. I'm feeling more at home,
like I really do belong here. It feels like . . ."

"Like what?"

"Like I've been here longer than just a couple of days. I can't
explain it, but things seem both familiar and strange."

"You're always welcome here in the stables," Drew offered.
"I've usually got the fire going, and a pot of tea on the stove. And
something stronger in the pantry if you're in need of it. Stop by
anytime, even if I'm not here. You'll need to get out of the house,
from time to time. Believe me. It does have a way of making you
feel that everything in the universe is contained within those brick
walls. You need to breathe the fresh air every now and then to remind yourself that the outside world exists."

I exhaled. He really was impossibly kind.

Suddenly, I remembered what I was doing there. I had been so
caught up in listening to Drew that I had almost forgotten. "Oh,
my goodness!" I said. "I came down here to tell you that Adrian is
hoping you can take the dogs and track those footprints, to see
where they came from."

He nodded. "I was planning to do that this morning, just as I
saw you, actually."

"Would you mind terribly if I went with you?" I asked.

"Wouldn't mind a bit." He smiled and unfolded himself from
his chair, crossing the room to the wall where he had hung our
jackets. "But only if you bundle up."

SEVENTEEN

We crunched together through the snow. As we neared the front door of Havenwood, the dogs took off running down the length of the patio and disappeared around the side of the house.

"Girls!" Drew called to them. "Come!" We waited for a moment, expecting them to bound back around the corner, but they didn't reappear.

He raised his eyebrows. "The girls don't so much obey commands as take them under advisement." He chuckled, starting off in the direction they had gone. "I wonder what they're after."

"An animal, maybe?" I offered, following him. We rounded the corner of the house and there they were, snouts to the ground in front of one of the bay windows, sniffing and scratching at the snow. Nearing them, Drew and I saw what had captured the dogs' attention. Footprints. And not the ones we had seen the night before. These were fresh, and in front of the drawing room window.

"Were you walking around out here earlier?" he asked me.

I shook my head. "I wasn't."

"Well, then it looks like our visitor was back," he said, furrowing his brow. "I wonder what this is about, then."

We walked around the house to the kitchen door, following the footprints all the way. Drew pointed to the trail, which snaked its way across the lawn, toward the forest beyond. I clearly saw what I couldn't in the darkness the night before—a person had come from the stand of trees, walked up to the house, and had gone back again. There was no doubt.

I remembered how trapped I had felt in my house in Chicago after the news broke of Jeremy's death—the media, his victims, and even curious gawkers were always lurking at my windows, trying to get a look at the grieving widow. And this was feeling all too familiar. I was beginning to believe that we hadn't attracted a curious villager when we were in town the day before. A chill shot through me when I thought of my house burning to the ground.

Was I endangering Havenwood and everyone in it just by being here?

"Are there tourists in the area this time of year?" I asked, grasping for any other explanation. "People who might be curious about the house? It is such an oddity, after all, this enormous estate in the middle of the wilderness."

He shook his head. "Not generally," he said. "The house isn't exactly in the guidebooks. People would have to know it's here, or stumble across it while hiking on the trails or canoeing on the river. And they don't do any of that in late November. This is our downtime. It's too cold for the summer sports but there's not enough snow for the cross-country skiers and snowmobilers."

He squinted at the trail of prints. "But then again, it's easy walking right now. Whoever it was didn't have to use snowshoes. Later on in the season, he never could have walked in the forest without them. He'd be up to his waist in snow. But now, all he'd need is a good pair of boots, and you certainly don't come to this area without those."

"So it's not out of the realm of possibility," I said, satisfied with that explanation and liking the innocence of it. I could imagine myself on a hike in the wilderness, stumbling across this massive estate, and simply having to come closer to get a better look.

"Come on," he said, setting off along the trail of footprints. "Let's see where this leads us."

He whistled for the dogs, and they came bounding from where they had been, one on either side of Drew and me, and one behind us. I was beginning to really like having their protection.

We walked in silence for a while, going deeper and deeper into the forest. The enormous pine trees reminded me of photos I'd seen of the giant redwoods in California. They towered above our heads and seemed to close in around us, partially blocking out the sun. I noticed the chill becoming more intense, the dogs' breath hanging in the air around them in tufts.

"These trees must be hundreds of years old," I said, my voice seeming to shatter the very stillness into tiny pieces.

"Red pines," he said. "The estate is one of the only areas around where there has never been any logging. It's quite wonderful, don't you think, to be able to see this forest just as it was, hundreds of years ago?"

I craned my neck to look upward, so mesmerized by the trees that I almost forgot we had another, darker purpose for being out there.

We followed the footprints through the forest until they led us to a clearing, where a lake appeared, seemingly from out of the blue. It wasn't yet frozen over but the water looked ice-cold, a slight mist rising from its surface and dissipating into the air.

"Look at this," Drew said, pointing down to the lakeshore. At first I didn't see what he was pointing to . . . and then I did. The remnants of a campfire, the snow around it fully packed down. Somebody had made camp here.

"It looks like our visitor spent the night," Drew said, kicking snow at the campfire ashes to make sure they were out. "And look here." He moved closer to the lakeshore and bent down.

I saw what he was pointing to. Tracks, as though somebody had pulled a boat—a canoe, likely—out of the water and onto shore.

Drew stood up and looked me in the face. "This wasn't some curious villager following us home, Julia. Whatever could this be about?"

In that moment, it became as clear to me as the water before us, lapping at the snowy shore.

I sat down on a nearby log and put my head in my hands. "Drew," I said, wishing I didn't have to say the words. "I think I know exactly what this is about. And it has nothing to do with Havenwood, and nothing to do with Mrs. Sinclair or Adrian, and nothing to do with you. It has to do with me."

"You?"

"Whoever this is, he's looking for me."

Drew squinted at me. "And, from your expression, I'm guessing he's not looking for you to deliver the Publishers Clearing House grand prize."

I managed a smile. "Not that, no. I'm afraid my being here is putting all of you, and Havenwood, in danger. I'm going to have to leave. Today."

The problem was I had no place to go.

EIGHTEEN

$\mathcal{I}$ got to my feet and started marching back through the forest the way we had come, the dogs close at my heels. It felt like the pines were closing in around me. I had thought I was finished with everything that had happened to me in the past year—I really had begun to leave it all behind. And yet, here it was again, refusing to let me go.

Tears stung at my eyes and began to stream down my face. I wiped them away with my mittened hands before they froze on my cheeks. I quickened my pace, trying to outrun the emotion.

Drew caught up with me, grabbing my arm and turning me around toward him. When he saw the tears, he gave me a look of such compassion and concern—and that was all it took. The floodgates opened, and I began to let it all out, my shoulders shaking with the force of it. Drew wrapped his arms around me and held me close, rubbing my back and whispering words I didn't quite understand.

I cried for the marriage I thought I had, for the friendships I had lost, for the funny, gentle man I thought I had married who turned out to be a sociopath, for the people he hurt. All the pain and frustration I had been holding inside for months bubbled to the surface.

As I pulled away, Drew handed me a handkerchief that had been in his pocket.

"I'm sorry," I said, taking off my mittens to blow my nose. "I didn't mean to do that. I must look a fright."

"Nonsense," he said, smiling down at me. "But you need to tell me what this is about, Julia. Right now. I want the truth, and believe me, I don't care what it is. I will have heard worse. You can tell me you murdered sixteen people in cold blood and I'd still be on your side."

"Sixteen? Really?"

His mouth curled into a grin. "I draw the line at seventeen."

I couldn't help but chuckle, despite it all.

"Seriously, Julia. You need to tell me everything, especially if you think your being here is putting Havenwood in danger."

So much for leaving my past behind. My blissful anonymity had lasted all of two days. I looked around me at the rugged pines and delicate snow cover, and realized that even here, in the pristine Havenwood wilderness, it wasn't possible to escape my past. The truth was too powerful.

I took a deep breath, and as we walked through the forest toward Havenwood, I told him everything. How Jeremy swindled me, our friends, and hundreds more out of their life savings. How all of our friends had abandoned me, thinking I was part of it. How the media hounded me relentlessly. How lawsuits were floating out there with my name on them. How the angry victims had threatened me. And how Adrian had promised to make all of it go away, if I would just come to Havenwood with him.

Now that I was talking about it, telling Drew the nightmare that had been my life for the past year, I couldn't stop. It was like a dam inside of me, the one that had kept my heartbreak and anger and frustration about this whole situation at bay, had burst. Finally, someone would listen to my side of things. And care. I couldn't stop if I tried.

"Holy Jesus," he said under his breath.

"And you haven't heard the worst of it yet," I said. "The day after I left Chicago for Havenwood, my house there burned to the ground. The police suspect it was arson."

"And you think whoever set your house afire is our visitor, here to do the same to Havenwood," he concluded.

I could see the edge of the forest in front of us, with Havenwood standing guard in the distance. The image of flames coming out of its windows, lapping at the stone facade, swirled in my brain. I stopped walking and looked at Drew.

"Yes. That's what I'm most afraid of. You all have been so kind to me. If anything were to happen to you—"

He held up a hand to stop my words. "Does Adrian know about the fire?"

"He was in Chicago at the time. He was there."

Drew nodded, as though this were nothing remarkable. It made me wonder, not for the first time, exactly who Adrian was.

"Good," he said. "I'll have to get with him straightaway to make a plan of action. I gather Mrs. Sinclair knows none of this?"

"She knows about my history, but that's all. Not about the fire."

"That's good as well. Let's keep it that way. I'm sure Adrian will agree with me. After dinner tonight when Mrs. Sinclair takes her leave, we'll sort this out. Adrian and I will take care of this."

He began walking toward the house. I called after him. "But isn't the best thing for me to just leave?"

He walked back to me and took me by the arms, his face so close to mine I could feel his breath on my cheeks.

"You cannot leave here, Julia," he whispered. "You just cannot. Not now."

I just stood there, my eyes locked with his. I couldn't move, or even breathe. Just being this close to him felt like magic and energy and whispers and danger were all around us. He smiled slightly, as though he were feeling it, too.

He leaned into me, and the air between us thickened. I knew he was going in for a kiss. And although part of me wanted nothing more than to throw my arms around him, my reason won out. I stiffened and pulled away.

"Please don't," I said.

He looked like he'd been stung. "I'm sorry," he said, taking a step back from me. "That was completely inappropriate. Please forgive me."

I smiled, wanting to lighten the mood. "Don't worry about it," I said. "Let's just get back to the house."

We began walking through the snow back toward Havenwood, the dogs bounding ahead of us at a run. It felt like we were leaving the possibility of a kiss behind, too.

When we reached the front door, we stood there for a moment.

"Remember, not a word about this to Mrs. Sinclair," he said, his voice low. "If she asks, let her know we followed the footprints into the forest and lost the trail, but that we thought it was heading back toward town. I'll find Adrian and apprise him of the situation."

"Okay," I said, feeling calmer with a plan in place.

"Okay," he said. "Now I've got to dig out my tuxedo for dinner." And then he smiled. "Or maybe this calls for my kilt, eh?"

"Only real men wear skirts in the snow."

"Challenge accepted. I'll see you at six thirty."

NINETEEN

I opened the door to my room to find Marion leaning over an enormous old trunk, which had not been there before.

"What's this?" I asked her.

She straightened up, putting a hand to her back. "Mrs. Sinclair asked me to have it moved into your room. It's full of dresses. She said she wasn't sure if you had brought sufficient formalwear for the dinners she's planning to have. Now that you're here, she's feeling a bit more"—she paused and searched for the right word—"festive than usual, I guess you could say."

"That's right, I only brought a couple of dresses, and casual ones at that," I said to her, glancing into the trunk at the taffeta and crinoline and silk. "I was wondering if I'd have to wear them over and over again. I really don't have the funds to buy any more."

Marion smiled. "Well, now you don't have to. There are so many dresses in here, all beautiful. And there's another trunk where this came from as well. Shall I hang these up in the closet for you and press something for dinner tonight?" She fingered the fabrics in the trunk and crinkled her nose. "It looks as though some of these need to be steamed."

I glanced at the clock. It was well after noon. Drew and I had been in the woods longer than I realized, and I felt a deep chill. I was craving a long, hot bath and a good book.

"Do you have time to tend to these dresses, Marion?" I asked, eyeing the trunk. "Don't you need to get dinner started?"

"The soup's on the stove and the roast is ready to go in the oven," she said, smoothing her apron.

"Then, if you don't mind, while you deal with these"—I pointed to the trunk—"I'm going to slip down to the library and grab a couple of books. I've been outside all morning and could use a good soak in a hot bath."

She nodded. "I'll run it for you," she said.

I padded my way through the house to the library, satisfied that I was finally learning my way through this maze. The halls, which had been so off-putting when I first arrived, were now becoming more familiar. But still, they felt empty. There were only four of us, along with several servants, in this massive house, after all. The chances of seeing someone else at any given time were very slim.

That was why, when I got to the library and began nosing around the shelves, I was surprised to hear noises coming from the east salon. Its doors were thrown open and light was streaming from them.

I crossed the room, my footsteps muffled by the Oriental rugs, and poked my head inside. A man dressed in a dark suit and two women in traditional black maids' uniforms were bustling about. One of the women was polishing the woodwork; the other was on a ladder washing the windows. The man was clearing the remnants of that long-ago meal from the table. None of them took any notice of me. I scanned the room and saw brooms and dustpans and all manner of cleaning supplies.

I cleared my throat. "Excuse me? What's going on?"

They all snapped their heads around to look at me at the same time.

The man straightened his jacket and gave me a slight bow of his head. "Hello, miss," he said. "We're straightening the room for tonight's festivities."

"Festivities?"

"At the lady of the house's request."

That was odd. I knew Mrs. Sinclair had kept this room shut off from the rest of the house for years, maybe decades. I wondered what these "festivities" would entail.

I stepped into the room and looked around—it was gleaming with freshness. Now that all the spiderwebs were brushed away and the dust was swept up, it looked quite beautiful.

My gaze shot over to the fireplace—but the wall above it was bare. Did someone take down that ghastly painting? Or had I just imagined the whole thing? I shuddered and realized the cleaning crew was staring at me with expectant eyes.

"You're doing a nice job," I said, clearing my throat, not knowing quite what else to say. Finally I came up with "Carry on!" and backed out of the room.

We'd likely be having our drinks in the east salon before or after dinner, I reasoned, hence the cleaning. At least that horrible painting that had come to life the day before was gone.

Back in the library, I was tempted to go to the first editions shelf but then thought better of it. I was planning to read in the tub and all I'd need would be to drop a priceless volume into the water. So I moved on to the other shelves on the first floor, noticing that they were set up like a regular bookstore—in sections. I ran a finger along the spines and saw biography, travel, history, the occult—I hurried past that one—and finally came to what I was looking for, fiction. As I studied the spines for titles that interested me, the books themselves seemed to be whispering and cooing, drawing me in.

I chose *The Hound of the Baskervilles*, *Wuthering Heights*, *Rebecca*, and a couple of modern-day mysteries that I hadn't yet read. But then I realized that I had chosen only eerie tales—my life itself was eerie enough these days—and I made a point of finding *The Shell Seekers* to balance things out. My arms loaded, I headed back out the door, excited to slip into a hot bath and lose myself in a good book.

But then I heard it again, the same small, singsongy voice, way off in the distance, as though it was coming from the past.

"Jack and Jill went up the hill / To fetch a pail of water . . ."

I snapped my head around to look toward the door of the east salon, and the image of a blond girl in a white gown was hovering there, in the air. But then she flickered and faded from view.

I stood there, frozen in terror. I didn't know if this was a hallucination or one of the ghosts Mrs. Sinclair told me was floating around Havenwood, but at that moment, I didn't care. Something inside of me snapped. I found my feet and pounded blindly down the hallway as though the devil himself were chasing me. I had to get out. I threw open the front door and ran outside, no coat, no boots, no gloves. I didn't care. I would've run all the way back to Chicago through the foreboding wilderness rather than go back inside that house of horrors.

"Julia!" It was Drew, coming around the side of the house. "What are you doing out here?"

I didn't stop. I didn't answer him. I hurried down the front steps and into the driveway, oblivious to the cold.

"Julia!" Drew called again.

He reached me in an instant, grabbing me by the arms and turning me around toward him. "What's the matter? Where are you going?"

I could barely catch my breath and leaned against him. "I saw something inside the house," I panted.

"Come on," he said gently, rubbing my arms. "You must be freezing. Let's get you back inside."

I shook my head. "No!" I cried, the image of the little girl floating through my mind. "I . . ." But my words trailed off. Looking into Drew's eyes, seeing his expression of gentle concern, I suddenly felt very silly. And, all at once, cold.

"Come on," he repeated, leading me back up the steps and through the still-open front door.

I shook my head. "I don't know what came over me," I said.

"You said you saw something?"

I took a deep breath, my pounding heart slowing as we walked together through the foyer. "I went into the library to get a couple of books," I said. "And I noticed people in the east salon."

"The east salon?" He furrowed his brow. "Are you sure?"

"They said they were opening it up, per Mrs. Sinclair's request."

He frowned. "And that frightened you?"

I didn't quite know how to go on. How was I going to tell this man I had seen, and heard, the apparition of a little girl?

"Not that, exactly," I began. "It's just, I don't know, Drew. Ever since I got to Havenwood, I think I'm seeing—and hearing—things that aren't there. It makes me feel like I'm going crazy."

He looked at me for a moment, opening his mouth as if to say something, and then closing it again. Finally, he spoke, his voice warm and gentle. "You're not crazy. Far from it. I mean, look at all of us here at Havenwood, Julia. We're a collection of oddities, the whole lot of us. You're the most normal person among us."

I thought of Mrs. Sinclair dressed in full riding gear the day before, and somehow managed a chuckle.

"But you did look terrified just now," he went on, leading me up the grand staircase. "And that's no laughing matter. I'll make you this promise, Julia. You are safe here at Havenwood. Whatever it was that you saw, or thought you saw, it's not going to hurt you."

Somehow, I believed him. This man I barely knew had such a way of making me feel calm and secure.

"You need to promise me something in return, however," he said.

"What's that?"

"No more running outside into the snow," he said. "Seriously, Julia. Night is falling. It's going to be below zero tonight, and you were out there without so much as a coat. What if I hadn't come upon you when I did?"

I truly didn't know the answer to that. I hadn't been thinking clearly; that was obvious. I wondered what sort of horrible situation I might have gotten myself into out there in the frozen woods, alone.

"You need to promise me you're not going to do that again," he pressed. "Please, Julia. This is why I made sure you knew you could come to the stable at any time. If ever you feel like you have to get out of this house, and believe me, we all feel that way at times, come to the stable. That's your refuge, night or day. Do not attempt to leave the property on your own. It's too dangerous. Can you promise me that?"

"I guess so," I said.

"If you really want to leave Havenwood," he continued, "I'll take you wherever you want to go. Agreed?"

I smiled at him. "Agreed."

By the time we reached my room on the third floor, I was completely calmed and feeling slightly chagrined.

"I'm really sorry about this," I said to him as we stood together in the hallway by my door. "You must think . . ." My words melted into a sigh.

"Not at all," he said, giving my arm a squeeze. "Are you going to be all right here? I've got some things to attend to before dinner."

"I'm fine," I said. "Thanks for coming to my rescue."

"Anytime, Julia. Anytime."

Back inside my room, I found that Marion had finished with the dresses and gone, somehow leaving a snack of crackers, cheeses, and figs and a pitcher of water with lemon on the nightstand. Perfect. I hadn't realized it, but I was starving.

I nibbled on some cheese and opened the door to the walk-in closet to take a look at the dresses—just the thing to put that embarrassing episode out of my mind. They were hanging in neat rows of teals, purples, blacks, and deep reds, each more beautiful than the last. They were old-fashioned and lovely, like something out of another place and time—which, I assumed, they were. Some were slim sheaths with plunging necklines and low backs, their fabrics glittering and shimmering. Others were more modest, with full skirts and cap sleeves. Accents of lace and pearls and embroidery adorned them. To me, they looked like something Grace Kelly or Audrey Hepburn would have worn—I had never owned anything like them. I hoped they'd be at least close to my size.

I noticed shoes standing beneath the dresses, delicate heels and flats. I slipped my foot into one of them—a perfect fit.

On top of the dresser sat a jewelry box that hadn't been there before. It was open, revealing strands of pearls, long silver chains, and dangling earrings.

I was excited to play dress-up in these clothes, whomever they had originally belonged to, and glide down the grand staircase to the formal dinner that awaited me in a few hours. It occurred to me that the same thing had been done at Havenwood for more than one hundred years—guests dressing for dinner and joining their hosts for drinks in front of the fire. It gave me a sense of timelessness that I couldn't quite define. I was at once in the present and the past, and they were both the same. I wondered if Havenwood had that effect on everyone.

I poured myself a glass of water, grabbed the copy of *Rebecca*, and headed to the bathroom, where I found a steaming-hot tub of scented water and several candles flickering here and there. Again, perfect. That Marion really had a knack of knowing just what to do, I thought. "Thank you, Marion," I whispered into the air, and peeled off my sweater and jeans.

Before I slipped into the claw-foot tub, a thought knocked at the corners of my mind, interrupting the serenity of the moment. Our "visitor." Had he got what he wanted? Would he be back?

I pushed aside the curtains and peeked out the bathroom window. I'm not sure what I was looking for—more footprints in the snow? A man lurking around? But what I saw surprised me.

Adrian and Drew were standing with a third man, whom I had never seen before. They were looking toward the forest where Drew and I had found the campsite, and Drew was talking to both of them. That was when I saw the third man was carrying a rifle. I watched as he walked off into the woods, and Drew and Adrian went their separate ways, Drew toward the stable and Adrian toward the house.

I slipped into the steaming water, wondering what all that was about.

TWENTY

The bath was perfect. The spicy scent of the water tickled my nose and filled my lungs with calmness. I breathed in and out, releasing the day's tension with each exhale. Whatever I had seen, or hadn't seen, in the east salon faded away. And I would think about our "visitor" another time. It looked as though Drew and Adrian had it handled, at least for the moment. I tried to put it out of my mind and relax.

I opened one of the books and began to read, but I made it through only a couple of chapters before my eyes started feeling heavy. Not wanting to drop the old volume in the water, I set it on the window ledge next to me and lay back, sinking down farther.

I closed my eyes and submerged, listening to the rush of water in my ears, the soft hum soothing me like a mantra.

But then the hum disappeared. I heard voices in its place. Or did I? I shot up and grabbed a hand towel for my face, and listened. Two female voices, I was sure of it. There were two people in my bedroom. And I hadn't locked the bathroom door.

Was it Marion, with another woman, back to tend further to the dresses? That had to be it. Still, I wasn't comfortable being in the bath with them on the other side of an unlocked door, so I slipped out of the water and into the plush terry cloth robe that was hanging on a hook nearby. As I wrapped it around me, I heard giggling.

"What will you wear tonight?"

"I am still unsure. The blue one? What do you think? Will I please him in this one?"

What was going on? That certainly wasn't Marion's voice. I opened the door to see two women, neither of whom I recognized. Several dresses were lying on the bed, and one of the women was holding a blue gown up to her face. "Does this favor my eyes?"

"Who are you?" I asked, stalking out into the bedroom in as threatening a manner as I could muster while wearing a bathrobe. "Why are you in my suite?"

The women both gasped when they saw me, one of them putting a hand to her mouth to muffle a scream. She dropped the blue dress . . . and then they were gone. They simply dissipated, like steam rising above a lake on a chilly morning. Just like the figures in the paintings.

I blinked several times, not quite knowing what I had just seen, and pulled the robe tighter around me. I had attributed these "sightings" to my going off my medication abruptly. But after the scene in the east salon . . . Was that what was going on? Or was it something else?

Somehow, the vision of these two women didn't frighten me like the others did—they were just two girls getting ready for a formal dinner, just like I'd be doing shortly. Maybe that was it, I reasoned. I had been feeling a sense of timelessness when Marion had brought me the dresses, and maybe, my imagination working overtime, combined with the lack of medication . . .

I sighed and didn't know what to think. One minute, I was fleeing in terror from this house after seeing something I couldn't explain. The next minute, a similar vision wasn't fazing me in the least. Maybe I was going crazy after all.

"Which one favors *my* eyes?" I said into the air. And then I headed back into the bathroom to finish my soak, careful to lock the door behind me.

★ ★ ★

$\mathcal{M}$uch too early to dress for dinner, I pulled on jeans and a turtleneck and slid my feet into my slippers. I thought I'd go looking for Adrian and ask him not only about what news, if any, he had heard about the fire, but also if he had found out anything about our intruder.

I slipped out the door and padded down the hallway toward the study I had found the day before. One peek inside revealed it was empty, but I did notice the black phone was gone. Marion's handiwork, no doubt. She didn't want me making calls, so she made sure I wouldn't be making them.

Where to look now? The drawing room, maybe? I made my way back down the hall to the grand stairway and intended to go to the main floor, but stopped at the second-floor landing. This was the floor where the family's rooms were located, I recalled. I knew Marion had told me to stay away from them, but maybe I could find Adrian in his personal study—if indeed he had one.

I took several hesitant steps down the dark hall when I heard a voice. Adrian? I followed it to what I thought was the end of the hall but discovered it actually turned a corner. Of course, like the third floor, this, too, was U-shaped. I peeked around the corner and saw a door was open about midway down the hall, light streaming from inside. As I got closer, I realized that it was indeed Adrian's voice I was hearing; he was speaking on the phone to someone. I intended to knock on the doorjamb to let him know I was there, but his side of the conversation stopped me short.

"I don't have to explain anything to you," he said, the anger in his voice hanging in the air. "This is no longer your affair."

"That's touching," the sarcasm whittled his voice to a hiss. "But considering what you've done, forgive me if—"

"No. Absolutely not. Not back there."

"The best place for her? That's absurd." His voice was louder now, angrier. "How can you even ask why? I fully blame you for the whole debacle, for everything that happened."

Was he talking about Mrs. Sinclair? I crept closer to the door.

"Those are your words, not mine. I would have chosen 'gross incompetence.'"

"Yes, I do mean it. And don't think for a moment my threat doesn't still stand. If this effort doesn't work, you *will* pay for what's happened to her."

"No, it is not dangerous, and no, I did not have to clear anything with you. Somebody had to do something. You certainly were of very little help."

Silence for a moment. And then he hissed: "She's already here, you fool. It has begun." I heard him slam down the receiver.

My blood ran cold. Was he talking about me? I waited outside the door for a few moments and then poked my head around the jamb and saw Adrian, his head in his hands, sitting at a desk strewn with papers.

I nearly spoke to him, wanting to ask what that conversation was about, but something about the way he was sitting with his shoulders slumped, head in his hands, made me think better of it. Obviously, he was upset by what had just transpired. I held my breath and backed away.

As I walked toward the grand staircase, I ran headlong into Marion. Why did she always turn up when I was in the wrong place at the wrong time?

"Marion!" I said. "I was just—"

She shook her head and smiled. "This house can be so confusing," she said, taking me by the arm and walking with me up the stairs. "No one blames you for losing your way."

Back in my room, I sat at the window and tried to piece together what I thought I had overheard, but nothing was making sense to me. It was just a one-sided conversation that may or may not have been about me. But . . . what if it *was* about me? What might it mean? Mrs. Sinclair had hinted at an "ulterior motive" for inviting me to Havenwood. Did the conversation have something to do with that?

As I thought about it, seeds of suspicion were taking root in my mind. Everyone had been so warm and welcoming to me—almost too warm. Too welcoming. Something about it was off. Wrong. But what?

And then I put my finger on it—they were too familiar with me. I had just met these people, and yet Adrian was always touching me, offering me his arm when we walked. Mrs. Sinclair was always calling me "darling" and "my dear." And really, when I thought more about it, I was just an employee. And a brand-new employee, at that. I didn't hear anyone referring to Marion as "darling." They were treating me like I was a family member who had finally come home.

I thought of asking them about it, but how does one say: "You people are being too nice to me and I demand to know the reason why!"

And then I thought of the papers strewn on the desk in Adrian's study, the ones I had seen when he had been on that call. Maybe they could shed some light on things.

*A*s six thirty neared, I looked at myself in the mirror. I had chosen a glittery black sleeveless sheath dress to wear and it fit like a glove. I wound a strand of pearls around my neck and put pearl drop earrings in my ears. It almost felt like a costume, truth be told, but one that I wouldn't mind wearing every evening of my life. Timeless elegance, here in this timeless house.

I slipped out the door, but instead of heading all the way down the grand staircase, I stole down the hallway on the second floor. I knew everyone would be in the drawing room having drinks and the ever-present Marion would be busy in the kitchen. It was the perfect time to get a look in Adrian's study.

I poked my head around the doorframe and saw the room was empty. Not wanting to turn on the overhead light—too bright—I flipped on the desk lamp and began to look around, my heart pounding so loudly that I was sure everyone could hear it downstairs.

The papers weren't on the desk as they had been, but a manila folder sat in Adrian's inbox. Might it be as easy as that? I opened it to find a business ledger. Not it. But underneath where the folder had been, I spied a stack of papers.

With shaking hands, I slipped them under the soft glow of the lamp and began to read. It was a handwritten letter.

Oak Lawn Sanitarium
May 28, 2003

> *The patient has progressed steadily, if slowly, from a state of extreme catatonia to being fully aware and alert. She is walking and talking, responding to questions. The patient has, however, suffered a psychotic break. Total amnesia of the event. While not typical, it is possible in those who have endured extreme trauma. The memories may return or they may remain hidden. The patient is nonviolent.*
>
> *I recommend no visitors at this time. Progress is tenuous but I will, of course, keep you informed. More as I have it.*

It was signed by a doctor—a psychiatrist?—along with his phone number.

I stood there holding that letter for a moment, and then the significance of it hit me. The date! Ten years earlier. That was right around the time Mrs. Sinclair "died." She must have been in a mental hospital after some traumatic event, and rather than let the public know about it, Adrian concocted the story that his mother had died. Perhaps the catatonia was so severe, he didn't think she'd come out of it.

So, the person Adrian was talking to earlier was probably her psychiatrist. That was why he got this letter out after all of these years. The phone number. Maybe she had had some sort of a relapse . . . ?

I put the letter back where I had found it and flipped off the light, feeling suddenly ashamed for snooping. Obviously, it wasn't something Mrs. Sinclair intended to have as public knowledge. And considering her rather eccentric behavior—the cowboy getup, her jogging suits, her seeming to have several personalities—and the way Adrian and Drew were so protective of her . . . It all made a sad sort of sense. This was the reason Adrian wanted a companion for his mother when he was away on business. He was worried about her mental state, and considering this new information, I could understand why. It didn't explain why I was the person he chose for the task, but at least one mystery of Havenwood was solved.

As I made my way down the stairs for dinner, I felt a wave of sympathy for Mrs. Sinclair. Catatonia, amnesia, winding up in a mental hospital . . . whatever had caused that, it had to be very bad. I vowed then and there to stop asking about it. I didn't need to know any more. If she wanted to tell me about it someday, that was one thing. But I was done pushing.

I found Marion waiting for me at the bottom of the stairs. "Mrs. Sinclair is in the drawing room," she said, motioning the way.

"Julia!" Mrs. Sinclair cooed as I entered the drawing room to find a fire blazing in the fireplace, candles flickering all around the room, and Adrian and Drew standing together at the sidebar. "You are breathtaking!"

Adrian and Drew turned to me then, each holding a lowball of, I assumed, Scotch. Adrian was smiling while Drew's mouth hung agape as he shook his head.

All eyes on me, I felt suddenly shy. "It's amazing what a bath and the right dress can do for a girl," I said, shrugging and moving toward the bar.

"My dear," Mrs. Sinclair said, floating toward me in a wispy teal-and-black gown that looked as if it were made of hundreds of silk handkerchiefs, "you must excuse my absence today. I was feeling rather tired from all of our adventures yesterday. I hope you had something to keep you busy." She looked at Drew with dancing eyes.

"I did indeed," I told her. "We went for a lovely walk in the woods."

Drew was pouring me a drink, and I whispered to him, not wanting a repeat of the night before, "Light on the gin, please." He nodded slightly, handed me a glass that was mostly tonic and lime, and came out from around the side of the bar.

My face broke into a wide grin. He was wearing a kilt with a green, blue, and black print and a sash of the same print over a white shirt, along with knee-high stockings and black shoes. His shoulders looked extraordinarily broad and his legs incredibly muscled, as though he had spent a lifetime, or several, working outdoors.

"Laird Andrew McCullough only breaks out the kilt on special occasions," Mrs. Sinclair said, beaming. She crossed the room and tousled his hair. "I think he should wear it all the time."

Adrian poured himself another drink and joined us in the middle of the room. "You two seem to have hit it off in my absence." I couldn't tell if his tone was humorous or not—he was so reserved at all times. He seemed to have an edge to him tonight, I thought, perhaps having to do with that phone call.

"Julia here is quite the horsewoman, so I've learned," Drew said, doing his best to deflect the comment. "She has braved the fierce Nelly, and won."

Laughter all around. We talked of other things until Marion came to summon us to dinner. Adrian was quick to offer me his arm, which I took somewhat reluctantly. Drew was right behind, escorting Mrs. Sinclair into the dining room.

We chatted idly over a dinner of spicy lentil soup, roast beef, asparagus with hollandaise sauce, and a crisp salad. Nobody asked Adrian about his business trip and I certainly didn't, either, considering what had occurred at my Chicago home. I wondered how much Mrs. Sinclair knew, but thought it best not to find out.

After dinner, Marion led us away from the drawing room and down the hall, to what I knew would be the east salon. We walked through the library in silence, Adrian and Drew exchanging worried glances, until we reached the room's doors, which were open.

We entered the east salon to find candles flickering everywhere, a fire blazing in the fireplace, and a bar set up with cognac, B&B, Scotch, and other liqueurs I wasn't familiar with. A tray of chocolates sat nearby.

The room was in beautiful contrast to how I had seen it before—first in disarray and then in stages of repair. The wood-paneled walls gleamed in the candlelight; a chandelier glittered above the round table. The sofas looked as good as new, and the floors shone with a fresh polish.

And yet, the very fact of setting foot in this room was making my stomach turn. Maybe it was the otherworldly experience I'd had earlier, but there was a sense of darkness here that made me want to run and hide.

"Mother," Adrian said, gazing around the room with a strange look on his face. "I can't believe it. You've opened it up again. Without consulting me."

"Oh, darling," she said, crossing the room and taking his hands in hers. "I thought it was time. Now, more than ever."

He shook off her embrace and took a few steps forward, anger bubbling up from under his usually reserved facade. "We said this room would never be used again. Not until—"

"I know, my darling," Mrs. Sinclair said, approaching him slowly, as though she were coming up on a wild animal. "But I realized yesterday that the only way is to open this room up. Now. I thought you were on board with this. You are the one who . . ."

But then everyone stopped talking. The silence hung around us like a tangible thing. I realized the others were staring at me. Drew's mouth was open, his eyes wide.

"What?" I said.

"The resemblance is amazing," Adrian murmured. "Seeing the two of them together like this, it's really quite something."

The painting was hanging back on the wall above the fireplace, where I had seen it before. There it was, in all of its ghastly glory, man with the severed head and all.

Mrs. Sinclair glided across the floor and took my hand. "Julia, darling," she cooed. "When you came to us, Adrian said he thought you bore a passing resemblance to one of Havenwood's most famous visitors." She gestured at the painting. "I wanted to come in here to see for myself."

"Who is she?" I wanted to know, staring at my mirror image.

"She is Seraphina, my dear."

"Seraphina?" I parroted. "From your novel?"

"Not quite," she said. "I patterned my character after her. This is the real Seraphina, the most gifted and famous medium of the Spiritualist Age."

I thought of the book I had found in the library. "The woman to whom Dickens gave the copy of *A Christmas Carol*?"

"The same," she said. "That's why I thought it so remarkable that, of all the books in the library, that's the one you were drawn to." She pointed up at the painting. "If you look closer, you'll recognize him. Second chap from the right."

I walked a few more steps into the room and squinted up at the painting—it did look like the photographs I had seen of Dickens.

"So, this is Christmastime 1867? Here at Havenwood?"

"It is indeed," Mrs. Sinclair said. "He came all the way from the East Coast just to see her."

"But . . ." I was having trouble formulating my thoughts. I wasn't familiar with the real Seraphina—I had no idea there *was* a real Seraphina until just now—but I certainly knew the novel of the same name written by Amaris Sinclair. It was about a psychic medium who opens the wrong door to the spirit world, a door she can never close again. It was a dark tale of possession and murder and sorrow, and it had always reminded me of a variation on the theme of Pandora's box.

I wondered if that same kind of evil in the novel was let loose here, at Havenwood, in this room, by the real Seraphina. Was that what inspired Mrs. Sinclair to write her most famous book? Was that what I was feeling when I stepped through the door?

As I looked at my twin hanging above the fireplace, a cloak of fear wrapped itself around me, making my skin tingle. I can't explain exactly why. What is so frightening about resembling a woman in a painting, after all? It's an oddity, a curiosity, not a nightmare. But something about the way they were all looking at me, coupled with what I had experienced in that room earlier, made me squirm. My breathing became shallow and quick, and my heart began thumping. I felt the fight-or-flight mechanism kicking in again, and *flight* seemed like a very good option. I wanted nothing more than to run away from Havenwood and all the secrets it contained. But I couldn't very well go running into the snow in my dress and heels. And I had promised Drew I wouldn't.

All at once, the conversation I had had with Mrs. Sinclair the day before began rapping at the back of my mind. What had she said? That she had an ulterior motive for inviting me to Havenwood? As I stood there with everyone looking from my face to the woman in the painting and back again, I got the terrible feeling that her ulterior motive had something to do with me being a dead ringer for a dead woman.

TWENTY-ONE

*Y*ou knew about this?" I asked Mrs. Sinclair, finally finding my voice. "About how much I resembled this woman in the painting?"

"Of course I knew about it," she said gently, recognizing, I supposed, the fear welling up in my eyes.

"So, you realized it that first day when you saw me at breakfast?"

She shook her head. "Long before that. The news reports on television, dear. Adrian spotted the resemblance right away."

I felt a chill, from the inside out. I thought back to the day Adrian appeared on my doorstep. Was this, finally, the reason they had sought me out? This resemblance was the ulterior motive?

Amaris Sinclair sighed, crossing the room to take a seat on one of the sofas.

"I knew this all was going to come out," she said, shaking her head. "But I didn't think it would happen so quickly."

That same cold breeze whooshed around me. And then it was gone.

"So, you saw me on the news and realized I look like this lady in the painting, Seraphina, and that's why you asked me to come here?"

"Now, Julia," Adrian said, crossing the room to take my hand. "Don't make too much of this. You're getting worked up over something very small."

I could feel the calmness he was trying to exude. And when

I thought about it rationally, what he said made sense. "It's just a resemblance to somebody who lived and died more than one hundred years ago," I said, looking from one to the other of them. I wasn't sure whom I was trying to convince. "It doesn't mean anything more than that. It's just an odd coincidence that doesn't have anything to do with me."

Mrs. Sinclair smiled. "Oh, but it does, my dear," she said. "It does."

"Mother—" Adrian began.

She waved a hand at him. "I think it's time she was told."

She was looking at me but not focusing on me, not really. Her eyes seemed to be seeing something that wasn't there. I noticed her hands were shaking, and remembered the letter from the psychiatrist I had seen before dinner. I followed her across the room and sat next to her, taking those shaking hands into my own. My skin tingled.

"Please," I said. "If you have something to tell me, just say it. Whatever it is, it'll be all right."

"Your resemblance to her is no coincidence, Julia," she said. "Seraphina was your great-great-grandmother."

TWENTY-TWO

I stared at her, not knowing quite how to respond to what she had just said to me. Was this an aftereffect of her illness? Was she psychotic? Or was she simply creating fiction, as she had done so often over the years in her novels?

I squeezed her hands. "Mrs. Sinclair, I'm sorry to tell you that you're mistaken," I said as gently as I could. "There may be quite a resemblance, but that's as far as it goes. This woman was not related to me."

"Oh, but she was." She nodded. "On your mother's side."

My mind raced back to what I knew about my family history. "I'm sorry, but that's just not right. I hate to disappoint you, but my grandmother was born in a small town in Wisconsin. Her parents were Scandinavian immigrants, like most of the people in that area. Her grandmother wasn't a famous medium and she certainly wasn't named Seraphina. Believe me, I would have heard about that."

I chuckled, looking at each of them in turn. None of them chuckled along with me.

"Family history is all too often revised and rewritten, Julia, especially when strange birds are perched on one's family tree," Mrs. Sinclair said.

The look on my face must have told her what I was feeling, because she said, "I can see you're unconvinced."

"There's just no way an exotic psychic who was famous and, I presume, wealthy was my great-great-grandmother. As I told you, my great-grandparents were Scandinavian immigrants. They came to this country to build a better life for themselves and they worked hard at it. They were by no means wealthy, just the opposite. So you see, it's just not possible that my great-grandmother's mother was Seraphina." I gestured toward the painting. "I mean, how could this woman's daughter have wound up as a poor immigrant eking out a living in rural Wisconsin? You have to see that one and one don't equal two here."

Mrs. Sinclair patted my knee before pushing herself up from the sofa where we had been sitting. "You're looking at this with your rational mind, Julia," she said, turning on her heel. "Look with your heart, and I think you'll begin to see things differently."

A chill crept its way up my spine as I watched her. *She wants me to be related to Seraphina despite all the facts I've told her to the contrary,* I thought. *Why?*

I decided not to push it—Adrian had hired me as a companion for his mother and obviously this sort of behavior was the reason she needed one. I didn't want to upset her by further denying her theory, so I stayed silent for the moment, looking to Adrian and Drew for support. Perhaps we could forget all about this Seraphina business and go on with our evening.

Mrs. Sinclair opened a drawer on the sideboard and withdrew a manila file folder.

"Adrian did the research before he sought you out, my dear," she said, handing it to me.

I opened it to find a sheet of paper. On it, a family tree. Mine. All the names were familiar, just as I knew them to be. My name, my mother's, my grandmother's. My eyes stung with the memories of those incredibly strong and loving women, now all gone. Had any of them been alive, I would have retreated to the safety of their embrace after the whole business with Jeremy came to light.

I wouldn't be here right now, at Havenwood. I stared at the tree for a moment, and then looked back at Mrs. Sinclair, confused as to what she was trying to prove by showing this to me.

"This says Juuli Herrala was my great-great-grandmother, just like I told you," I said, putting the sheet on the table and pointing to her name. "See? It's right there. I was named after her."

Mrs. Sinclair nodded. "Exactly my point, dear. Juuli Herrala was Seraphina's real name."

I blinked at her several times. "How do you know that?"

"It is a historical fact."

"Don't think for a moment that I believe any of what you say is true," I said, the words catching in the air by a tendril of doubt. "But just for the sake of argument, let's say you're right. Seraphina was my great-great-grandmother. How in the world would her descendants wind up in northern Wisconsin scraping by on farms or working in the mines?"

"I don't know what happened to Seraphina after she left this house. She was lost to history. But I can tell you that what happened to her on that last, terrible night must have frightened her deeply. Deeply enough to cause her to give up her career, drop out of sight, and disappear." She gave me a wry look. "I know exactly what that feels like, and I dare say you do, too."

I sighed. She did have a point about that.

"And if she wanted to disappear, to get away from the fame and celebrity that surrounded her, what better place to run to than a rural community populated by those who knew absolutely nothing about her old life?"

I slumped into an armchair. She was describing exactly the same reason I had come to Havenwood.

Still. It seemed as though she had a lot invested in me being this Seraphina's descendant—it was the very reason she had brought me here. Whether I believed it or not, it occurred to me at that moment that I might do well to play along. My old life was gone. This was my reality now. What might she do if she realized she was wrong, that I wasn't Seraphina's descendant? The psychiatrist's letter flashed into my mind. *The patient is nonviolent.* Had she been violent? Was that the reason she was institutionalized?

"I can see you're having trouble with all of this," Mrs. Sinclair said to me as she reached over and took my hand in hers. "Maybe we've had enough talk about Seraphina for one evening, hmm? Let's have some drinks and talk about something more pleasant."

They certainly had a way of changing the subject with rapid-fire speed here at Havenwood, I thought, as Adrian poured another drink and began talking about whether it was supposed to snow that evening. As I looked from one person to the next, it occurred to me that we were all hiding something. Adrian and Drew didn't want Mrs. Sinclair to know about our "visitor." I didn't want any of them to know about my hallucinations. And Mrs. Sinclair was probably hiding the most of us all.

Havenwood was indeed a den of secrets, I thought as I sipped my drink. I wondered what else was lurking just out of sight.

TWENTY-THREE

$\mathcal{I}$ retreated to my room shortly after that. I had no wish to drink as much as we all did the night before, and I was equally unwilling to broach the Seraphina subject again. I felt like one of those "see no evil, hear no evil, speak no evil" monkeys. If she was my ancestor, and if that was the reason Adrian brought me here, I didn't want to know about it, at least not right then.

As I undressed, I thought about the strange dichotomy that was Havenwood. At once it felt safe and welcoming, and at the same time, there was an undercurrent of—what? Malice? Danger? Fear?—bubbling just below the surface. Yes, I was free to leave. I could've bundled up and had Drew take me away at that very moment . . . but the very thought of it made me shiver. God only knows what we'd encounter out there in the dark night in those millions of acres of wilderness. Mountain lions. Wolves. The person who had spied on us the night before. That was *real* danger. But here, beyond the eccentricities of a strange and potentially insane old lady? I might be imagining it all. Paintings coming to life, floating apparitions, party-going girls from the past back to try on dresses—all of it, every last thing, might be brought on by drug withdrawal. And what if it wasn't? A couple of giggling ghosts of society girls in taffeta weren't exactly the great undead. What was the worst they could do? Spill champagne on me? Hide my pearls?

I realized, as I hung the dress up carefully in the closet, slipped the shoes back into place, and returned the necklace and earrings to the jewelry box where I had found them, that I didn't want to leave Havenwood, not really. I had already become quite fond of Mrs. Sinclair and her velour jogging suits and gotten used to the rhythm of life here. The horses. The dogs. It all felt right somehow. And further, it felt as though I had been here not just a few days, but forever, that my place at this table had been set long ago.

It was like my old life had dissipated into my distant past. Shopping on Michigan Avenue seemed as long ago and far away as my childhood.

I was pulling on my pajamas when I heard a scratching at my door. What was this? Another hallucination?

It was light at first, then louder. And then a low bark. I opened the door a crack to find all three dogs standing there, tails up, ears perked. I opened the door wider, and they filed into my room and paced about, sniffing here and there, before turning in circles a few times and laying down in front of the fireplace, tails wrapped around their snouts.

"It looks like you're in for the night," I said to them, shutting the door behind me.

The dogs looked enormous in this setting—seeing them outside with the backdrop of the vast wilderness was one thing, but here, I got the full image of just how big they actually were. I moved carefully around them to the bathroom, where I washed my face and brushed my teeth.

"You might want water," I said aloud, peering out the door into my room at the sleeping giants. I looked under the vanity and found a large plastic basin, which I rinsed out and filled from the cold water tap and set onto the tiled floor, figuring the dogs would find it if they wanted it.

I made my way back across the room, stepping gingerly over the dogs, and turned out the light before slipping under the covers. Just as my head hit the pillow, Molly, the red dog that had greeted me so enthusiastically in the field, jumped onto the bed, turned in a circle a few times, and curled up next to me. I held my breath, not knowing quite what to do: Could I move? What if I nudged her in my sleep? But soon, the slow, steady rhythm of her breathing calmed me, and I drifted off to sleep feeling safer than I ever had.

My dreams that night were convoluted and eerie. I vaguely remembered the dogs growling low and steady at something floating in the corner of my room—the little girl I had seen?—but my limbs felt like deadweight and my eyes felt so heavy that I couldn't move to get away. That, too, may have been a dream.

Whatever it was, I awoke the next morning refreshed and full of energy, if somewhat perplexed to see that the dogs were nowhere to be seen. Had the omnipresent Marion let them out of my room? I wasn't sure.

I padded over to the window and opened the curtains to find a fury of white outside. A real Minnesota blizzard! I hadn't seen one of those since I left home years before. It evoked such a sweet sense of nostalgia that I thought my heart would burst from the joy of it. When I was a child and a blizzard descended, school would be canceled and we'd have a snow day. This was a more exciting treat than even Christmas morning. We couldn't wait for the snow to finally stop so we could burst out into the cold to build elaborate forts inside the drifts, have endless snowball fights, or simply fall backward and extend our arms and legs to make perfect snow angels, before rushing inside, faces red and stinging from the cold, for tomato soup and grilled cheese sandwiches, which we gobbled up in front of the television. I don't know how long I stood there, those sweet days of childhood swirling around me as furiously as the snow outside.

As I headed down the grand staircase toward breakfast, buoyed by my memories, a resolution hit me, growing stronger with each step I took. Strange visions notwithstanding, I liked it here at Havenwood. I didn't want to leave. But I needed to resolve this sinister undercurrent—or what I *thought* was a sinister undercurrent. And that meant I had to get to the bottom of Mrs. Sinclair's ulterior motive for bringing me here.

TWENTY-FOUR

$\mathscr{I}$ pushed open the door of the breakfast room to find Adrian standing in front of the window, gazing out into the swirling whiteness. He was wearing faded jeans and a well-worn fisherman's knit sweater. I had never seen him in anything but a perfectly tailored suit and tie. It felt a bit like coming upon Prince Charles wearing a Green Bay Packers sweatshirt.

"Well, look at you," I said, trying to stifle a laugh. "No suit today?"

He turned to me, grinning, his arms outstretched, palms up. "No need. I'm not going anywhere. It's a snow day!"

"It certainly is," I said, joining him at the window. "I was just thinking about snow days when I was a kid."

"I never had that treat," he said. "English boarding schools and all that. But growing up here, you must have experienced it often."

I nodded. "There was nothing so exciting as watching television in the morning when there had been a big snowfall overnight and seeing the list of schools that were closed, holding your breath until you saw your school's name," I said, staring out into the whiteness. "One year, we had so many snow days that they had to add two weeks on to the end of the school year to make up for it. Of course, we thought ourselves very ill used when June rolled around and we were still in the classroom."

Adrian and I shared a chuckle as Marion clattered into the

room pushing a cart with a coffeepot and cups and a basket filled with something that smelled like cinnamon and spice.

"Coffee and muffins to tide you over until breakfast is ready," she said, pouring both of us cups of coffee and splashing cream into mine. "Mrs. Sinclair will be another twenty minutes or so. She's running behind this morning."

"Thank you, Marion," Adrian said. Once she had left the room and gone back into the kitchen, he gestured toward the table.

"Good," he said, sinking into a chair. "This will give us a few minutes to talk."

I sat in my usual place and sipped my coffee. "I assume this is about our visitor?"

He nodded. "Yes, you rushed off to bed so quickly last night . . ." His thought hung in midair and then changed direction. "I'm sorry about that, by the way."

"About what?"

"The whole Seraphina business. We were terribly rude, all of us, gaping at you like that."

I took a deep breath. Could it be resolved as easily as this? "Adrian," I began, "is that why I'm here?"

"Is *what* why you're here?"

"Seraphina. My resemblance to her. The fact that your mother thinks I'm related to her."

He shook his head. "Certainly not."

"But your mother said—"

He reached across the table and put his hand over mine and spoke gently. "I know what she said. And I'd have cleared this up last night, but I didn't want to upset her. Whatever my mother has cooked up in her own mind, the only motive, ulterior or otherwise, was finding a suitable companion she wouldn't throw out into the street the minute I left the house."

I nodded, unconvinced. "But the family tree . . ."

He held my gaze for a moment, and I got the feeling he understood I wasn't going to let this go so easily. "Listen to me, Julia. I'll

admit that when I saw you on the news, you looked familiar to
me. Remember, none of us had been in that room for years and
years."

That hadn't occurred to me. The east salon had been shut up
tight. He was telling the truth.

"Did I research your background? Of course. You'd do the same,
bringing someone into your house to care for your mother. I'm
afraid that when she saw the name of your great-great-grandmother,
she cooked up this whole story. You mustn't make too much of
her ramblings. She is a novelist, after all. Surely you have become
familiar with her eccentricities by now."

"Well . . . ," I began. I didn't want to let on that I knew her "eccentricities" might be much more than that. "I suppose there's no
harm in her thinking I'm related to Seraphina."

He smiled. "That's the spirit! Now, quickly, before my mother
seizes the day. I wanted to touch base with you about, as you called
him, our 'visitor.' Drew and I have talked. I know what you found
in the woods, and I've got a man on it.

"But now, with the snow," he said, turning his head toward
the window, "I don't think we have anything to worry about, at
least for the time being. We're supposed to get upward of two feet
out of this blizzard when all is said and done, and after that, the
wind will drift the snow much higher than that. The roads won't
be plowed for a few days, and coming through the woods on foot
will be highly difficult, if not impossible."

I nodded and took a sip of my coffee. "I told Drew I was prepared to leave Havenwood," I said. "If this is related to me somehow, I don't want to be the cause of any potential harm coming to
you or Mrs. Sinclair. I can leave after the snow—"

"Nonsense," he interrupted. "There is every chance that it's
nothing but a curious tourist, here to gawk at the castle in the
wilderness. But if it is someone from your past, even the arsonist,
he won't get what he's come for. Havenwood has stood fast against
worse evil than a disgruntled investor, believe me."

As if on cue, Mrs. Sinclair burst through the door. She was wearing jeans and a sweatshirt in a Northwoodsy print of bears, moose, and loons. I couldn't help but grin, and Adrian laughed aloud.

"What, darlings?" she said. "It's a snow day!"

TWENTY-FIVE

*L*ater that morning, after we had finished our breakfasts and Mrs. Sinclair and Adrian each went off to parts unknown, I made my way to the west salon. I wanted to sit in front of its floor-to-ceiling wall of windows and watch the snowfall. The room was fast becoming my favorite in the house.

When I got there, I found its doors opened, a fire in the fire-place, and the books I had selected from the library the day before on an end table next to a legal pad and several pens. A cup of steaming hot chocolate laced, I discovered as I sipped it, with Baileys Irish Cream was the perfect addition. Marion's handiwork, no doubt. I was beginning to believe she was more than a little bit psychic.

I settled into one of the armchairs and stared out the window, mesmerized by the snow for I don't know how long, until Marion's voice startled me out of my trance.

"More hot chocolate, miss?" She was standing there with a Thermos.

I held my cup aloft. "Thank you," I said, smiling up at her. "And thank you for opening up the room and starting a fire. How did you know I was going to come in here?"

Marion looked very pleased with herself. "Spend as long as I have tending to the needs of the residents of Havenwood, and you'll start to get a sixth sense."

I guessed she was right.

"Also, miss, I wanted to let you know that the power is out."

I looked around the room. "Really? I've been sitting here in front of the window and didn't even realize the lights were off."

"There's no telling how long it will be out," she said. "With heavy snowfall like this, it can be out for days. I've had the girls move most of the perishables to the icebox—"

This struck me as odd. "Icebox?"

She nodded. "It's original. We keep it down in the basement kitchen. It comes in handy during times like this."

"I guess there's no shortage of ice for it outside," I offered, thinking that I didn't even know there was a basement kitchen and wondering what else about Havenwood I didn't know.

"Quite. I know you're not in the habit of venturing into the kitchen yourself, but I just thought I'd mention that it's best not to open the refrigerator until the power comes back on. There isn't room in the icebox for everything, so we need to keep as much cold in the refrigerator as we can, and that means not opening the door."

I nodded. "Got it."

"And," she continued, gesturing to a small kerosene lantern on one of the tables, "you'll want to use that to get around the house, especially as night falls. This house is dark as a tomb without the lights."

I looked around the room and felt a shudder pass through me. I had no desire to be wandering the corridors in the inky blackness of an almost two-hundred-year-old house.

"Of course, we have flashlights, but it's best not to waste the battery power if we can help it," she said, smoothing her apron. "Do you need anything else?"

"I don't think so." I smiled at her. "Thank you, Marion."

She turned and walked to the door, stopping just before she went through it.

"Will you be staying in the west salon today?" she asked me.

"I think so," I said.

"Then I'll bring your lunch to you here," she told me. "Mrs.

Sinclair likes to stay in her suite when the power is out." She gazed about the room. "This salon is so bright and cheery, it's a good place for you to be on a day like this."

With that, she disappeared into the dark hallway.

I curled my legs under me and covered my lap with an afghan that had been slung over the back of the chair. I opened my book to the passage where I had left off. I had a fire in the fireplace, plenty of light to read by, and a freshly refilled cup of Baileys and hot chocolate. What did it matter to me if the power was out? I had everything I needed, right there.

I read for a while, but my eyes kept turning to the pad of paper on the end table. I hadn't written in so long, but maybe I would find inspiration here.

Another thought hit me then. I realized I hadn't done a whole lot of thinking about my future. I had left my past behind and was here at Havenwood for the time being, but I really didn't know how long I wanted to stay—or how long I'd be welcome to stay—and I had no idea what I'd do when I left. Adrian had promised to give me a fresh start with a new identity, and fortuitously enough, the fire had ensured that nobody would come looking for me once I left Havenwood for good. But there was still the matter of making a living. I'd have to earn my keep, new identity or not. The last job I'd had was at Jeremy's firm, and I wasn't exactly going to be touting that on a résumé. But I had enjoyed modest success with the one novel I wrote, way back when. Maybe I could catch lightning in a bottle a second time, under a different name, of course. I closed the book I was reading and picked up the legal pad and pen.

But what would I write about? I started jotting down notes of things that had happened to me, or struck me, since I came to Havenwood, in an effort to crystallize my thoughts into possible plot lines or themes. *Aging novelist. Haunted mansion. Dark hallways. Paintings come to life. Dog protectors. Horseback rides through the wilderness.*

But one subject kept coming up, over and over again. *Seraphina.* I couldn't deny that I was fascinated by my resemblance to the woman in the painting, to Seraphina, the greatest psychic medium who ever lived. I had denied it so vehemently, but the possibility of it kept floating through my mind. Was she really my great-great-grandmother? Could it be?

I wrote until Marion materialized with lunch—split pea soup with ham and crusty bread, which I devoured. After that, I made several false starts trying to get interested in my book again, but I could not stop thinking about the previous night's oddity. I closed the book and set it on my lap, staring outside at the snow, which was whipping sideways in the stiff wind.

Everyone had made so much of the resemblance between Seraphina and me the night before. Why was Mrs. Sinclair so fixated on that? The fact that Adrian had tried so clumsily to convince me it was nothing told me it was *something*. As I sat there, mesmerized by the snowflakes that were darting through the air like millions of tiny beings, I let my imagination soar with them, this way and that.

Whether she was related to me or not, Seraphina had been a visitor in this house more than a century earlier. Maybe, somewhere in her story, I could find a tale that I'd like to tell the world. Maybe she'd be my inspiration, just like she was an inspiration for Mrs. Sinclair. And there was only one place in the house where I could find out more about her. So I gathered up my books and pad of paper, lit the kerosene lantern with the matches Marion had left beside it, and set off for the library to do a little sleuthing.

Despite the soft glow of the lantern, the corridors were as dark as night, and as I walked, the sound of my footsteps echoed, bouncing off the walls and ceiling. It was a strange sensation, being plunged into such darkness when I knew it wasn't much past one o'clock. But with the snow blocking out the sun and the construction of the hallways themselves as internal corridors with rooms on either side and windows only on each end, it made for an almost total blackout. Marion was right; I had no desire to find myself here with no light to guide my way.

I was very glad that I'd had several days to familiarize myself with Havenwood's layout. But even as it was, I inched my way down the corridors and through the salons and finally found myself on the opposite side of the house, grateful I hadn't run into any otherworldly denizens.

I pushed open the library doors, and after a futile attempt to switch on the lights—I rolled my eyes at myself—I stepped into the room. Even though I had just come from a dim hallway, it took a few moments for my eyes to adjust to the darkness there. It was as though the books themselves were soaking up even the faint light coming through the stained-glass windows. I tried not to look into the blackness and instead focused on the light coming from my lantern, but every so often the corners of my eyes would catch a figure—nothing more ominous than a chair here and a table there—but in that darkness it seemed to be a creature, crouching and ready to strike.

I began to wonder if I shouldn't just come back when the lights were on, but then thought better of it. "You're here," I said aloud, my voice reverberating through the cavernous room, "you might as well get what you came for."

So I began to search the shelves, holding the lantern in front of me to illuminate the spines of the books. I saw biographies, history books, classics from literature, my hallowed first editions shelf, travel stories, fairy tales, political tomes, and much, much more before I finally found the section I was seeking—the occult. I had seen it when I had been in the library before and quickly passed by it, but if this library contained any books about Seraphina, I knew this was where they would reside.

As I ran my finger from spine to spine, words like "spells" and "magic" and "tarot" and "Spiritualism" seemed to illuminate themselves and hover just above the spines, and more than that, they seemed to be whispering, hissing, even floating on the air around me. I could faintly hear them beckoning me to choose them, to pull their books off the shelf and open the pages.

And then I saw what I had come for. *Seraphina: The Most Famous Psychic Medium of the Spiritualist Age.*

I intended to simply take the book, leave the library, and find my way back to the west salon's brightness, but I just couldn't wait to see what it contained. I slid the slim volume off the shelf and sat down at the table nearest the door, set my lantern on the table, and opened the book.

On the very first page I found a photograph of a woman in a long, dark dress, sitting in an ornately carved chair next to a fireplace in what looked to be a fancy drawing room. I took a quick breath in when I realized that the painting I had seen of Seraphina didn't do her, or my resemblance to her, justice. It was like looking at a picture of myself dressed up in the costume of another age. I flipped back to the title page to make sure—it was published in 1890—and then I turned back to the photo of Seraphina.

I don't know how long I sat there staring her. It was as though she had reached out of the page and pulled me in. I found myself imagining all sorts of things. I thought about the room where she was sitting—what color were the walls? Blue? Yes. Definitely blue. What other furniture might have been there? A fainting couch? Who else was with her? Was this photo taken in Seraphina's home? And if so, where was that home?

I was holding the book up closer to my eyes to get a better look at the photo in the dim light of the room, when something dropped out of it. A letter, its envelope yellowed, the front addressed in neat handwriting that was fading with age.

Havenwood Estate
Grand Marais, Minnesota

What was this? I was so mesmerized by this letter from the past that I didn't even hear him come in. At least, that was what I told myself later, when I came back to myself and was thinking clearly.

I had just begun to take the letter out of its envelope, when I felt someone's breath on my neck. Panting softly, as though he had been holding his breath awhile and finally let it out. I grabbed the lantern and shot up, wheeling the light around in a circle and knocking the chair to the ground.

"Who's there?" I shouted. "Drew? Adrian?" Silence. I turned again, shining the light in a wide circle around me. I didn't see anyone.

A hallucination? Or was it one of Havenwood's wayward, benign ghosts that slipped from a painting into real life? I wasn't sure, but I wasn't going to stick around to find out. I grabbed the book, stuffed the letter back where I had found it, and slipped the volume into the pocket of my cardigan, when just then, I heard it.

Laughter, slow and low, and decidedly not full of mirth. It was unquestionably a man's voice, but it didn't sound like Drew or Adrian.

"Show yourself!" I yelled, my own voice cracking despite my attempt at bravado. "You're really a big man, standing in the dark and trying to scare a woman. How about coming into the light and trying the same thing?" I had no idea what I'd do if he took me up on the offer.

I shone the light around my little corner of the room again. Books. The table. Chairs. Nothing else. No ghosts, and certainly no real-life people. I gathered up my wits and marched toward the door.

I had just reached it and grabbed the handle when I heard the voice again.

"Julia."

TWENTY-SIX

I shoved the library door open with all of my might and ran down the hallway at full speed, the lantern swaying before me, casting strange and macabre shadows on the walls.

I didn't stop running until I heard a familiar voice.

"Julia! Hey, what's the matter?"

I snapped my head around to see Drew, his face full of concern. He was at my side instantly.

"What's happened?" he said, taking hold of my arms and looking into my eyes, his voice low and soothing. "You look like you've seen a ghost."

I took a few deep breaths in. "Worse than that," I huffed. "I think somebody is in the house."

He shook his head. "That's impossible."

"No," I said, still trying to catch my breath. "No, Drew. I was just in the library, and somebody was in there with me."

He smiled slightly. "This house can play tricks on you, Julia. Especially when the lights are out. Is it the same thing you saw yesterday?"

I shook my head and pulled away from him. "No, you don't understand. This wasn't a hallucination or anything otherworldly. Somebody—a man!—was standing right behind me. I felt his breath on my neck and then he said—"

"What did he say?"

I could barely get the words out. "He said my name," I whispered. "Whoever this is, he's here for me, Drew."

He looked at me seriously for a moment and then took me by the arm. "Come on. Let's go into the drawing room where we can talk."

"No!" I said, looking back down the dark hallway, my voice a harsh whisper. "There's somebody in the library! We need to tell Adrian. Or call the police. Or something. But whatever it is, we need to do it now!"

"I know," he said, his grip firm on my arm. "Come with me." And we walked down the corridor together, my heart beating hard and fast in my chest.

"He said my name, Drew. You believe me, don't you?"

He nodded slightly. "Of course I do."

He steered me into the drawing room, where someone had lit a blazing fire in the fireplace. Dozens of candles in stained-glass holders were glittering on end tables and on the hearth, casting a warm light throughout the room. The whole effect was soothing and comforting, exactly what I needed.

"It looks like a church alcove in here," I said, exhaling for what seemed to be the first time in a very long time.

He smiled. "Electricity is overrated."

I sunk down onto the leather sofa in front of the fire, and Drew made his way over to the sideboard and opened a bottle of wine.

"What's that they say?" He smiled as he handed me a glass. "It's five o'clock somewhere? Anyway, I thought you could use this."

I reached out for the glass with shaking hands, which he noticed. "You really did have a fright, didn't you?"

"Listen, we need to call the police. Somebody is in the house and—"

He put up a hand to stop me. "Nobody is in the house, Julia."

I shook my head. "Yes, there is! I heard—"

Just then, Adrian materialized under the archway. "What's this about somebody being in the house?"

Drew walked back to the sideboard and poured Adrian a drink, holding it out to him. "I think Julia just met Gideon."

"Are you all right?" Adrian asked, coming toward me.

"I was terrified, actually," I said. "Who's Gideon?"

"I thought he was gone," Drew said, more to Adrian than to me.

"So did I," Adrian mused, looking into the fire. "Wishful thinking, apparently. Does Mother know?"

Drew shook his head. "I think it's best we don't tell her. Not yet."

"Agreed."

"Are you two going to tell *me* what you're talking about?" I said, moving closer to them. "Who's Gideon? A servant? The groundskeeper?" But the cramp in my stomach told me I didn't want to know the answer.

Adrian and Drew exchanged a charged glance, but I couldn't tell exactly what it was charged with—worry? Fear? Embarrassment?

"Okay," I said, setting my drink down on the table a bit too forcefully. "One of you needs to start talking right now. All I know is, I was in the library, and somebody was in there with me. He said my name. Obviously you two know who it was, and you need to tell me right now."

"You're right, Julia—" Drew began, but I cut him off.

"Damn right I'm right! And I really don't like the idea of this guy creeping around here. He scared the life out of me, and he enjoyed it. I need to know if I should be locking my door at night." I took a breath. "And what's this about not telling Mrs. Sinclair?"

Adrian smiled. "You don't need to lock your door unless you want to, and you don't need to worry about Gideon, not really." He shot a look at Drew, who shrugged his shoulders. "We're not telling Mother because she tends to make more out of this kind of thing than there is."

"More of what kind of thing?"

"The fact is, Julia, we don't quite know who Gideon is," Adrian said. "Or I guess the proper word is 'was.'"

We stood in silence for a moment. "*Was*. So you're saying that Gideon is a ghost?"

All of my strange experiences since I had come to Havenwood rushed into my mind, from the paintings coming to life to floating, singing apparitions to the girls in my room trying on dresses. I had been holding out some kind of hope that those visions had been induced by my stopping my medication so abruptly, but now—was it something else?

"I guess I'm not surprised," Drew said to Adrian more than to me. "What with opening up the east salon again."

"I was afraid it might happen." Adrian sighed. "I had no idea she was going to open that room so soon."

"I'm going to give you about five seconds to tell me what this is all about or I'm going to . . ." My words trailed off as I realized I had no threat to make, not really. "Seriously. What's going on? You're scaring me."

Adrian just stared into the fire and shook his head.

"You need to tell me what this is all about," I said. "Trust me enough to do that, please."

"I do trust you, my dear." Adrian half smiled at me.

"Then tell me the truth. I can understand you wanting to shield your mother from things, but if I'm going to be living in this house I need to know what's going on. I don't want another surprise like the one I had in the library just now."

"Well, then," Adrian began, "I suggest we all freshen our drinks and settle in. This is going to take a while."

Drew came around and filled our glasses as Adrian sunk into an armchair by the fire and crossed his legs. I sat on the sofa opposite him, and Drew slid in beside me.

"Adrian, listen," I said. "If you're going to tell me Havenwood is haunted, I've got news for you: I already know. I've known from the first day. I thought I was seeing things, but now—"

He shook his head. "I'm afraid there's much more to it than that," he said. "You've been asking and wondering why my mother chose to drop out of sight and stop writing, all of those years ago. It's time you knew the truth about the vanishing of Amaris Sinclair. Especially because you have just come face-to-face with it."

TWENTY-SEVEN

*T*he fire blazed and the candles flickered as I sat in the drawing room, waiting for Adrian to begin his tale. He seemed to be gathering his thoughts, or his courage, and was clearly elsewhere—not there in the room with us in front of the fire, but back to whatever time and place this story occurred. I looked at Drew, and from his furrowed brow, I understood that he knew the tale Adrian was about to tell all too well. I got a knot it my stomach when I saw how serious both of their faces were. This was the reason Mrs. Sinclair had ended up in that psychiatric hospital, I could feel it. Suddenly, I wanted to stop what I had started.

"Listen," I said, breaking the silence and surprising Adrian out of whatever thoughts he had retreated into. "I know I was the one insisting I be told what's going on here at Havenwood, but from the looks of both of you right now, I'm not sure I want to know."

We sat in silence for a moment. I had the distinct feeling that I had stirred up a hornet's nest, and wanted very much to calm it back down. "If this is Mrs. Sinclair's story, maybe she should be the one who tells it to me," I offered. I didn't want to admit to knowing at least part of the story already.

"I suppose," Adrian said, "that with any good story, it's best to start at the very beginning." He smiled and raised his glass. "My mother bought Havenwood when I was no more than a boy. She had been here as a child and had fallen in love with the place, especially the library."

I nodded. "I know that. She told me."

"So you must also know the house's history."

"I do. Built by Andrew McCullough in the 1800s, patterned after his family home in Scotland."

"Very good. And you've heard Andrew's strange tale?" He eyed Drew.

"About the Windigo? Yes, she told me about it."

At the mention of this, I could see a shudder pass through Drew.

"Well, my dear, this house has a history of strange things happening within it, starting with old Andrew but not ending there, I'm afraid. You know he was a patron of the arts, and invited musicians and writers and painters and dancers and all manner of artistic types here to this house, in the middle of the wilderness. And they came."

Drew took up the tale at this point, leaning in toward me. "But one visitor stood out in Andrew's mind, above all the others. Seraphina."

I fingered the slim volume about her life in my sweater pocket. Why did all roads seem to lead back to her?

"What was it about her that intrigued him so?" I wanted to know.

"Well, she was beautiful and mysterious, and Andrew was never one to let a pretty woman go unnoticed"—Drew smiled at me—"at least that's what family lore tells us. But more than her looks, Andrew was obsessed with her gift."

"The psychic medium business," I said.

He nodded. "You must remember, Julia, this was the height of the Spiritualist Age in this country. You couldn't walk down the street, any street in any big city, and not see signs for psychic tearooms and séances and mediums.

"It became an obsession for the wealthy," he continued. "The poor and working classes had much to occupy their daily lives—making a living, putting food on the table, just simply surviving in a harsh world. Especially the recent immigrants to this land. Oh, our Andrew had it easy—he had the foundation of a family fortune underneath him. But the average people? They didn't have time for such nonsense."

"But the wealthy did," I said.

He nodded, taking a sip of his Scotch. "Indeed. When you've got food on the table and a fire to keep you warm and no worry of either of those things ever going away, then it's time to think about things like the great beyond. And people wanted to know about the afterlife, whether their loved ones were safe and happy, and what lay beyond the veil."

"I remember Houdini was into it, wasn't he? And Arthur Conan Doyle?" I asked.

"Conan Doyle, famously so," Drew said. "Others in literature and entertainment as well. But where there is a rich old widow who is willing to pay to talk to her dearly departed husband, there's a charlatan waiting to take her money and run."

"There were a lot of charlatans, then?"

"The movement was full of them," Drew said. "It was a disgrace, really. People in the most important houses in New York City and Boston and places like that would have Spiritualist salons, and a whole cottage industry of fakers sprung up as a result. The rapping on the tables, the levitation of the chairs—all of that, or most of it anyway, was faked."

"Are you saying Seraphina was one of those fakers?"

Drew shook his head. "Just the opposite, Julia. Seraphina was the real thing. Astonishingly real. With her, there was no sideshow, no big production of going into a 'trance,' or calling of spirits, or dimming of the lights. She'd simply talk to the dead as easily and naturally as we are talking here, now.

"She would fill theaters all over Europe and on the East Coast, where she would walk out onto the stage with no fanfare whatsoever, and begin to relay messages to members of the audience from their loved ones who had died."

I nodded. All of it sounded familiar. I'd seen modern-day psychics do the same thing.

"It was astonishing; she was a true phenomenon. The messages were real and easily verified. In one very famous incident, she accused an audience member of murder. Of course he had done it—his dead wife was there, telling Seraphina the whole story. She also told Seraphina where to find the murder weapon, a fact Seraphina relayed to the police. The man went to prison. She did quite a bit of work with law enforcement after that.

"Andrew had heard about her and was intrigued. He had lost both of his parents, remember, and would've loved nothing more than to hear from them again. He invited her to Havenwood. She came. Several times. And brought many other people with her, artists and writers—"

"Charles Dickens!" I added. "I saw a book he inscribed to her."

"Indeed."

"I wonder if she was ever able to bring Andrew any messages from his parents," I mused, staring into the fire. I felt a knot in my throat and a stinging behind my eyes at the thought of my own parents, both gone almost two decades now. I would've given anything to have heard from them somehow during the past few years of my life. I wondered if I'd have made different choices, had they been here to guide me. I quickly wiped away the tears that threatened to fall and cleared my throat, and realized for the first time what easy prey the grieving wealthy must have been.

Drew seemed to sense what I was thinking. "The story is that yes, she did help Andrew communicate with his parents. I think that's why he kept asking her back. That, and the fact that he was in love with her."

"In love? Are you sure? I thought he married a local girl and had a family. Besides, from what I've read, Seraphina was married, too."

"Love doesn't always follow the rules, Julia," Drew said, smiling rather sadly, I thought. "Any soap opera will confirm that for you."

I looked at him. "Are you telling me they were having an affair? How could you possibly know that?"

Drew shifted in his seat and took a sip of Scotch. "Andrew's journal. We found it in what had been his study during a renovation of the third floor. It's pretty clear they were in love with each other. What they did with that love—that's their business, I guess. In any case, after the night we're telling you about, all of that was over. For all we know, they never saw each other again."

I took a sip of wine and considered what they were telling me. "But what does her story have to do with Mrs. Sinclair? That's what we're talking about, right? I mean, Seraphina couldn't very well have caused her to stop writing and drop out of sight."

"Ah, that's where you're wrong, my dear," Adrian said, taking up the tale. "Seraphina's story and my mother's are completely intertwined.

"As Drew said, Seraphina had no trouble talking to the dead. As I understood it, she had had the gift since childhood. But this particular night in the east salon at Havenwood was different. Several people sat around the table, all of whom were looking for messages from their dearly departed. But Seraphina couldn't hear anything. No voices, no messages of any kind. Only an eerie silence. An emptiness. She couldn't figure it out. She knew full well the people around this table had lost loved ones, but no matter what she tried, she could not conjure up any sort of communication from beyond the veil, so to speak."

I was confused. "That doesn't sound so dire," I said. "So, she couldn't talk to that dead that night. So what?"

Adrian took a sip of his Scotch. "Have you ever heard of something called the Devil's Toy Box, my dear?"

I hadn't. I shook my head. "Doesn't ring a bell."

"I'm very glad it doesn't. It's not something anyone should play around with. It's a very, very dangerous object. But Seraphina didn't know that when she brought it here to Havenwood."

"What is it?"

"It's a box with a tight-fitting lid, made of ancient wood. It usually has symbols and inscriptions on the outside. The inside is covered with mirrors."

"What is it for?"

"It's for trapping spirits, my dear."

At this, Drew pushed himself up from the sofa and made his way to the sideboard. "I think this calls for a refill, don't you, Adrian?" He poured Scotch into his own glass and Adrian's and crossed the room with the wine bottle for me.

"Thanks," I said to him, catching his eye. I didn't know if all this talk of spirits was something he believed in or disdained, but I couldn't tell from his expression. The conversation was definitely veering off into the absurd.

"This box sounds like some sort of parlor trick," I said, sipping my wine. "I thought you said Seraphina didn't need any of those kinds of things."

"She didn't, at least not until this particular night," Adrian said. "And the Devil's Toy Box is all too real. It's no trick. But the tragedy of the whole story is Seraphina didn't know what it was, not really. She had no idea what she was doing when she opened that box. I firmly believe she'd have never opened it, had she known."

"So, what happened, exactly?"

"It was during this particular séance, in the east salon, the one in which Seraphina was having trouble communicating with the other side. As the story goes, she was getting frustrated and angry. She didn't want to disappoint the people who had come all of this way to see her and communicate with their departed loved ones. But she just wasn't getting any sort of messages at all.

"So she thought she'd try something she had never tried before. Her husband had been traveling in the Far East and had brought back a small box covered with strange symbols."

"The Devil's Toy Box."

"Yes. A shaman of sorts sold it to him, and he took a liking to it, thinking it might be useful to his wife in her stage act. So he brought it home and gave it to her. She put it in her bag and didn't think much more about it, until that particular night here at Havenwood. That night, in an effort to jump-start things, she lit a few candles and then remembered the box, and thought she'd put it on the table and open it, to see if that might not coax a few spirits out of wherever they were hiding. She thought she'd put a candle inside, and the mirrors reflecting it would cast an interesting glow. She had no idea."

"So, she opened the box?"

"She opened the box."

Adrian and Drew shared a look.

"I know this is going to sound fantastic," Adrian said, a sheepish expression on his face. "And to tell you the truth, I wouldn't have believed it myself, if not for what happened later. But when Seraphina opened that box, she unleashed something monstrous and strange. Not the spirit of someone who had died, but something else. Something evil and dark that was better left hidden and alone.

"One man attending the séance that night died. It may have been a heart attack, but others who were there reported that it was like someone was choking the life out of him. People were scratched and beaten—it was a hellish scene."

"So, you're telling me that something was trapped in the box, Seraphina opened it, and whatever it was got out."

"That's exactly what we're telling you," Adrian said.

"Was Andrew there?" I asked.

"He was indeed there," Drew said. "It terrified him."

"What happened after that?" I wanted to know.

"Seraphina left Havenwood and never came back. Nobody knows where she went or whatever became of her. She never held another séance that we know of and never appeared on the stage again. It was as though she fell off the face of the earth. And Andrew never held another séance or had anything to do with Spiritualism ever again."

"But what happened after that? It's not like Havenwood is some sort of house of horrors. I mean, a few ghosts here and there? Sure. What hundred-year-old house doesn't have them? But there's nothing evil here, not really."

Adrian stiffened. "I'm afraid there is. And you came upon it tonight, my dear."

I looked from Adrian's face to Drew's and back again. Their whole story sounded preposterous, and yet their expressions were deadly serious.

"Gideon?" I asked.

"Indeed," Adrian said.

I wasn't quite sure what to make of this tale, but the mention of Gideon made my stomach turn. My head began to pound.

"Are you all right?" Drew asked.

"I am," I said, rubbing my temples. "I'm just not feeling all that great right now."

Drew and Adrian exchanged a worried look.

"Maybe that's enough talk about this for one day," Adrian said.

"No," I said. "You said this thing was evil. What is it?"

"We're not sure what he is, Julia," Adrian admitted. "Usually, this isn't a problem. Not at all. You said it yourself; Havenwood is full of spirits. But this . . . this is something different."

I didn't like where this conversation was going. "You said something about opening up the east salon."

Adrian nodded. "Yes. It has been closed for some years."

"Ever since that night with Seraphina?"

"No." Adrian's eyes glistened with tears, and he shook his head as if to shake them away. "There was another night. Much more recently."

Drew got up to stoke the fire, and a wave of realization washed over me.

"It has to do with why Mrs. Sinclair dropped out of sight and stopped writing."

"That's right," Adrian said, taking a sip of his drink. "You needed to hear about the last night Seraphina was ever here at Haven-wood to understand my mother's story. As I said, the two are intertwined. My mother's tale wouldn't have existed without Seraphina's."

"What are you three talking about?" Mrs. Sinclair's voice pierced the tense atmosphere in the room and made everyone jump.

"Mother!" Adrian scrambled to his feet and crossed the room toward her. "What are you doing out of your suite?"

She tousled his hair. "Can't an old dowager take a little walk around her own house?"

"But the hallways are pitch-black," he protested. "Mother, I don't want you hurting yourself. You might have fallen down the stairs!"

"Oh, for goodness' sake, I'm not going to fall down the stairs," she said, holding up a lantern similar to the one Marion had given me. "He treats me like I'm a hothouse flower," she said to Drew and me, shaking her head.

"Now," she said, crossing the room and pouring herself a drink at the sideboard. "What are we talking about? You three look absolutely caught up in something."

"Oh, we're just sharing stories," Adrian said, shooting me a look. I understood: we wouldn't be finishing the tale, at least not right then. I slumped against the back of the sofa, wishing she hadn't come in here.

"Actually, Amaris, I was telling Julia here about the fact that old Andrew was in love with Seraphina, back in the day," Drew said, pushing himself out of his seat on the couch and crossing the room to freshen his drink.

"Ooh, there's nothing like century-old gossip to liven up an afternoon!" she cooed. "Yes, Julia, it's true. Did he tell you about us finding the journal?"

I nodded, clearing my throat. "That must've been quite exciting."

"Indeed it was," she said, her eyes twinkling. "A communication from another place and time. It was like looking through a window into the past. Drew, you've got it out in the stables, yes? Maybe you can show it to our dear Julia someday soon."

"I'd like that," I said.

And then our conversation turned to other things—the blizzard and the power outage, mostly—until Marion came into the room and announced dinner was served. We were all following her to the dining room when I felt Adrian's hand on my arm pulling me back. He waited until Drew had escorted his mother through the archway before he locked eyes with me and spoke.

"Thank you for not saying anything to Mother about what we were discussing," he said, his voice low.

"Of course," I said, but truthfully, I wondered about the reason for the secrecy. "But if it's on the loose—"

"I don't want you to worry about that," he said.

"But," I pressed, "I really do want to hear the rest of this story, especially considering the fact that I ran headlong into this thing." My stomach tightened at the thought of it.

"Yes," he said, "and you will. But for the time being, I think it's best for you to simply stay out of the library and especially the east salon. Gideon is contained there, somehow. He has never appeared in the rest of the house."

"How is that possible?" I asked, my voice dropping to a low whisper.

Adrian shook his head. "We really don't know. We've speculated that Seraphina put some sort of a shield around the rooms before she left."

"That's why you left the east salon closed?"

"That's right."

"But, knowing all of this, why would your mother have opened it again?"

"Julia," he said, taking me by the arm. "You're asking questions that I just can't answer right now. Another time. Let's catch up with Mother before she comes looking for us."

"Of course. But, Adrian . . . ," I began, not quite knowing how to finish my thought. The familiar gnarling in the pit of my stomach told me something just wasn't right. The deep, dark woods were looking better and better.

"You're going to ask if you're safe here."

"Well, yes. It's just that, I don't know the whole story. I'm sure the unknown is far worse than whatever is really going on."

He took my hands in his and smiled. "I wouldn't be too sure about that, Julia. But I can assure you of one thing: no harm will come to you, not if I can help it. Did the dogs sleep in your room last night?"

I nodded.

"Good. Expect them again. Neither man nor beast will bother you with those girls by your side."

As we walked down the dark hallway toward the dining room, I felt good about the "man" part of that sentence. It was the "beast" comment that was tying my stomach into knots.

TWENTY-EIGHT

*D*uring dinner, as the others were chatting about this and that, I wasn't really listening. I was thinking about the tale Adrian and Drew had just told me. I had no doubt they believed what they were saying, but they seemed to be alluding to the fact that what I had encountered in the library earlier in the day was . . . what? That same evil and monstrous thing?

It just didn't ring true. It seemed rather—well, "ridiculous" is a harsh word, but that was how it seemed to me at the time. As I was sitting there in Havenwood's beautiful dining room eating off fine china on an exquisitely set table, candles glittering everywhere, the whole story seemed far-fetched, to put it mildly.

I had no doubt the place was full of spirits. But the idea that something evil had been lurking in the east salon since Seraphina released it all those years ago? Not only was it far-fetched, but it just didn't make sense. After all, Andrew McCullough married and raised his children here. They then married and raised children of their own here. Mrs. Sinclair had been living at Havenwood for decades. Even Marion and the rest of the staff—they'd been here for all of that time, too. Generations of the same family would hardly reside for decade upon decade in another *Amityville Horror* house, infested with evil. If what Adrian had told me was true, why wouldn't the family simply have left?

Adrian had said that whatever caused Mrs. Sinclair to drop out of sight was related to what happened with Seraphina. Without knowing the rest of the story, I couldn't pass judgment on that. But I knew one thing for sure: what I had discovered in the library was flesh and blood. I had felt his breath on my neck. I'm no expert, but I didn't think ghosts, even evil ones, did a whole lot of breathing.

No. The only explanation had to be that someone was in the house.

As the certainty of this took hold, I felt a chill. What was I going to do now? Adrian had specifically asked me not to mention either my "encounter" or anything about the fire to Mrs. Sinclair, but . . . someone had broken into the house! It might be the Chicago arsonist, for all I knew. I pictured flames against the night sky. How could anyone, especially Mrs. Sinclair, get out of a burning Havenwood? I was desperate to warn her. But how?

"Say," I began, after I had finished the last of my icy sorbet and Marion was pouring coffee for us all. "We haven't talked much about our 'visitor' from the other night."

"You're right, dear!" Mrs. Sinclair said. "I'd almost forgotten about it, to tell you the truth." She turned to her son. "Any progress on that front?"

Adrian scowled at me. Obviously this line of conversation annoyed him. So be it. I was going to push further.

"I was wondering the same thing," I said to him. "You mentioned you had a man on it?"

"I do," Adrian said, drawing out the words as though he were grasping in the air for what to say next. "He was tracked into the forest; then the trail went cold. But it's nothing to worry about, not unless he makes another appearance. This blizzard obliterated any possibility of him coming back. There's no way a person could make it through this blinding snow."

Unless he came to the house and settled in before it started, I thought.

"This man you have on it," I continued, "is he an employee here at Havenwood?"

Adrian nodded and took a sip of his coffee. "Mr. Tucker from the groundskeeping staff."

"Is he here now, during the blizzard?"

"Yes," Adrian said. "We have a staff of—what is it now, Mother? Twenty? Most live in the village, but some, including Mr. Tucker, live on-site."

This was news to me. "Twenty staff people?" I had seen only Marion, a couple of girls in the kitchen, and the people who had cleaned the east salon the day before. It was hard to believe there were so many others.

Mrs. Sinclair beamed. "Most are cleaning staff who take care of the house," she explained. "They do their work early in the morning, before any of us are up. It simply wouldn't do to be hearing Hoovers and smelling cleaning solutions."

I steered the conversation back to the topic at hand. "This Mr. Tucker. Might you ask him, and maybe a couple of his colleagues, to patrol the house at night, just until we're certain any possible danger had passed?"

Adrian shot me a look. "I hardly think that's necessary," he sniffed.

"You're probably right," I said. "But all the same, I'd hate to think of someone prowling around the house while we're all sleeping. Heaven only knows what a person like that might do."

"I couldn't agree more, my dear," Mrs. Sinclair said, setting her coffee cup on the table with an air of finality. "Adrian, make it happen."

"Of course, Mother." He smiled at her. "Anything you say."

"I'll take a little stroll myself from room to room tonight," Drew offered. "Believe me, Julia, if anyone is hiding in this house, he'll wish he wasn't."

After dinner, as Mrs. Sinclair was leading everyone back into the drawing room for a nightcap, I pulled Adrian aside.

"I'm sorry about that," I said.

"Julia, you know it wasn't some man in the library," he whispered. "I wish I had been able to tell you the entire story."

I shook my head. "I'm not trying to stir up trouble where there isn't any, but please. Just think about it from my perspective. My house was burned to the ground by an arsonist, and there's a strange man looking into our windows the very next night. I'm terrified that I'm going to bring ruin upon you all, that the man who was here is the arsonist, and that he's going to set fire to Havenwood to finish the job he started in Chicago."

He looked at me with such a tender expression that I almost burst into tears.

"Listen to me, my dear. There's not going to be any fire, and I'm fairly certain there's not an intruder lurking here at Havenwood. But on the off chance you're right and you encountered a living human being in the library tonight, let's just pray that Mr. Tucker catches him before Drew McCullough does." He gave me a slight smile. "Woe be unto any poor soul who trespasses on the land of a Scotsman."

I tried to smile in return, but my eyes remained tearful. "I suppose you're right," I offered.

He nodded. "All the same. Lock your door tonight, Julia. And I'll send the dogs up with you. You have absolutely nothing to fear."

As we walked out of the dining room to join the others, I didn't have the heart to tell Adrian that I didn't fear an intruder creeping into my room. That I could handle. It was the idea of a fire that terrified me. As we walked down the hallway, my eyes darted this way and that, but I didn't see what I was looking for. It occurred to me that I'd never seen a smoke detector anywhere at Havenwood.

TWENTY-NINE

We sat for a while in the drawing room after dinner. The candles were blazing, the fire in the fireplace crackling, casting shadows on the walls that danced and swayed like revelers at a ball. Mrs. Sinclair was talking about something or other, but my thoughts were dancing around in my head with the shadows.

"You look troubled, my dear," she said, turning to me and jolting me out of my imaginings. "Still worried about our visitor?"

"I'll feel better when we've either caught whoever it is, or confirmed that I'm wrong and nobody is lurking around the house," I said, staring at the flames, willing them to stay confined to the fireplace.

"Agreed," Mrs. Sinclair said. "But for now, piglets, I'm going to retire. I've got a collection of good books in my suite and I plan to curl up for a few hours and read."

Adrian pushed himself to his feet. "Let me walk you upstairs, Mother," he said. "I know you've got a lantern but these hallways are so dark when the power is out."

She took his arm and looked back at me, a twinkle in her eye. "He's such a good boy, isn't he?" They walked through the archway together. "Good night, all!" she sang over her shoulder. And then they disappeared into the dark corridor.

I eyed Drew across the room. Electricity seemed to charge the air between us.

"And then there were two," he said, getting up to stoke the fire. "Would you like another brandy?"

"I'm good," I said, swirling the liquid in my snifter. I didn't want a repeat performance of the other night, tempting as the outcome may have been.

He refilled his glass and joined me on the sofa. We sat together in silence for a while, staring at the fire.

"You believe what you heard tonight in the library was the person looking in the kitchen window, the one we tracked into the woods," he said finally, still gazing into the flames.

"I do," I admitted. "I know what you and Adrian said, but—"

He held up a hand to cut me off. "You may well be right," he said. "I didn't want to jump into the fray between you and Adrian, but ghost in the library or no ghost in the library, there's no doubt that someone was lurking outside of Havenwood and may well have found his way inside. If that's the case, then whoever it was had to have gotten in before the blizzard, because there's no way anyone could have made his way here during it."

I nodded. "That's exactly what I've been thinking. So, what do we do now?"

"We? Nothing. Adrian is talking to Mr. Tucker and his cohorts, and they'll patrol the house tonight. I am planning a walkabout of my own. But you? If this is someone who is here to do you harm, there is no way short of dying that I'm allowing you to come into contact with him."

At first, the comment prickled my insides a bit. Who was he to "allow" me to do anything? But at the same time, I felt secure in a way that I hadn't felt in a very long time, if ever. I couldn't help but smile.

"I meant what I said out in the woods, Julia." He smiled back at me, a slight shyness showing on his face. "I'm very glad you came to Havenwood. I hope you're glad, too."

I could feel my own face redden. "I am. Very glad to be here, and to have met you." I stumbled over my words, quickly adding: "All of you."

"You've brought a liveliness to this house that we haven't seen in years," he said, moving a bit closer to me. "It's an old saying, but it really fits in this case. You're a breath of fresh air."

"It's funny. I've only been here a few days, but it feels like forever. My old life seems very far away and almost unreal. Like it was a dream I was having in my bedroom upstairs."

He nodded. "I know what you mean. This place has a way of enveloping a person, doesn't it? Taking over and blocking everything else out."

I took a sip of the spicy amber liquid and felt it warm me from the inside out. "I don't mind telling you that I've had some pretty strange things happen to me since I've been here," I said, remembering the paintings. "Other than the guy in the library, I mean."

"Havenwood is one big ghost story; that's for certain. Just like one of Mrs. Sinclair's stories. That's not going to scare you away, I hope."

I stared into the fire and shook my head. "I know it should probably bother me more than it does. I'm sort of taking the ghosts in stride. I think I'd have been more surprised if a house like this didn't have some dearly departed residents."

"Oh, Havenwood has its share of those, no doubt," he said, taking a sip of his Scotch and swirling the ice around in his glass.

"I'm more afraid of a real-life, flesh-and-blood intruder," I said. "Especially if he's come here for me."

"You have nothing to fear, Julia," he said, draping an arm across the back of the sofa and turning toward me. "There was only one set of tracks in the snow, remember? If this is true, if this same person has doubled back somehow after we tracked him and is now inside Havenwood, he's just one man. He doesn't stand a chance."

He held my gaze for a moment. The air thickened between us and I was struck by the kindness of his face, the slight lines around his eyes betraying years of laughter. I imagined myself sliding over and wrapping my arms around him—why not? We were alone in a candlelit room, the brandy was working its magic, we were both single as far as I knew, and even though I had been trying to tell myself otherwise, there was something about this Scotsman that tempted me to follow where the moment, if not sensibility, was leading.

But I didn't. I can't quite explain why, but I chose that moment to jump up and pour myself another brandy.

"I guess I will have a bit more after all," I said, my words coming out too fast and tripping all over one another. Whatever had been brewing between us disintegrated and fell to the floor.

Drew smiled and shook his head, downing the last drops from his glass: "Well, it's been a long day. I guess it's about time for me to turn in."

The words I failed to say were scratching at the back of my throat, the kiss that I denied stinging my lips. "You're not going to the stables in this storm, are you?"

He shook his head. "No, I'll retreat to my rooms here in the main house tonight." He pushed himself off the sofa and stretched. "But, before I do, may I walk you upstairs? Those hallways are pitch-black."

"That would be great," I said, taking a big sip of my brandy and putting the glass on the table. "I really have no wish to venture out into a darkened Havenwood alone. God only knows what might be lurking."

He smiled and offered his arm. I took it and we set off together, the lantern casting a delicate glow before us. As we walked, I could swear I heard muffled voices in the darkness, and I imagined it was the paintings murmuring and whispering as we passed.

"Andrew's got a girl," I clearly heard, the voice crackling like the sound of an old record on a gramophone.

"It's about time," another voice said, wispy and light, like wind through pine needles.

I let out a giggle and Drew turned to me. "Something's funny?"

"You don't hear that?"

"The only thing I've heard is our footsteps, and I seriously doubt that's tickling your funny bone."

I smiled and held tighter to his arm. "It's nothing," I said. "Just the walls talking."

He chuckled. "If any walls had stories to tell, it would be these."

We reached the grand staircase and started up. Marion was right: the place was as dark as a tomb now that the sun was down. I shuddered. Anything could be out there, in the darkness, waiting.

We finally reached my room, where I saw the three dogs curled up in front of the door, their tails thumping in unison, their faces full of expectant joy.

"Girls!" Drew said, bending down to tousle fur and scratch ears. He stood up and smiled at me, leaning against the wall. "I see you've got your bodyguards for the evening."

"I do," I said, grasping in the dark for the next word, worried my heart was thumping as loudly as the dogs' tails. I held the lantern out to him. "I suppose you'll be needing this."

He took it, and I found myself suddenly all too aware of my hands. Should I clasp them together? Let them dangle at my sides? Finally I stuffed one of them in my pocket and pushed a tendril of hair behind my ear with the other.

"Going on your rounds now?" I asked him, my voice a little higher than I expected.

"Off to protect Havenwood," he said, pushing himself away from the wall. "It's been my duty for some time now, you know."

"I can see we're all in good hands," I said, fingering the doorknob. "I suppose I should . . ."

"Sleep well, then," he said. His gaze fell to the floor and then rose up to me again. "Good night, Julia."

"Good night," I said with a gulp.

I stood there for a moment, watching him walk down the dark hallway, the light of his lantern bouncing off the walls. I was just about to open my door when it stopped.

"Oh, bloody hell," I heard him mutter before turning around and making his way back down the hallway toward me.

Did he forget something? Was there a problem? I didn't get a chance to ask him because he wrapped an arm around me and pulled me close into him, and before I knew what was happening, his mouth was on mine. Despite what my common sense was shouting at me from inside my brain, I slid my arms around his neck and leaned into him.

"I've been wanting to do that ever since I first laid eyes on you," Drew whispered.

"Me, too," I admitted, to myself as much as to him.

"I was intending to tell you my feelings tonight in the drawing room, but I got the distinct impression you didn't want to hear it, not right then," he said, his hand stroking the back of my neck. I could feel his breath on my cheeks.

"I do want to hear it," I whispered. "But not right now." I leaned in closer, hoping he wasn't going to dissipate like he did that night on the stairs. He didn't.

He pulled back and ran a hand through my hair, gazing at me with an intensity I could feel throughout my whole body. It was as though we were looking at each other through the eyes of two people who had been together for generations. I can't explain it, but I got the distinct feeling, as we stood there in this ancient house, that I was looking at him through Seraphina's eyes, gazing at her lover, Andrew. I wondered if their energies or spirits were hovering nearby, perhaps even inside of us. Somehow, in the darkness of Havenwood that night, that thought didn't seem as outlandish as it might have during the light of day. That night, I was willing to entertain all sorts of possibilities.

One of those possibilities, however, would have to wait.

"I'd love to invite you in, but—"

He shook his head. "You don't have to say it. I don't want to rush this, either. It feels too . . . important. I don't want to mess it up. We have all the time in the world to get it right."

He kissed me again, pulling me close. I felt my knees go weak with the force of it, and I hoped I wouldn't fall to the ground.

"Wow," I said, smiling up at him.

"Wow, indeed."

We stood there smiling at each other for a moment, and then he cleared his throat.

"I suppose I really should be going this time," he said. "I've got an intruder to catch tonight."

"Adrian said that he hopes Mr. Tucker catches him first."

"I daresay the intruder hopes that, too," Drew said. "I don't take a liking to anyone who is lurking around my house scaring a woman like you."

"Be careful, though," I whispered.

He nodded, taking my hand and kissing it. "I'll see you at breakfast, then."

I opened my door to let the dogs in, and stood in the doorway watching Drew walk back down the hallway. Halfway toward the stairs, he turned around.

"Lock your door behind you, Julia," he said.

"I will."

He went on his way then, until the darkness swallowed him up.

I closed and locked the door behind me to find a fire blazing and candles placed here and there. Marion's handiwork again. I was grateful for the cozy welcome to my room, especially that night. I also saw she had brought a snifter of brandy along with my usual carafe of water, and had placed both on the nightstand.

I washed my face, changed into my pajamas, and curled up in the armchair in front of the fire with the snifter of brandy, letting my thoughts drift back into the hallway, remembering the taste of his mouth on mine. I closed my eyes and exhaled.

THIRTY

I tossed and turned, but try as I might, sleep would not come. Even the hypnotic rhythm of the dogs' breathing didn't calm me the way it had the night before. I couldn't stop thinking about Drew prowling the corridors alone. If what I suspected was true— that one of Jeremy's victims who had set fire to my house in Chicago had indeed followed me here—then Drew might well be walking into danger because of me. I knew what he had told me to do, stay in my room behind a locked door, but my entire body was vibrating with the guilt that I had placed him, and everyone else here at Havenwood, at risk.

Maybe I could find him. I crawled out of bed, pulled my robe around me, and lit the lantern. I slipped out the door, the dogs close behind me. I hoped they knew me well enough to spring to my aid if I were threatened.

We crept down the grand staircase, the lantern casting a soft glow that bobbed from side to side as we made our way along. The house was deathly quiet. As we moved through the inky corridors, the only sound I could hear was my own breathing.

I had no intention of venturing anywhere near the library and the east salon, no intention at all. Adrian had warned me about that. But as I glanced down the hallway, I saw light coming from under the library's closed doors. But . . . how could that be? We were still without power, as far as I knew.

I stood there, peering down the hall for a few moments.

"Who's in the library, girls?" I whispered to the dogs, now sitting at my feet. "What are they doing?"

Maybe it was Drew. Or Mr. Tucker. Maybe they had found our visitor. Maybe it was the visitor himself. I decided to make my way down the hall to find out.

As soon as we reached the door, I heard rumblings from the dogs. Not growls, exactly, but yowls, almost like speech, soft and low. It was as though they were talking to one another, getting their plans straight for whatever might be coming next. I pulled open the doors, wholly unprepared for what I would find awaiting me there.

The room was ablaze with light from what seemed to be a thousand candles that had been set all around, casting their warm glow as far as the third-floor balcony, the books on the shelves illuminated so that their spines shone with color. A fire roared in the fireplace. And in an armchair in front of that fire sat Mrs. Sinclair, wearing her robe and slippers. She was staring into the flames and obviously had not heard me come into the room.

"Mrs. Sinclair?" I said. "What are you doing down here, out of bed at this hour?"

But she didn't respond to me. She didn't even look away from the fire. It was as though she didn't hear me at all. Was this one of her "episodes" that Adrian had spoken of? Part of her psychosis?

I took a step toward her, intending to put a hand on her shoulder and let her know I was there, but I didn't get the chance to do that because the dogs stood directly in my path. Molly locked eyes with me and let out a low, short growl. I understood perfectly. She was telling me not to move. I did as I was told.

Tundra and Tika were staring at Mrs. Sinclair, their heads down, their ears on high alert. Their tails, normally held high and curled, slowly dropped. At the same time, I noticed the fur on their backs bristle and stand up.

And then all three of them began to bark. Their massive chests produced a sound that might have come from a bear or a lion—a deep, threatening, snarling, terrifying sound loud enough to shake Havenwood's very foundations. Loud enough to wake the dead. But not Mrs. Sinclair. She didn't turn around; she didn't even look at us. She didn't have any idea three 140-pound animals were barking at her.

I wanted to go over to where she was sitting—maybe she was asleep?—and shake her. She needed help getting back upstairs to her suite, obviously. Where was the omnipresent Marion? But I couldn't move. The dogs had positioned themselves between Mrs. Sinclair and me, and there was no way I could get around them without losing an arm.

"Mrs. Sinclair!" I cried, hoping she could hear me above the din. "Amaris! It's Julia!"

At this, she turned her head slowly toward me. She was smiling. "Julia," she said.

"Mrs. Sinclair, what are you doing here? Can I help you back to bed?"

She turned her body toward me and gently eased herself off the couch.

At first, I didn't realize what I was seeing. Had she spilled something on herself? Tea, maybe? But then the realization hit me like an icy wave. The front of her white robe was red. She was covered in blood. It was dripping off her and pooling on the floor.

I dropped my lantern as my hands flew to my mouth. "Oh my God, Mrs. Sinclair! You're hurt!" I wanted to rush to her side, to help her, to stop the bleeding, but I still couldn't move. "What's happened?"

She took a step or two toward me, and the dogs stopped barking. Now they were growling, teeth bared. They looked like a pack of giant wolves, ready to take down a bull moose. Mrs. Sinclair didn't seem to notice them. She seemingly had no idea her life was in danger.

"Julia," she said again, a slight smile curling up the edges of her lips.

And that was when I realized she wasn't hurt at all.

As the dogs snarled, standing firm between Mrs. Sinclair and me, I looked into her eyes. They were inky black, devoid of expression. Not the dancing green eyes of the woman I had come to love over the past several days. I had no idea who was in the library with me, but it wasn't Mrs. Sinclair.

She just stood there, smiling a terrifying smile, the smile of a killer very much enjoying the moment just before it strikes its prey. The smile of someone who loves eliciting fear.

"Julia," she said. "Juuli."

While Tundra and Tika stood their ground, heads low, ears back, growling terrible growls at Mrs. Sinclair, Molly turned to me. In one awful moment I thought she was going to bite, but she nudged me backward, yowling in the way only sled dogs can, staring directly into my eyes. Again, I understood perfectly. She was herding me toward the door.

I backed up, one unsteady foot after another, keeping my eyes on Mrs. Sinclair all the while. When I reached the door and pulled it open, the other two dogs turned and followed us, and once they were through the door behind me, I slammed it shut.

I tore off down the pitch-black hallway—I had dropped my lantern in the library so I couldn't see an inch in front of my face—but I could hear Molly in front of me and the other two dogs behind me. My heart was pounding and my breath was coming in short bursts. I think I was crying but I don't quite remember because all I could think of was that terrible thing that was masquerading as Mrs. Sinclair. I was running full out down what I knew to be the hallway past the empty rooms, which would lead to the main foyer and grand staircase. I had been in this house long enough; I didn't need to see to know where I was going.

But then, down at the other end of the hall, I saw the soft light of a lantern. It had to be Drew or Mr. Tucker.

"Hey!" I cried out, my voice shredded by the terror that was gripping me. "Help!"

"Julia?" I heard in the darkness. "Is that you?"

"Yes! Yes, it's me and the dogs!" I ran toward the lantern's glow and soon Adrian's face came into view. I finally reached him and threw my arms around him, sobbing into his chest. The dogs paced around us nervously.

He pushed me back and looked me in the face. "My God, Julia. What's happened?"

I bent at the waist, trying to catch my breath. "I've never been so glad to see anybody in my whole life," I said to him.

He took hold of my arms. "You look like you've seen a ghost."

My body wouldn't stop shaking. "Worse than that," I managed to squeak out. I took a deep breath and held his gaze. "Adrian, there's something in the library."

He nodded, furrowing his brow. "Yes. We talked about this earlier."

I shook my head. "No! No, we didn't talk about this earlier. Adrian, whatever is in the library, it looks just like your mother."

He squinted at me. "I don't understand, Julia."

I took another deep breath, trying to calm my racing heart. "Drew told me he was going to patrol Havenwood tonight," I said, my voice still vibrating with fear. "I started feeling a little guilty about that, because if someone is here, it's because of me. So I thought I'd try to find Drew and help. Maybe we could patrol together."

"Okay," Adrian said. "What happened then?"

"I was walking around, the dogs at my heels, and didn't see anything until I got to the hallway leading to the library," I said, turning my head to look behind me. "I saw light coming from the library doors. I went to investigate because I thought it might be Drew. It wasn't."

"You're saying it was Mother?" His face went blank.

I nodded. "It looked like her, but Adrian, it wasn't her. At first she didn't hear us come in, but my God. The dogs were snarling and barking—"

He put a hand up. "The dogs were barking at Mother?"

"I thought they were going to tear her apart!" I told him. "They were barking and snarling and stood between me and Mrs. Sinclair. But she didn't even hear them."

"Didn't hear them?"

I shook my head. "They were barking at her and she didn't even look up. She just stared into the fireplace. That's what I'm telling you, Adrian. It looked like her, but it wasn't her. It wasn't until I said, 'It's Julia,' that she turned to me. And then she just kept saying my name over and over. Julia, Julia, Julia."

His eyes grew wide. "Where is she, did you say? The library?"

I nodded.

"Can you get back up to your room by yourself?" he asked me.

"I think so."

"Good. Take the dogs and lock your door. And for heaven's sake, Julia, do as you're told this time and don't come out again until morning."

With that, he turned to make his way down the hall.

I reached out and grabbed his arm. "Adrian!"

He looked into my eyes. "What is it?"

"She was covered in blood."

I saw the color drain from his face. "Is she hurt?" His voice was small and very far away.

I shook my head. "She didn't seem to be hurt." My voice dropped to a whisper. "But, Adrian, I have the awful feeling that she hurt someone else. Where else would all of that blood have come from?"

He closed his eyes and swallowed, hard. "Julia, do as I say. Go back up to your room. Lock the door. And don't come out again until morning. I'll handle this."

"No!" I protested. "I don't know what's in the library, but it's not your mother. Its eyes were black, Adrian. It just kept smiling and repeating my name. I'm not going to let you do battle with whatever that is on your own. We should find Drew and Mr. Tucker and get whatever kinds of weapons exist in this house and, I don't know, maybe call the police and—"

But Adrian's tentative smile stopped my words. "Please, Julia. Do as I say now."

And then he turned and was gone, swallowed up by the gloom. As I stood there watching him until he disappeared into the darkness, my stomach seized so violently that I was afraid my dinner was about to make its way back up. The blood on Mrs. Sinclair's robe was all I could see, my vision red with the thought of it. Whom had she—or whatever that creature was—hurt?

THIRTY-ONE

$\mathcal{I}$ tried to block out that thought, knowing that if I simply made my way upstairs, I could find my room and be safe on the other side of a locked door in very short order. But someone in this house was hurt, perhaps even dying. I couldn't go back to my room in the face of that.

I had to find a way to get in touch with Drew and Marion and everyone else at Havenwood to make sure they were okay. But how? Go from room to room in this enormous house in the dark, without so much as a candle to light my way?

I closed my eyes and opened them again, trying to get my bearings. I was standing in the middle of the foyer—the grand staircase behind me, the maze leading to the kitchen and breakfast room on one side. Then I remembered seeing Marion produce a flashlight from a kitchen cupboard a few nights previous. If I could get there, I figured at least I would have a source of light to help me get upstairs, if I didn't find anything else first.

"We can make it," I said to the dogs.

We set off through the blackness, staying close to one wall so I could feel my way along.

Slowly, my eyes became accustomed to the darkness, and I began to see shapes. A chair here, a sideboard there, even outlines of the frames holding the paintings on the walls.

They are certainly quiet, I sniffed to myself. Ever since I had arrived at Havenwood, the paintings had shimmered with life. And now, when I needed some help, they were silent.

But then Mrs. Sinclair's own words echoed in my head—something she had said to me days before—and a chill descended around me and held me where I stood:

Don't be surprised to encounter the odd spirit wafting down the hall-ways here, Julia. Be surprised when you don't. That means something a bit more sinister is at work.

Something more sinister. Is that what I had just seen? Were the very spirits of Havenwood afraid of whatever had Mrs. Sinclair in its thrall?

I tried to put those thoughts out of my mind and hurried toward the kitchen, pushing open its swinging doors with such force they thudded against the wall.

"Marion!" I called out, my voice shattering the silence of the house and echoing through the emptiness. "Hello! Are you here?"

I realized she was probably in her room for the night, and I had no idea where it was. Off the kitchen? Upstairs on the third floor?

No matter. With or without her, I needed a source of light. I began rummaging through the drawers, not quite remembering where Marion had found the flashlight, when my eyes fell on something standing in the middle of the countertop. A lantern! I picked it up and turned it on, and sure enough, its soft glow illuminated the room. I held it up and turned toward the door, and only then did I see her.

It was Marion, standing in the opposite doorway. Her hair wasn't in her usual severe bun, but down and loose at her shoulders. She was wearing a white cotton nightgown, and there in the soft light of the lantern, she looked much younger somehow, her skin un-lined and glowing. I jumped back, holding the lantern in front of me, its light shaking to and fro like a strobe.

"Do you need something, miss?" she said. "I heard you calling."

I exhaled, bending over at the waist and placing one hand on the counter for support. "Marion, you scared the life out of me," I said to her, managing a slight chuckle.

But when I looked up at her again, she had disappeared. Nobody was in the opposite doorway. That door was closed tight.

"Marion?" I whispered, knowing full well nobody was going to respond.

"Oka-a-a-y," I said aloud. "I'm done." All thoughts of finding others to warn them about what I had seen in the library vanished. The only thing I wanted was to be back upstairs in the safety of my room. I should have known better than to creep through the halls of Havenwood at night, especially that night. What was I thinking? I should have listened to Drew and Adrian when they told me to stay behind my own locked door.

I hurried through the maze of rooms and up the grand staircase holding the lantern in front of me, the dogs behind me, hoping nothing was lurking in the darkness. When I reached my hallway, I saw light coming from under the door of my room, and first the dogs, then I, took off at a run toward the sanctuary I imagined it would provide. I fumbled with the knob and slipped inside the door, closing and locking it behind me.

I watched as the dogs made for their water dishes right away—I supposed all of that barking and growling had left them thirsty. After drinking their fill, they did a few circles near my fireplace and slumped to the ground with a thud, tails curled around their noses. I wondered how they felt about seeing Mrs. Sinclair—their mistress—like that, defending me from her. They weren't my dogs, after all; they were hers.

I took a long sip of brandy before draping my robe over a chair and curling down under the covers. The fire in the fireplace was still crackling, and I stacked my pillows behind me so I could watch the flames. The wind seemed to be picking up outside, rushing around the exterior corners of the house, whooshing and whooping like a banshee.

Every time I closed my eyes, Mrs. Sinclair's ghoulish face floated through my field of vision. Adrian had said whatever I saw in the library was part of the story he had begun to tell me earlier in the evening. Was it somehow related to the reason why she had stopped writing and ended up in that mental institution? Did she kill someone? Or was it more than that? If it truly was Mrs. Sinclair in the library earlier, she seemed—I hesitated to even formulate the word—"possessed" by something dark and horrible and monstrous. When I looked into the face of whatever it was in the library, I did not see the Mrs. Sinclair that I knew. It was as if the eccentric, sweet-natured lady had vanished and something dark and menacing had taken her place.

The whole evening was like something out of my worst nightmares. Was that what I had chosen by coming to Havenwood? To live in a nightmare?

THIRTY-TWO

Somehow, sleep managed to capture me and take hold. But I kept fighting it, tossing and turning, strange thoughts taking my dreams hostage to macabre places. Once, I was rustled awake by the sound of the telephone ringing at the end of the hallway, but I put my hands over my ears to muffle the noise, and before I knew it, I drifted off to sleep again. I knew better than to venture out of my room alone on this night again. And the last person I wanted to hear from was Jeremy.

Soon enough, I was opening my eyes to a bright and sunny morning, and all thoughts of otherworldly phone calls and nightmares were drifting back into the ethers from which they came.

But then I remembered Mrs. Sinclair and the strange specter that seemed to be Marion, and I curled back under the covers, shivering.

I was perfectly safe, or I thought I was, in my room. I toyed with the idea of simply staying there all day. Unlike the night before, I had no compelling urge to venture out into the hallways to find what was awaiting me there. I didn't want to know.

But my blissful isolation was not to be. The dogs saw that I was awake and were pacing back and forth, nudging me with their noses, one even going so far as to jump up on the bed and place her great head on my chest. Her yellow eyes staring intently into mine told me the girls wanted their breakfast and a walk outside.

I could hardly keep them cooped up in the bedroom with me, as much as I might have wanted to do so.

I didn't even bother to shower. I washed my face and brushed my teeth, ran a brush through my hair—not perfect but it would have to do—and pulled on a warm cable-knit sweater and jeans, along with the thickest socks I could find. I had stashed my boots and jacket in the closet downstairs, and I prayed that I could get there without seeing anyone. I needed some time to think and I knew just where I wanted to do it.

I slipped down the grand staircase, the dogs at my heels, through the foyer, and toward the front door, holding my breath all the while. I saw no one. The house was as quiet as it had been the night before. Tears stung my eyes when I thought of my strange encounter with Marion, and I hoped it didn't mean what I thought it meant, that she was buzzing around getting ready for breakfast, as usual, and not lying somewhere with a knife in her chest. I looked over my shoulder toward the kitchen and almost marched back there to see for myself, but I couldn't bring myself to move closer. I did not want to find an empty kitchen, not when I was alone.

So, after bundling up, I headed outside and into the wind.

The dogs bounded into the air as though they were jumping into a warm pool of water, but it hit me like a thousand icy pinpricks on my face and neck, pulling the breath out of my lungs. I had grown up with Minnesota winters, but I couldn't remember feeling anything like this. *It must be double digits below zero*, I thought, pulling my hood up and snapping it around my neck. I held my gloves over the exposed part of my face, put my head down, and started trudging forward.

It had snowed more than two feet during the blizzard, but someone had already shoveled a path between the main house and the stable. The dogs didn't pay it any mind; they bounded and jumped through the drifts, yowling and barking with glee. By the time I got to the stable, they had already done a few laps around it and were huffing and puffing at the door. I knocked. No answer. I knocked again, louder this time. Nothing. My heart sunk.

I tried the door, and when I found it unlocked, I pushed it open, just a crack. "Drew?" I called inside. "Are you there?"

The dogs nudged me out of the way and nosed the door open, the heat from the room colliding with the cold where I stood. I poked my head into the warmth. "Hey!" I called. "It's Julia!"

I took a few steps inside and shut the door behind me. The stable was as warm and welcoming as it had been when I had first seen it. The dogs were circling their food dishes, and after opening several cabinets to no avail, I found an enormous bucket with a lid on it. Their reactions told me it was dog food, so I poured a couple of scoopfuls into each of their dishes and they started gobbling up their meals.

"Well, hello there."

I whirled around to see Drew standing in the doorway to his quarters, wearing sweatpants, a T-shirt, and mocs. His hair was wet.

"You've caught me just out of the shower, I'm afraid." He smiled.

My throat seized up. He was all right, then. Whoever's blood was covering Mrs. Sinclair the night before, it wasn't his. I gulped in air but couldn't get a deep breath. I wanted to fall to my knees to give thanks, or at the very least rush over and throw my arms around him, but my feet were frozen to the floor. "Hi" was all I managed.

"I see you brought the girls for their breakfast," he said, glancing toward the dogs and running a hand through his hair.

"Yes." Why wasn't I able to formulate more than a few words?

"Come on in." He nodded toward his quarters. "I've got the kettle on. We have some time before we've got to get up to the main house. Let's have a cup of tea."

I followed him into his suite. "I'm not sure there's going to be any breakfast," I said. I unzipped my jacket with shaking hands and slipped out of my gloves before slumping down onto the leather sofa.

He handed me a cup of sweet-smelling tea. "What's happened, Julia?" he said, sitting beside me.

I set the tea on the end table and looked into his face, so concerned, so loving. And then the tears came. He enveloped me in his arms, holding me while I shook with the force of everything I had experienced the night before.

"I thought I had lost you," I said, my voice wavering.

"That's not possible," he said, pushing a strand of hair behind my ear. "You're not going to lose me. Remember what I said about the seventeen people? It still stands."

"I thought it was sixteen." I managed a chuckle.

"Who's counting? Now," he said, pushing a box of tissues in my direction, "why don't you tell me exactly what's going on?"

I blew my nose and took a sip of the steaming tea. It seemed to calm me from the inside out, somehow. In a moment, I was together enough to tell him what had happened. It was, after all, why I'd come.

"I knew you were in the house last night, but I thought you'd be out here checking on the horses this morning," I began. "At least I hoped you would be."

"You thought right," he said. "I needed to make sure they were okay after yesterday's blizzard. They were fine, if a bit hungry."

"I came to tell you about something that happened to me in the house last night," I said. "You will not believe it."

He crossed the room and poured a cup of tea for himself. "Oh, I'll wager I will."

I took a deep breath. "Well, I started feeling guilty about you prowling around the house alone," I said.

"Don't tell me you went searching for me."

I nodded, looking up at him like a guilty child might look at a parent, and took another sip of tea. "I don't quite know how to say this," I started. "I was wandering through the house looking for you, and I saw some light coming from the library. So I went in there, and that's where I found her."

"Found who?"

"Mrs. Sinclair," I said. I reached for my tea but put my hands down into my lap when I saw how much they were shaking. "Only, it wasn't Mrs. Sinclair."

"Go on," he said, clearing his throat.

"Drew, she was covered with blood. I thought it was yours. She was talking in this weird voice and her eyes . . . they weren't her eyes at all. They were black, for one thing, and it was like she saw me, but didn't see me, not really."

"And then what happened?" he whispered, his eyes wide.

"The dogs started barking at her. Ferociously! I took that moment to get out of there, they followed, and we ran headlong into Adrian."

"So, he knows about this."

I nodded and took another sip of my tea. "He said he'd handle it. Whatever that meant."

I opened my mouth to tell Drew about the Marion business, but closed it again when a chill began to work its way up my spine. Drew was just sitting there, looking at me with the calmest of faces. I had just told him of a nightmarish encounter, and he was reacting as though I was talking to him about the weather or saying that the dogs needed a walk.

I pushed myself up from the sofa, clutching my jacket and gloves. I walked out into the main stable, wanting the dogs near me.

"Hey," he said, following me. "Where are you going? What's the matter?"

I whirled around. "None of this surprises you! I don't get it. I tell you that the woman who owns this house is running around covered in blood and you react like I'm telling you Marion burned the scones."

"Julia," he said, his voice low and soothing. He was walking toward me like he would approach a skittish horse, palms up. "You need to calm down."

"And *you* need to explain to me what's going on here," I said, my heart beating so fast that I found myself gulping air into my lungs in an effort to quiet it.

"Okay," he said, his palms still up in the air as though he were trying to push something away.

I nodded, not saying anything. It was up to him now.

"Listen," he said, looking down at his T-shirt and slippers, "give me a few minutes to change. Then we'll go up to the main house together and we'll sort all of this out. We'll find Adrian and he'll tell us exactly what happened. It's about time for breakfast, so we know just where he'll be."

"Breakfast?" I could scarcely believe what I was hearing. "I have no idea if anyone is still alive in the house after last night; that's what I'm trying to tell you. And you haven't even heard about Marion yet!"

"What about Marion?"

"I was looking in the kitchen for a flashlight and she appeared there—and then she was gone! Considering the fact that Mrs. Sinclair was doused in blood, and the blood obviously wasn't yours . . ." I took a deep breath and finally said the words: "I'm terrified that, what with all the ghosts I've been seeing around Havenwood, Marion's now one of them. What other explanation could there be?"

"This is Havenwood, lassie," he said. "There are limitless amounts of explanations for otherworldly things happening around here. Now, promise you'll wait for me while I throw on something a little more presentable?"

What else was I to do? I certainly wasn't planning on venturing back into the house by myself. "I'll wait," I said.

While Drew changed, I wandered through the stable, stopping for a moment at Nelly's stall. She came right up to me and I stroked her head, her gentle eyes calming my frayed nerves.

"Do you remember me, girl?" I said to her.

Drew appeared through the doorway and smiled. "You can give her a carrot if you'd like," he said, handing one to me.

I put it in my palm and held it out to her. She gobbled it up, careful not to touch my hand with her teeth. I could feel the calmness and strength she was exuding, almost as if she knew I needed it.

"We'll go riding again once the weather warms up a bit," he said.

I wondered if I'd be at Havenwood that long.

"Now," he said, grabbing his coat and hat, "bundle up. We'll head on up to the main house and get to the bottom of whatever went on last night. I promise."

"Come on, girls," I called to the dogs as I zipped up my jacket and pulled on my gloves. "We're going outside!"

Drew shot me a look. "They're happy out here, you know," he said. "The stables are heated and they can come and go into the field through their doggie door."

"Not a chance," I said, whistling again. "I'm not going back into that house without these dogs by my side."

I was convinced they saved me last night from whatever I encountered in the library. It was still there for all I knew. I wasn't going to take any chances.

The dogs stretched and yawned but were at my side within a few seconds. We all went through the doors together and out into the sunshine.

We trudged through the snow, my anxiety growing with every step. Why was I going back into that house when I knew what might be lurking there? I gazed into the distance and wondered if I could make it the three miles to town on my own. Frigid, yes, but in that moment, I tried to convince myself that I preferred a little frostbite to the threat of what might be waiting for me inside the house.

In the end, though, I followed where Drew was leading. What

other real choice did I have? The bears might be hibernating this time of year, but the wolves, mountain lions, and lynx were active in the winter woods. And probably hungry.

We peeled off our coats and boots in the foyer, and Drew started off toward the kitchen. I intended to go with him, but my feet wouldn't move. The dogs stayed by my side, pacing around me.

Drew poked his head around the archway. "Coming?"

The look of fear on my face must have spoken volumes, because he crossed the room and took my hands in his.

"I promise you, Julia, this house isn't any different today than it was yesterday at this time," he said, running a hand through my hair.

I exhaled. "Then I feel very naive about yesterday."

"No, you weren't," he said, shaking his head. "I would not allow you to remain in a dangerous situation. And I wouldn't have let Adrian bring anybody into this house if there were any chance . . ." His words trailed off, and I got the feeling he thought better of what he was going to say.

"Any chance of what?" I prodded.

The look on his face almost seemed to be pleading with me. "Will you just come to breakfast?" he asked, his voice wavering. "You need to know, Julia, that there is no way short of dying that I'm going to let any harm come to you."

"That's what I'm afraid of," I whispered.

"Come on," he said, "coffee and scones await. Marion will have fits if we keep Mrs. Sinclair waiting."

At the mention of her name, my stomach dropped. Would she be buzzing around the kitchen as she usually was? I didn't want to find out. I wanted to run back upstairs to my room and hide under the covers, but Drew took me by the hand and we set off, the dogs following close behind, our footsteps echoing through the house.

When we got to the threshold of the breakfast room, I locked eyes with Drew for a second and then pushed open the door. The room was empty, despite our lateness. No Mrs. Sinclair. No Marion buzzing about. Only silence. I knew this was what we'd find.

My hands flew to my mouth, muffling a cry.

Just then, Marion came through the kitchen door holding the coffeepot. I blinked a few times and then stared at her, open-mouthed.

"Oh, Marion, thank God," I said, my voice cracking.

"Is something wrong, Miss Julia?" she asked, placing the pot on the sideboard warmer next to the cream and sugar. "You look positively ashen."

I squinted at her. No mention of the night before? Did I even see what I thought I had seen?

"I'm just a little tired, I guess," I said, pulling my chair out from the table and slumping into it. Drew took the seat opposite me and smiled.

"Well," Marion said, pouring cups of coffee for Drew and me, "the good news is our power's back on."

The room was so bright; I hadn't noticed. She set the cups down in front of each of us, and then shuttled the cream and sugar to the table from the sideboard.

"Breakfast will be in a few minutes," she said over her shoulder, as she pushed open the kitchen's swinging door. "Omelets, sausage, fruit, and yogurt today. We're a little behind our time this morning, I'm afraid."

The door swung shut, and we were once again alone in the room. I looked at Drew, placing my hands on the table, palms up. "I have no idea what—" But I didn't get to finish that thought.

"Good morning, children!" It was Mrs. Sinclair, dressed in her familiar dark green jogging suit. "How are you both on this fine day? Thank goodness it stopped snowing!" She floated over to the sideboard to pour herself a cup of coffee, and I turned to Drew, shaking my head and mouthing: "What is this?"

He gave a swift shake of his head and scowled at me. I got the message. Obviously, I wasn't to bring up what had happened the night before. Obviously, this was just the way things were around here. I took another sip of my coffee.

Adrian came through the door next.

"Hello, all!" he said, pulling out his chair and sliding gently onto it. "I understand our power has been restored. Excellent!"

I didn't hear much of the conversation after that, or rather, it didn't register with me. All I could think about was the monstrous thing I had witnessed the previous night, and how nobody was talking about it now. Breakfast was going on as it usually did, with small talk about the weather and the day's events. Nobody mentioned the strange occurrence in the library, nobody mentioned the fact that Mrs. Sinclair was covered in blood, nobody mentioned Marion floating around like a specter. It was like it never happened.

Or—I asked myself as I looked at these people around the table nibbling at their omelets and scones, sipping their coffees with cream, casual, unconcerned expressions on their faces—was it that the previous night was an altogether ordinary occurrence here at Havenwood?

I held my fork aloft and looked from one to the next. Only Drew seemed to sense my growing unease, an almost hidden look of alarm creeping across his face, betrayed solely in his eyes. He shook his head so slightly that I almost didn't catch it, his eyes pleading.

It was all too much for me, suddenly and completely.

"Adrian," I said, my fork clattering on the side of my plate. "May I see you out in the hallway? For a word?"

I pushed my chair back from the table and stood up, depositing my napkin as I did so.

He didn't say anything in response. The three of them just sat there, staring at me.

"Please?" I said, and walked out of the room, the door swinging shut behind me. I stood waiting for him in the hallway for a moment, not quite knowing what I'd do if he didn't follow me. Thankfully, he did.

"What is it, Julia?" he said, still carrying his napkin from the table, his brow furrowed. "This is rather unusual."

"I know," I said, my voice wavering. "But when I came to Havenwood, you said you'd help me when it was time to leave. A new identity, money, things like that."

He nodded. "Of course."

"Well," I said, taking a deep breath in, "I think it's time. I want to leave."

He stood there, blinking at me, shaking his head slightly. "But you've only just arrived!"

"I know that," I said, running a hand through my hair and pacing back and forth in the hallway.

"Aren't you happy here, Julia?"

"Yes," I told him. "I am happy here."

"So, whyever would you want to leave?"

I stopped pacing and looked him square in the eyes. "Isn't it obvious, Adrian?" I let out a slight chuckle. "Do you really expect me to stay after what happened last night? I run into some kind of monster in the library, covered in blood no less, and then today, here at breakfast, you're all acting like it's nothing! I don't have any idea what I've walked into, but whatever it is, I don't like it. I don't feel safe here anymore. I feel—"

He put his hands up, the same as Drew had done. "Stop, Julia. Please listen."

"You keep saying that!" I cried, a bit too loudly. "Drew keeps saying that! I'm listening, Adrian, I've been listening. I'm just not hearing anything."

He took a few steps toward me and grasped my arms with both hands. "Julia," he said, his voice soft and soothing. "Please calm down."

"But . . ." I looked into his eyes. They were pleading with me, just as Drew's had been.

"Let's go back and finish our meals. That way Mother will toddle off to her room for her 'meditation time' and we can retreat somewhere and have a chat. Hear me out, Julia, before you make any decisions about leaving Havenwood. You owe me that much."

He was right. I did.

"I know it feels like you've walked into a nightmare," he said, his voice gentle. "But when you hear the whole story, it will make sense to you. As much sense as a story like this can make. And then, after you've heard it all, if you still want to leave us, I will arrange for you to do so with everything you'll need to start over. A new name, driver's license, passport, and money. Agreed?"

That sounded reasonable to me. The first reasonable thing I'd heard in a while. I took a deep breath. "Agreed."

Adrian pushed the breakfast room door open and held it as we walked through. We found Drew staring into his coffee cup and Mrs. Sinclair absorbed in watching a scene unfold outside the window: two cardinals flitting back and forth from one snowy pine branch to another. She turned to us as we each pulled out our chairs and slid back into our places.

"The children have returned." She smiled, holding her coffee cup aloft. "And what was this crisis about? Are you all right, Julia, dear?" She and Adrian exchanged a concerned look.

I opened my mouth to respond to her, but then closed it again.

"Julia is a bit homesick; that's all," Adrian said, clearing his throat before taking a sip of his coffee.

Mrs. Sinclair turned to me with such a look of compassion on her face that I could feel my heart squeezing with remorse. She laid one gnarled hand on mine. "Of course you are, my dear," she said. "We tend to forget you're a newcomer, because it feels to me—to all of us—as though you've been here at Havenwood with us forever. You're such a part of this place already that it's hard for us to remember you've only just arrived."

She looked from Adrian to Drew and back to me again. "Isn't that right, boys?"

"It's true, it's true," Drew said, his voice husky and rough.

"And what may we do for you, Julia, to help?" Mrs. Sinclair asked me.

Now it was my turn to look to Drew and Adrian, my eyes pleading with either of them to jump in and save me. But neither did, not right then.

"Well . . ." I began, grasping for ideas, but Mrs. Sinclair squeezed my hand, stopping me.

"I know!" she said, her green eyes dancing with delight. "I'll have Marion cook your favorite dish for dinner! Something you loved having at home in Chicago." She rapped the table with her hand. "That's settled, then! You have a think about it, and let Marion know what you'd like her to make. She may have to do some improvising with what she has in the pantry, so let her know early."

I couldn't help but smile. This woman wasn't anything like that creature in the library. She was her same, quirky, dynamic self. I couldn't imagine what had made her so changed, so horrible, so monstrous. I didn't want to imagine.

"Thank you, Mrs. Sinclair," I said, twisting my napkin in my lap.

"Chicago is known for its pizza, is it not?" Drew's eyes smiled at me over the rim of his coffee cup.

I raised my eyebrows. "That it is. Deep dish. The cheesier, the better."

Mrs. Sinclair let out a guffaw. "Marion just might walk out of here for good if we ask her to whip that up," she said. "A meat pie, yes. A pizza pie? I'm not sure!"

The conversation turned to other things, then. I watched as the three people around the table talked and laughed, but I couldn't take part in it, not really. I felt as though I were detached, separate, not really even there.

THIRTY-THREE

As Marion was clearing the breakfast dishes, she put a hand on Adrian's shoulder. "Mr. Tucker's wanting a word with you, Mr. Sinclair," she said, and then glanced over at Drew. "With the both of you."

My stomach dropped.

"Do you think he's corralled our visitor?" Mrs. Sinclair asked.

"I don't know," Adrian said, using his napkin to wipe the corners of his mouth before laying it on his plate and pushing his chair away from the table. "But we'll find out, now, won't we?"

He turned to Mrs. Sinclair. "Shall I escort you up to your suite, Mother?"

"No need, my darling." She laid a hand gently on his arm. "I plan to meditate and do some yoga to recharge for the rest of the day." She turned to me. "Later, Julia, I thought we might go down to the stables and visit the horses. I know it's still cold but maybe we could have a short ride, just around the property at least. How does that sound?"

"Wonderful," I said, taking a deep breath and trying to make my body feel what my words were describing. It wasn't working.

Adrian shot me a look and scowled at his mother. "You know I don't want you riding."

She laughed and squeezed his arm. "There's two feet of new snow! If I fall off, it'll be like falling into a pillow."

As Adrian steered his mother out the door, he looked back at me and winked. And then they were gone.

"We'll reconvene in Adrian's office after we're done with Mr. Tucker," Drew said, taking a last sip of his coffee and pushing his chair away from the table. "Where will you be until then?"

"Can I come with you?" I asked him. "If Mr. Tucker did find somebody, and if that somebody is here for me . . ."

Drew shook his head. "I don't think that's a good idea."

"Okay." I sighed, not having the strength for yet another fight. "But you'll tell me what he's found, if anything?"

"Of course we will," Drew said.

"I guess I'll just go back up to my room, then."

He put a hand on my back and steered me toward the door, my whole body tingling. "Would you like me to take you upstairs?"

I looked around for the dogs, and only then did I realize they weren't in the room with us. I wondered if they had gone with Mrs. Sinclair. Quite a change from the night before, when they might have ripped her throat out.

"Well, since my posse seems to have abandoned me . . ." I smiled at him and shrugged, and we walked through the door together.

We made our way through the empty rooms toward the grand staircase. Neither of us said anything. I was just enjoying being so close to him, smelling the fresh scent of soap mixed with the muskiness of the stable, hay and feed and fire.

We reached my room and stood outside the door. I leaned back against it.

"This is getting to be somewhat of a routine, isn't it?" he asked, his voice low and deep, moving in so close to me that I could feel his breath on my neck. "The dead last thing I want to do right now is go away from you to talk to Mr. bloody Tucker." Drew smiled.

"But we want to know what, if anything, he found, don't we?" I said.

"Right," he said, clearing his throat. "I will come back to get you, after we're finished with him."

I watched him walk down the hall away from me until he had turned the corner to the stairs. After he had gone and I was inside my room, I prayed that Adrian would clear up all of my fears and concerns. I was getting frustrated with these delays. It seemed as though they were forever starting a story but never finishing it. Always putting off really telling the truth about what was going on. Still, I had no choice but to wait until Drew and Adrian came back.

But what to do until then? Look out the window? Sit in front of the fire? Then I remembered the reason I had first gone into the library the previous day. The biography! In all the excitement, I had completely forgotten about it.

I found my cardigan in the closet, and sure enough, the slim volume about Seraphina was still in the pocket. Just the thing to pass the hours on a cold winter's morning. I settled into the arm-chair by the window, opened the book, and began to read.

> *At the Winter Palace, Seraphina warns the Romanovs . . .*
> *During a reading in the south of France for Victor Hugo,*
> *Seraphina channels his daughter Léopoldine . . . Onstage in*
> *London, Seraphina helps a wife confront the specter of her dead*
> *husband . . .*

It was mostly a collection of accounts of her readings. Interesting, yes, but it didn't tell me much of anything I didn't already know. She was a famous Spiritualist psychic who rose to great acclaim and traveled worldwide to help people communicate with their dearly departed loved ones, bringing messages of hope and of sorrow, warnings of impending doom and predictions of triumphs, or simply the knowledge that those on the "other side" were okay, happy, and, above all, still there.

Then I came to the chapter titled "Early Life." I held my breath and took in the words on the page.

The most famous psychic of the Spiritualist Age didn't material-ize onto the stage like one of the specters with which she communicated. Seraphina began life in a remote Finnish village.

My stomach flipped. She was Finnish, just like my ancestors. I read on. But the further I read, the more disappointed I became. The biography really didn't tell me much, beyond her having the gift of "sight" from a very early age. It also told of how she married a traveling merchant who came through her village. He was the one who exploited her gift and got her onto a world stage, or so it said. Interesting, sure, but not what I was looking for. I wanted some sort of proof that she was or wasn't my great-great-grandmother, and, of course, I wasn't going to find it here. I sighed, wondering how Mrs. Sinclair came up with this fantasy in the first place.

I scanned the rest of the pages until I got to the back of the book, and a word caught my eye. "Havenwood."

Seraphina traveled often to Havenwood, the remote estate of fur and lumber baron Andrew McCullough, who reproduced his family's ancient Scottish manor house in the Minnesota wilderness. McCullough was reportedly obsessed with Spiritual-ism, his parents having been tragically killed in a stagecoach accident while he was in America tending to his father's fur business. He took every opportunity to invite the young psychic to his home in an effort to receive messages from his mother and father.

It is after one of these visits that Seraphina vanished from history. She was last seen arriving at the Havenwood estate in one of McCullough's carriages that he famously had pulled by a team of eight horses. As was his habit whenever Seraphina

visited, McCullough had invited several prominent people to the
estate for a séance. The psychic likely had no idea it was to be
her last.

Rumors circulated for years about exactly what went on
inside the Havenwood estate that evening, but accounts from
servants hinted at danger, bodily harm, and even death.
Medical records from the doctor's office in the nearby town
reflect that two people were transported from the estate in need
of medical attention—one man received treatment for a heart
ailment and another for burns on his arm, but both men insisted
that nothing untoward had happened. The heart ailment was
something that flared up from time to time and the burns were
simply from carelessness with a candle, so the matter was
dropped and police did not investigate further. As to the death, it
could not be confirmed.

That was wrong. Or, at least, not complete. I thought of the Devil's
Toy Box that Adrian had mentioned and noticed that there was no
reference to it in the book I was holding.

Seraphina disappeared after that night. She never again
performed on the stage, nor is there any record of her conducting
any private séances. Local police, becoming suspicious after
repeated inquiries from her husband, investigated the possibility
that Seraphina had died on the estate that night, until receiving
a letter, postmarked from Chicago, stating that she was
alive and well and wished to be left alone. That ended the
matter, and it was the last anyone ever heard from Seraphina,
whose disappearance was as mysterious as her séances.

As I sat there gazing out the window, the closed volume sitting in
my lap, something was nagging at me and wouldn't let up until I
realized what it was. Nowhere in this book, the only one about
Seraphina in Havenwood's library, did it say her real name. Yet

Mrs. Sinclair had tried to convince me that Seraphina's real name was a "historical fact," and furthermore, that it was my great-great-grandmother's name. Juuli Herrala. How could she possibly have come to this conclusion if history itself was in the dark about Seraphina's real identity?

Then I remembered the letter I had stashed in the back of the book. I had nearly forgotten about it in all the excitement. I flipped to the last page, and there it was, right where I had left it.

It was addressed to Andrew McCullough at Havenwood, the handwriting delicate and precise. I turned the envelope over and over in my hands, my stomach seemingly turning with it, at the thought of what it might contain.

Finally I pulled the letter out of the envelope and unfolded it, smoothing the pages with great care. I took a breath in and began to read.

My dearest Andrew,

I do not know how I can possibly begin to apologize for the horror that was unleashed at your beautiful Havenwood at my hands. How does one make amends for waking the dead? How does one atone for taking a life? It simply cannot be done. There are no amends, there is no atonement for an act as heinous as mine. I shall carry the guilt and remorse, born on that night, throughout the rest of my life and longer than that, I fear.

My only defense, and it is really no defense at all, is ignorance. I fervently hope you know I would never intentionally have released such evil in your home, or anywhere.

I have had this "gift"—although I would not call it that now—for as long as I can remember, and I truly did not know that anything as monstrous as what we encountered at Havenwood existed in this world or any other. It has crumbled the very foundations of my life. When I was a child, I spoke of this gift to no one, fearing it would be branded witchcraft. But the

man who would become my husband told me this was not true,
that I could use my peculiar gift to help the bereaved by communicating with their departed loved ones.

But what we all endured at Havenwood has convinced me of
two undeniable facts: those who feared this gift were correct,
that it is not a gift at all but a curse, and my husband was, as
you tried so valiantly to convince me, in league with evil. It is he
who gave me the box. That I took money for this . . . I'm so
ashamed.

I am writing this letter not to elicit forgiveness, for I do not
deserve it. I am writing to let you know that I have put my
"gift" away forever. These words are my solemn vow to you—I
will never again communicate with the dead, never again hold a
séance, never again take a cent from a grieving widow. Seraphina is no more.

Furthermore, I will never again lay eyes on the face of the
man who enticed me into this life of wickedness. Although I
believe he, too, was ignorant of the power held in the Devil's Toy
Box when he found it in the Far East, I cannot forgive him for
bringing it into our lives. I only opened it that night because, for
the first time, no spirits responded when I attempted to contact
them. I had grieving people around the table that night—you
included—and I was desperate to help them find solace. I hope
you can believe, despite the horror I unleashed by opening the
box, that I meant no harm.

I have left him, and all of our ill-gotten gains, behind. He
does not know where to find me, nor will you. I will only say
this because I can, even now, feel your concern for my welfare. I
have traveled to live with my sister, who came to this country
some ten years ago. She lives a small but wonderful life and has
welcomed me with open arms. Best of all, the townspeople know
me only as Juuli, sister of Maija.

You begged me to stay at Havenwood that night, saying the
words that no married woman should ever hear from another

man. I longed to say them to you in return. One's feelings are not bound by marriage vows. But actions are. You must know that what you suggested was, and remains, impossible, no matter how much both of us would wish this were not the case. Your wife is a good woman who has been impossibly kind to me. I would never betray her in this way. So I have chosen instead to disappear and start a new life, so you can carry on with yours.

Our parting was so chaotic; I choose not to think on it. Instead, I remember our sweet conversations by the firelight, and the magic that passed between us as we walked through the woods to the shimmering river. I will hold those memories, and you, my dear Andrew, in my heart forever.

Yours,
Juuli Herrala

So this was where Mrs. Sinclair found out Seraphina's real name, in this letter, I thought. Undoubtedly, she had discovered it somewhere on the estate in Andrew's personal belongings and put it in the biography when she was doing preliminary research for her novel.

Not only was Seraphina's real name the same as my great-great-grandmother's, but I also knew full well that my great-great-great-aunt's name was Maija.

I stared out the window and shook my head. It just couldn't be. But . . . those names, and my uncanny resemblance to the woman in the painting in the east salon, were too much of a coincidence. There could be no other explanation. The most famous psychic of the Spiritualist Age was my great-great-grandmother.

My hands were shaking as I refolded the letter and slipped it back into the envelope where it had rested for so many years. I turned my gaze back out to the vast white landscape and imagined her walking toward the stream with her beloved, just as I had done days before with Drew. We were the descendants of two remarkable people who, if this letter was any indication, had fallen deeply in love here at Havenwood. Drew had said his great-great-grandfather's journals were full of references to her.

I wished that was all there was to it, the sweet and wistful romance of impossible love, but there was a dark side to their story. They had experienced something monstrous and—dare I think it?—murderous together. And now, here I was, in the same house and, if Adrian's story was to be believed, that evil was still haunting the dark corridors of Havenwood, all of these years later. And I had found it in the library the night before.

Unexpectedly, my stomach began to churn. A wave of nausea sent me running to the bathroom, where I vomited up that morning's breakfast. I coughed the last of it up and sat on the tile floor for a while, getting my bearings, before pushing myself to my feet, my knees knocking. I splashed cool water onto my face and looked at myself in the mirror, wondering what in the world *that* was about. I ran some water onto a washcloth, squeezed out the excess, and took the cloth with me back to my bedroom.

Something about the breakfast that morning didn't agree with me, I reasoned, as I slid onto my bed on top of the bedspread, chills shaking me from the inside out, my stomach tensing into tight cramps. I kicked off my shoes and pulled an afghan over me, snuggling down on my nest of pillows. I closed my eyes and placed the washcloth over them, trying to will away the nausea. I thought of ringing for Marion to bring up an antacid, but then I remembered I had some in my travel kit. I tried to rise to get it, but the effort proved too great, and in the end I slumped back down, grateful for the comfort of goose down pillows and a cozy afghan. The antacid could wait.

I don't remember lying there even one minute longer; I fell immediately into a deep sleep. My dreams were a collage of images: a man with searing dark eyes looking into my soul, spirits whirling around me, people whispering their innermost thoughts and feelings, reindeer in a snowy field, green taffeta crinkling as I walked. The images flashed through my dreams like a slide show, one after another after another until finally a loud knocking jolted me awake.

"Julia!" I heard, far off in the distance, as though the sound were coming from another place and time. And then the knocking, going on and on and on.

My eyelids were heavy, so heavy I could hardly get them open. But when I finally did, I saw Drew's face. He was sitting at my bedside, gently shaking me.

"Hey," he said, pushing the hair out of my eyes, his hand lingering on my cheek. "I was worried when I couldn't wake you."

"Oh," I mumbled, my eyelids struggling to stay open. "What took you so long? I've been waiting for you forever."

I could feel him gently stroking my hair, way off in the distance.

"I've been waiting for you longer than that," he whispered, curling down next to me. I rolled into his arms and snuggled my head onto his chest.

"It's about time you got here," I murmured, just before I stopped fighting the sleep that wanted so much to overtake me.

THIRTY-FOUR

My eyes fluttered open to find Drew sitting in the armchair by the window.

"Hello," he said.

"Hello," I said, my receding dreams making a jumble of my thoughts.

I glanced at the clock on my bedside table. When I registered what it said, I bolted upright. "Noon?"

Drew stretched. "You've been out awhile."

"My goodness, what—" I didn't finish my thought, remembering the unfortunate incident in the bathroom earlier. "I think something in today's breakfast didn't agree with me."

He shook his head. "It wasn't the breakfast, I'll wager. You've had quite the frightening time of it, last night in particular. You've hardly slept at all, from what you've told me about your exploits. No wonder your body is reacting to the stress and lack of sleep. I think this is Havenwood, catching up with you. You need the rest, Julia."

I thought of standing up, but fell back against the pillows instead. "Mrs. Sinclair is expecting me for lunch."

"She isn't." He smiled. "I've let her know you're not feeling well. You've got the whole day free."

"But what about Adrian—" I started.

"Adrian can wait."

"Oh," I mumbled, rubbing my temples. Then I remembered our conversation of that morning. "Did you see Mr. Tucker?"

Drew nodded. "I did."

"And?"

"He didn't find anything," he said. "Not a shred of evidence that someone was inside this house."

"So, whatever I heard in the library—"

"Wasn't our visitor from the other night, back to do you harm." I exhaled.

"There's something else, too," he said. "Adrian was going to tell you after breakfast, but . . ."

"But my little outburst put an end to that."

"Well, yes. Anyway, he's heard from his sources in Chicago. They've found the person responsible for the fire."

I sat up. "Who was it?"

"Chap by the name of Carson. Michael Carson."

I squinted at him. "That doesn't ring a bell. Should it?"

"He was one of your husband's clients. Lost everything in the scheme, including his wife, who left him. He had invested his parents' money and his brother's; they lost everything, too. His whole family was wiped out."

"That's horrible," I said, aching for them and for everyone Jeremy swindled. "So, is he in custody? Did he admit setting the fire?"

"Yes to the admission, no to the custody. He left a note before swallowing a bottle of pills."

My hands flew to my mouth. "Oh my God!"

"Don't feel too badly. In the end I'm glad the bastard is dead."

I shook my head, not knowing quite what to say to that.

"Julia, his intent was to kill you, not just burn down your house. He thought you were inside. He said he saw someone in the upstairs window—of course he couldn't have, but that's what he thought. He wrote all about it in his note."

"If Adrian hadn't come to me when he did—"

"But he did. And you're here now."

I exhaled. "How do you know all of this? Was it in the newspaper?"

Drew shook his head. "Adrian has sources inside the Chicago Police Department. He made some inquiries and got the whole story."

I digested this for a moment, turning the facts over in my mind. It sounded true, but one aspect didn't make sense. "If it wasn't the man who set my house on fire, who was looking in the kitchen window that night? We know someone was there. We followed his tracks."

Drew shrugged his shoulders. "I don't know, Julia. We can speculate about it, but we have no way of knowing unless he comes back."

A knock on the door. Drew hopped up to answer it and found Marion, pushing a wheeled silver trolley containing what looked like lunch.

"Chicken soup and crackers for you, miss," she said to me, lifting a silver lid off a steaming bowl and setting the bowl on the table by the window. She turned to Drew. "I brought a sandwich and soup for you as well."

She slipped back out the door, and I pushed myself up, pausing at the edge of the bed for a moment to make sure I'd be steady on my feet. I had no more nausea, thank goodness, and the smell of the soup was restorative.

Drew pushed a couple of chairs over to the table and held mine out for me as I slipped onto it.

"How in the world did she get that trolley up the grand staircase?" I asked him.

"Elevator," he said, taking a bite of his sandwich. "It's in the back of the house, near the servants' stairs."

Elevator? I hadn't even seen the back area of the house or the servants' stairs.

After we finished our lunch, Drew pushed the trolley out of the room and into the hallway, where, presumably, Marion or one of her assistants would fetch it. Then he turned to me.

"How are you feeling? The soup seemed to go down okay."

"I feel just fine. I think those extra hours of sleep were just what I needed." I thought of him in the chair beside me when I woke up. "You didn't sit here all morning with me, did you?"

He shook his head. "While watching you sleep was lovely, I had a few other things to take care of. I slipped out to tell the rest of the household that you weren't feeling well, tended to the horses, that sort of thing."

"And then you came back."

"And then I came back." He smiled. "I didn't want you waking up alone, especially if you were off your game."

The memories of Jeremy that I was fighting so hard to contain rattled around in my brain. The police had told me, over and over, that I had been married to a sociopath. I refused to believe it, even after everything I knew.

But now, looking into the impossibly kind face of the man standing across the room from me—a man whom I was just getting to know, a man who, upon finding me under the weather, had jumped up to arrange for chicken soup and all the rest—I realized what the police had told me was true. Drew had taken better care of me that morning than Jeremy ever had during our entire marriage. I had forgotten what it felt like to be cared for.

"I have an idea," Drew said as he took his seat next to me, startling me from my musings.

"Do you, now?"

"I do. Would you care to hear it?"

"I'm dying to hear it."

"Do you feel up to a short walk to the stable?"

I wondered what was on his mind. "I think so. Like I said, the sleep really seems to have done the trick. I feel pretty good, especially after that soup."

"I was thinking we could go down to my little hideaway and watch a couple of movies this afternoon. You've probably noticed the lack of modern technology in the main house, but I've got a flat-screen TV and loads of films. And I've already told you

Mrs. Sinclair isn't expecting your company today. So, what do you say?"

"Really?" I asked him. "Don't you have better things to do than babysit me?"

As those words escaped my lips, a snake of icy suspicion slithered its way up my spine and took hold. I squinted at him. "That's not what you're doing, is it? Babysitting me? Please tell me Adrian didn't put you up to this because I threatened to leave."

His smile dropped and he sighed heavily. "Julia, I know the guy you were married to turned out to be a total bastard," he said, mirroring my thoughts of just a few minutes earlier. "But I'm not that guy."

I could feel the heat rising to my face. What had I been thinking? "I'm sorry for saying that," I said, my words tumbling out too fast. "It's just . . . I'm sorry. I'm just being paranoid. I know you're not that guy. You're not even close to being that guy."

He smiled. "Listen, your life has been upended. You're adjusting to a whole new world. It must seem like you've walked into the haunted house at the amusement park and gotten stuck there for good."

This elicited a chuckle. "Can we just forget I said anything?"

"Consider it forgotten," he said, hopping to his feet. "Now, what about those movies?"

I slipped into the bathroom to freshen up. But even though I tried to silence it, my suspicion remained. I had fallen ill right after breakfast . . . and right after I told Adrian I wanted to leave Havenwood. I had left the breakfast room briefly. Any one of them could've put something in my coffee to ensure that I physically couldn't leave, at least not right then.

And now here was Drew, babysitting me all afternoon.

I ran a brush through my hair and tried to shake those dark thoughts out of my head. I didn't need this, not now. Not after everything I had been through during the last year. Havenwood was supposed to be my way out. Why was I beginning to suspect it was even more of a prison than the one I had been facing?

THIRTY-FIVE

*D*rew and I trudged through the snow toward the stable, the dogs running in joyful circles around us. In the end, I took him up on his offer of movies. What else was I going to do? Prowl around the house alone? Stare at the four walls of my room?

I felt even better about it after we ran into Mrs. Sinclair on our way through the foyer.

"Oh, Julia, darling!" she said, walking toward me with her arms outstretched, pulling me into an embrace when she reached me. "You're up and about! I was so worried."

I let myself fold into her arms, taking in her powdery perfume. "I'm feeling much better," I told her. "A few hours of sleep really did the trick."

"I understand you're going to have an afternoon at the cinema, so to speak," she said, winking at Drew.

"That's the plan." I smiled at her. "If you don't need me. I'm feeling perfectly fine, so—"

"Absolutely not, darling," she interrupted. "You need some downtime. Besides, Adrian has promised to spend the day with his mother. I may give him fits by suggesting I drive into town!" Her giggle infected all of us. "We will reconvene at dinner if you're feeling up to it."

"I'm sure I will," I said.

"But it's not going to be formal," she continued, waggling a finger at me. "Jeans and sweaters. Slippers if you must. There's nothing worse than dressing in formalwear if one isn't feeling up to par. No, comfort is the name of the game!"

We parted, then, with promises to meet at six thirty in the drawing room. Drew and I headed toward the door and Mrs. Sinclair went on her way to find her son.

A fierce, protective sort of love bubbled up inside of me for the eccentric, charismatic woman I was watching walk away. I had been so concerned about myself, I hadn't even considered what sort of horrific nightmare she herself had gone through.

I watched her walk through the foyer until she was out of sight, and all we could hear was the clicking of her heels, echoing off the walls.

Soon afterward, the snowy trudge behind us, Drew and I were in the stable peeling off our jackets and pulling off our boots.

"Tea?" he asked over his shoulder as he hung our jackets up on the wrought-iron hooks near the fireplace.

"That would be lovely," I said.

"Let's migrate into my quarters," he said, leading me through the doorway from the main stable. "As delightful as the horses are, there can be a certain aroma in this part of the building from time to time."

I laughed and stepped into his apartment, a tingling coursing through me. We were well and truly alone. No Marion to intrude, no Mrs. Sinclair to summon us. I wondered, for the first time, what the afternoon might bring.

His eyes were full of an intensity that almost frightened me, just a bit. I wanted nothing more than to throw my arms around him and see where the afternoon might take us from there, but at the same time, I barely knew this man.

I thought he was going to pull me into a kiss, but instead he pulled away and walked to the kitchen area, a grin on his face. He filled up the kettle and set it on the stove.

"Julia, Julia," he said, looking at the kettle and shaking his head slightly. "Being alone with you has me thinking things I shouldn't."

I grasped around in my mind for a witty response to that, but all I could think of was the heat that was rushing to my face and the tingling in my hands. I wasn't exactly prepared to jump into bed with a man I'd only known for a few days. And yet. There was a timelessness to my brand-new relationship with Andrew McCullough that I didn't quite understand, but felt just the same, deep in my soul. And it made me want to be as close as possible with him. Yet I wasn't sure why. I watched him as he stood over the kettle until it boiled.

"I didn't agree to come down here to seduce you, you know." I smiled as he handed me a cup of tea and slid down next to me on the sofa. "I thought we were just going to watch a movie."

"Make no mistake, Julia," he said, his voice low. "If I'm ever lucky enough to coax you into my bedroom, it will be for one reason and one reason only."

"What's that?"

"True love."

The room seemed to shimmer and sway, then, my peripheral vision blurring. All I could see was Andrew's face, his eyes gazing into mine. Tears began to sting around their edges, and the sheer force of what I felt for this man washed over me like a wave.

"I found the letter," I whispered.

"What letter?" His voice was a rasp.

"The one from Seraphina to Andrew."

"The one she wrote to him after what happened at that last séance?"

I nodded.

"Where did you find it?" he wanted to know.

"In her biography," I told him. "That's the reason I went into the library in the first place, to find that book. I wanted to learn more about her. The letter was there, in the back of the book."

"So that's where it got to," he said, his expression far away, as though he were looking directly into the past. "Mrs. Sinclair must've put it there when she was doing her research."

I leaned back against the sofa. "You've seen it before?"

"Aye," he said, taking a deep breath and letting it out in a long sigh. "Andrew kept it with his private papers."

"So you know that it's true, all of it," I said, my voice wavering. "Seraphina was my great-great-grandmother."

"I know. The name might have been a coincidence, and the name of her sister and your great-great-great-aunt being the same might have been a coincidence. But when I took one look at you, I knew it was true."

"So, you also know they were deeply in love, my great-great-grandmother and your great-great-grandfather."

He ran a hand through my hair, letting it rest on my shoulder. "Oh, I know that, too." He was looking deeply into my eyes.

"Did true love find them, I wonder?" I whispered.

"I think we can be altogether sure of that, Julia," he said, pushing me deeper into the back of the sofa and kissing me with an urgency I had never before felt, as though he himself had been waiting for this moment for more than a century. We slid down until we were lying together on the couch, his hands reaching under my sweater and burning hot on my bare skin.

I fully expected we were going to give in to what was obviously happening between us, despite what we had said just moments before. But he pushed himself away and sat up.

"I think I need some water," he said, his voice gravelly and rough. He stood up and walked toward the kitchen. "You?"

"Okay," I said, gathering myself and curling my legs up beneath me, my whole body shaking.

He handed me a glass and slid back down next to me. "I'm sorry, Julia."

"What for?"

"I've not been altogether honest with you," he said, his eyes crinkling.

Not him. Not now. I took a sip of the cool water and tensed for what was coming. "Okay."

"I told you that I didn't want to, ah, take advantage of our alone-ness but I didn't tell you why," he said, clearing his throat.

My stomach seized up. These types of conversations didn't tend to go well. "Okay," I said again.

"You threatened to leave Havenwood," he said, averting his eyes from mine. "I wouldn't blame you if you did. But I'm not go-ing anywhere. This is my home and I'm here for the duration. If you do decide to leave us, it's going to be hard enough to lose you when I've well and truly fallen for you." His voice was shredded with the emotion of it all.

My spine tingled. *He's well and truly fallen for me?* While part of me liked that idea, I had just met this man a few days ago. It seemed a little soon for this kind of a declaration, didn't it? Although . . . was it, really? Our feelings were obviously leading somewhere, given what nearly happened a few moments before. He struck me as an honest man who wouldn't abide any game playing. Maybe he was the kind of man who would say what he felt when he felt it, chips fall where they may. *Okay,* I thought. *That's something new.*

"So you see," he said, moving a bit closer to me. "If we were to continue this conversation in my bedroom, and you decide later to leave, I couldn't bear it. I just couldn't lose you like that." Tears were shimmering in his eyes and he cleared his throat and shook his head, willing them away.

Sure, things were heating up between us, but tears? I didn't quite understand the depth of his emotion. Maybe he was just a guy who fell hard and fast?

But, perplexing intensity aside, I knew he was right. If I did decide to leave Havenwood, it would be hard enough to leave him as it was. I was beginning to have feelings for this man. And I wasn't at all sure how long I'd be staying.

And so, with the fire crackling in the fireplace and snow lightly falling outside, we snuggled down onto the sofa and put our feet up on the ottoman. We spent the afternoon watching movies. I sunk into the soft leather and exhaled, wrapped in the blissful normalcy of it all.

THIRTY-SIX

As the afternoon faded into twilight, I knew our perfect day was coming to an end.

I stretched and pushed myself up off the couch. "I should probably head back to the house and get ready for dinner."

"I suppose you should," he said, putting his arms behind his head and leaning back.

I smiled at him. "It has been wonderful to just kick back and do nothing at all. I can't remember when I've been so relaxed. It has literally been months."

"The first time you were here I told you that you'd need to get out of the main house from time to time," he said. "Now you see why I had this place renovated."

"I do," I said, pulling on my boots. He jumped up and grabbed my jacket from the hook by the fireplace and held it as I slipped my arms inside. "It really is a little island of tranquillity on this strange and otherworldly estate."

I thought about that as I trudged through the snow back to the main house, wondering what sort of "strange and otherworldly" things awaited me on the inside.

I had some time before dinner, so I hopped into the shower. After my long nap and day of lounging with Drew, I relished the warm cascade for as long as I could. After drying off, I wrapped my robe around me and sunk into the armchair by the window and watched the twilight turn into evening, wondering what *my* evening would bring.

As six thirty neared, I pulled on a black turtleneck and jeans—Mrs. Sinclair had said tonight would be an informal dinner—and closed my bedroom door behind me, descending the stairs one by one, my heart seeming to pound harder the closer I got to the main floor.

I found everyone waiting for me in the drawing room.

"Hello, darling!" Mrs. Sinclair sang out as I appeared in the archway. "What can I get you to drink? Wine? A cocktail?"

"Just water for me tonight," I said. "My stomach is still a little queasy." This was a lie, but I had no wish to be dulled by alcohol. And, I hated to think of it, but one of them might have slipped something into my coffee that morning. Best to be on my guard.

"How was your film festival this afternoon?" she asked, handing me a glass.

"It was nice," I said, smiling shyly at Drew. "I can't remember the last time I was so relaxed."

"Wonderful!" she said. "I'm glad you had a chance to rest."

I took a seat by the fireplace and the evening began. We had our drinks, and after a bit of small talk, Marion materialized to let us know she was about to serve dinner in the dining room.

"Roast chicken and mashed potatoes tonight," Marion said to me, uncovering her serving trays. "I didn't want to do anything too adventurous, what with you not feeling well and all."

I thanked her and she smiled a warm smile. Looking around the room, I saw that everyone was smiling at me. But their smiles didn't extend to their eyes, not really. It seemed to me that they were being a bit too nice, a bit too caring. That was always it with these people—too familiar, too intense, too caring. I began to squirm, my skin itching.

We lingered a bit longer than usual over the dessert, but soon enough the time had come. Mrs. Sinclair pushed her chair away from the table and cleared her throat.

"All right, children," she said. "Let us reconvene to the east salon, shall we?"

THIRTY-SEVEN

I avoided looking at the library altogether, and peeked around the east salon's doorframe before following the others inside. I saw candles placed here and there, along with a roaring fire in the fireplace and drinks set up on the sideboard. Standard fare at Havenwood, I was coming to learn. It was what I didn't see that caused me to exhale and step through the door. No hovering spirits floating from the painting, no lurking demons, only a room that looked warm and welcoming.

"Well, let's get our drinks and get settled, shall we?" Mrs. Sinclair said.

Tension floated in the air while Drew poured drinks for everyone. The clinking of glasses and bottles was the only noise in the room apart from the crackling fire. I supposed the others were as lost in their own thoughts as I was. Adrian kept stealing glances at me and at his mother, his face a mask of worry and concern.

Mrs. Sinclair took a seat in one of the wing chairs next to the fireplace; Adrian slid into the other. I sunk onto the sofa facing them, while Drew hovered at the sideboard, clinking the ice cubes in his ample glass of Scotch. I finally let my eyes drift up to the painting above the fireplace—my mirror image, surrounded by unspeakable horror. I wondered if life was imitating art at that moment as I glanced at Mrs. Sinclair, whose face had become so dear and familiar to me in just a few days, and yet, as I learned in the library the night before, also harbored something monstrous and—dare I think it?—insane.

"All right, my darling," she began, crossing her legs and holding my gaze, "you know I'm a master storyteller, adept at telling dark and macabre tales."

"You certainly are." I smiled at her and took a sip of water.

"Well, this is the darkest of them all." She took a deep breath and turned her eyes to her son. "I suppose it's best to just get on with it."

A pang sizzled through my stomach, just as it had earlier in the day. I shifted in my seat and hoped it would go away. I had no wish for a repeat performance of what had happened that morning.

"Are you ready to hear it?" she asked.

I wanted to know the story behind the horror of the previous night—*please let there be a rational explanation*—but I had the feeling it had something to do with what happened ten years prior, when she was sent to the mental hospital. Suddenly, I was afraid to hear what she had to say.

"Mrs. Sinclair, you don't owe me any explanations," I said.

She smiled sadly. "Oh, but I do, darling," she said. "I do."

"Well, in that case, maybe I should have a brandy," I said, crossing the room to the sideboard. Drew poured a generous shot into a glass, and I carried it with me as I settled into an armchair and crossed my legs, knowing I was going to hear a story by the great Amaris Sinclair.

"It all started one cold winter's night, not too different from this one, when Seraphina held a séance in this very room," Mrs. Sinclair said, her voice low and melodious.

As she spoke, retelling the story of the psychic and the Devil's Toy Box, how opening it had unleashed evil here at Havenwood, how one man died and several other people were injured, the room seemed to fall away. I could see the events of that night, the frightened faces of the bereaved who simply wanted a word from a departed loved one and were confronted with evil instead; I could hear their screams and even smell the oil from the lamps placed around the room.

By now, I knew the story so well it felt like I'd lived it. A chill shuddered through me and I wondered if, combined with the stomach cramps, it signaled I was coming down with something. I took another sip of my brandy, hoping it would settle my stomach as it always had when I was younger.

"I knew nothing about that event before I came to Havenwood," Mrs. Sinclair went on. "I had had some success as a writer at that time and was thrilled to move into this home with the agreement that I'd be presiding over Havenwood for my lifetime"—she winked at Drew—"until the rightful heir took the reins once again. In any case, once I got here and got settled, Havenwood began to work its magic on me."

"I can understand that," I said, savoring the heat as the brandy began to warm me from the inside out.

"I imagine you can, my dear," she said. "I imagine you can. I was a young woman in those days, as young as you are now. And I was filled with excitement about where my life was heading. I had a successful novel, the house of my dreams, the best son anyone could ask for." She smiled at Adrian and then gazed into the fire. "I had it all."

"It sounds wonderful," I said to her.

"Oh, it was," she said, a wistful tone in her voice. "It was wonderful for many years. I wrote some of my best work here, enjoyed great success, and was so proud of my boy as he made his way through school, and then to university." She sighed. "But then I got greedy, and I threw it all away."

Adrian was staring intently at his mother, while Drew seemed to be absorbed in his drink. It was as though he wanted to be as far away from this conversation as possible.

It seemed that Mrs. Sinclair was waiting for me to prompt her, but I couldn't seem to get the words out. Finally, she continued.

"It all began with this painting," she said, gesturing upward. "I was entranced by it. And when I learned it depicted a real event in this house and a real person, Seraphina, I became ensnared. I had had no idea a famous psychic had ever been to Havenwood! The more I learned about her, the more interested I became. 'Obsession' wouldn't have been too strong a word for it, Julia. I'll admit that. I was obsessed with her story, and even with Seraphina herself. The fact that this exotic woman had been at Havenwood and attracted the likes of Charles Dickens and Arthur Conan Doyle and people from all walks of life who wanted to touch the spirit world . . . it was a story that enthralled the novelist in me."

"Of course it did," I said, imagining how excited she must have been to have discovered this mystery.

"I dug up all the information I could about her," Mrs. Sinclair went on. "When I was on my book tours, visiting various cities around the country, I'd make it a point to stop at antiquarian bookstores to see if I could find a biography, or a book on Spiritualism that had her in it. I came upon plenty of information—she was famous and well regarded in Spiritualist circles—but I wanted more. Finally, as I was browsing the occult section of a dusty used bookstore in Baltimore, I found what I was looking for—the biography that we now have here at Havenwood."

She sighed and took a sip of her drink, gazing into the fire. The flames crackled and danced.

"And that's when I learned of the séance that went so horribly wrong," she said. "The séance that ended the magnificent career of this magnificent woman, and caused her to disappear from history. That it was held here at Havenwood—it was almost more than I could bear."

I glanced from Adrian to Drew and back again. Both men were staring at Mrs. Sinclair, seemingly rapt by her words.

"Is that when you wrote the novel about her?" I asked, remembering reading it when I was in school. I had no idea that it was true to life or that I'd be walking into its haunted pages years later.

"It is indeed, my dear," she said, her voice papery and thin.

"But that's not all I did, I'm afraid." A tear escaped one eye and she brushed it away, shaking her head and turning her gaze once again to the flames. She seemed to be lost in them, watching their dances and sways.

"You said something about being greedy?" I prompted her.

"Yes," she said, turning her head slowly to me. "I had great success, more than anyone should hope for in one lifetime. But it wasn't enough. I wanted more. I had to have more."

She pushed herself up from her chair and walked over to the sideboard where Drew was standing. He freshened her drink and squeezed her arm, palpable concern on his face. She laid a hand on his cheek and smiled, her sadness radiating from her like an aura.

"It's all right, Mother," Adrian said, shifting in his chair. "Nobody blames you."

"But, my dear, the sad fact is I am to blame for all of it, for what happened to our darling Audra."

Saying the name of this Audra, Mrs. Sinclair's voice broke into tiny pieces. Her hand flew to her mouth and she stifled a cry, turning to Drew, who wrapped his arms around her and pulled her close.

"Shh," he said to her, patting her back and eyeing me over her shoulder. "It's going to be all right. Please believe that." I wondered if he was speaking to me or to Mrs. Sinclair. Or to us both.

Adrian was on his feet in a second. His mother folded herself into his arms, looking as tiny and fragile as a baby bird.

"I haven't so much as said her name in so many years," she sputtered out, her shoulders shaking with the sobs that were overtaking her body. "Audra, my darling girl."

That same feeling of nausea growled in my stomach, threatening to bubble up. Who was Audra? And why did the very mention of her name cause my blood to run cold?

THIRTY-EIGHT

I'm sorry, my dear," Mrs. Sinclair said to me, after blowing her nose and wiping her eyes. "This is not an easy story to tell."

She grasped my hand and squeezed it on her way back to her chair. She sunk into it and crossed her legs, and took a deep breath.

"But I must tell it," she went on. "I owe that to you. And to Audra. It is her story, too."

"Who is Audra, Mrs. Sinclair?" I asked as gently as I could. Saying her name out loud caused that same chill to run through me. My head was beginning to pound.

She turned her eyes to her son.

"Audra is my daughter," Adrian said, swirling the ice in his Scotch, his eyes brimming with tears. "Was. She was my daughter."

I gasped. He had never once spoken of a daughter. He and his mother held each other's gaze across the room. Drew was looking out the window into the darkness, sipping on his drink. Nobody was saying anything, as the fire crackled and snapped.

"What happened to her?" I finally asked, knowing for certain I wouldn't like the answer.

"That, my dear, is the heart of this story." Mrs. Sinclair sighed deeply.

"Only when you're ready, Mother," Adrian said. "Take your time. It has been ten years. It can wait a bit longer."

In fact, if they were to ask me, it could wait forever. Suddenly, I wanted to hear no more of this story. "I can see this is upsetting you, Mrs. Sinclair," I tried. "We can wait to talk about this another day."

She shook her head. "No," she said. "Thank you for that, darling. But I have begun the tale, and shall continue the telling. It needs to be told and you need to hear it.

"We were speaking about greed, and wanting more and more, despite having it all. It is a dangerous thing, my dear, unbridled ambition. It brings out the worst. It certainly did here, and in me." She took a deep breath before continuing. "My novel about Seraphina was published to worldwide acclaim. Bestseller lists, millions of copies sold. I traveled all over the world doing readings and book signings. It was a wonderful, happy time, it really was."

She smiled at Adrian, who took over the tale when his mother's voice faltered. "It was during this time, Julia, that I married a woman I had met at university. The lovely Katherine." He smiled at the thought of her, a faraway look in his eyes. "After our honeymoon, I brought my new wife here, to Havenwood, to begin our life together. I had the affairs of this estate to run, my mother's investment portfolio to manage, that sort of thing. She's right; it was a happy time. Made all the happier by the news, about a year after we moved to Havenwood, that Katherine was expecting."

"I was over the moon about it," Mrs. Sinclair said, beaming. "A grandchild!"

"And there was no more doting a grandmother than Amaris Sinclair," Adrian said, chuckling softly. "Audra was on horseback almost as soon as she could walk, courtesy of my mother. We had several Shetland ponies at that time, and little Audra couldn't get enough of them. Do you remember, Mother?"

"Seeing Audra go around and around in the field on the back of a pony is one of my most cherished memories," Mrs. Sinclair said. "The look on her face—sheer joy. I try to think of that when the images of what came later haunt me."

Drew slid onto the couch next to me and crossed his legs. "Those are beautiful memories," he said to Mrs. Sinclair. "I'd love to leave the story there, with wee Audra flying around the field on horseback."

"Indeed," she said, nodding. "But we all know that's not to be. The crux of this tale happened when our girl was just a child."

"Sing a song of sixpence / A pocket full of rye . . ."

There it was again: a child's voice singing softly in my ear. I snapped my head around toward the door, looking for the ghostly girl with the wispy blond hair. But nothing was there. And then it occurred to me: Was this Audra, come out to play?

"Julia," Mrs. Sinclair said, bringing me back into the room. "Are you all right, dear?"

"Yes," I said, nodding. "I was just . . . thinking about how lovely the little girl must have been. That's all."

"She was indeed," she said, holding my gaze. "I was so busy doting on my granddaughter, I hadn't written a novel for some time. There were a couple after *Seraphina*, as you know, but the fact was it was such a happy time around Havenwood during those years that I didn't feel much like delving into the sorts of dark topics that were the hallmarks of my novels."

"Why didn't you write about something else? A romance, maybe?" I asked.

She shook her head. "Oh, that's not done. Nobody would want to read a happy story by Amaris Sinclair. No, my readers were looking for a good scare, and I was bound to give that to them. In fact, my publisher was pressuring me for a new novel. The problem was I couldn't conjure it up, no matter how I tried. Those sorts of plots and characters just weren't coming to me."

"It was about that time the letter surfaced," Drew said.

"The letter?" I asked.

"The one you came across, in the back of the biography," he said to me. "The letter from Seraphina to Andrew."

"Oh?" Mrs. Sinclair looked at me, her eyes shining. "You've seen it?"

"I have," I said.

She nodded. "You see, my dear, when I wrote the novel about Seraphina, all I knew—all history knew—about her last séance at Havenwood was that it went horribly wrong, people got hurt, and that it scared her enough to leave that life completely. So I embellished and took artistic license in the book. That's because nobody knew exactly what happened that night, so I had to use my imagination. But when we got our hands on that letter and found out that something called the Devil's Toy Box was the cause . . . What is it they say about ignorance?"

Mrs. Sinclair cleared her throat and continued. "I had no idea what a Devil's Toy Box was. Who did? But it sounded dark and horrible and frightening—perfect for one of my novels, don't you think? The idea of it consumed me. Finally, I had a kernel around which to build a new novel. I contacted my publisher right away, and he was thrilled, to say the least. So I started working."

I furrowed my brow. "I don't remember one of your novels dealing with a Devil's Toy Box," I said.

She smiled and shook her head. "That's because I never wrote it. As I said, I didn't know the first thing about such a device. So, I began my research here at Havenwood, in the library. I didn't come up with anything. I traveled back to Baltimore, to the same antiquarian bookstore where I found Seraphina's biography years earlier. I knew it had a huge occult section with several first edition Poe novels, and the owner of the shop was quite an odd duck himself, so I thought if anybody would know about the Devil's Toy Box, it would be him.

"Over the course of one's life, Julia, there are actions that pave the way for everything else that comes after, good or bad. Simple moments: Turning right instead of left on the street and running headlong into the man you'll marry. Choosing a ham sandwich instead of soup at the deli and choking on it. Diving into a pool of water and cracking your head on the bottom, paralyzing yourself for life. One of those moments, for me, came when I walked across the threshold of that bookstore. That simple action changed my life forever, Julia. It changed Adrian's life. And Audra's. And Katherine's. And, I'm sorry to say, yours. If I hadn't gone into Ravenspoint Books that bleak and rainy afternoon, we'd all be doing something else right now. Adrian might be attending his daughter's graduation. I might be on a book tour, enjoying the success of another novel. And you, darling, you would have never come to Havenwood."

A dark thought hovered around me, then. I'd be dead. The worst thing ever to happen in the lives of the Sinclairs had saved my life. She told me it was tied to the reason she brought me here, and because of that, I wasn't in my house in Chicago when it was set afire. If not for whatever tragedy unfolded all those years ago, I'd have burned along with all of my belongings. I could feel Adrian's stare boring a hole in my skull, and I knew he was thinking the same thing.

THIRTY-NINE

$\mathcal{M}$rs. Sinclair shifted in her chair and took a sip of her drink before continuing.

"Rain was drizzling down and fog hung in the air, and all of that gloom seemed to swirl inside the bookstore before I could close the door behind me. I'll never forget those dusty shelves, books stacked haphazardly throughout, some on the floor here, some piled on a chair there. Cases were filled with ancient volumes, but there was no real order to things. Sixteenth-century Bibles sat next to first edition copies of *The Raven* next to original versions of *Poor Richard's Almanack*. Papers were piled high behind the counter, and several resident cats prowled the shelves. I could never figure out if the store was a refuge for lovers of old books or the result of one madman's lifelong collecting of random volumes.

"That madman, the owner, a peculiar sort of man with wild gray hair that jutted out in all directions and little round glasses that were always perched on the end of his nose, was expecting me. I had called him months previously and asked him to keep his eye out for a box.

"'I think you're going to like this very much,' he said to me, shuffling into the back room. I waited for what seemed to be forever until he reemerged with a box in his hands. The sight of it made me gasp. It was slightly taller than it was wide, with a pyramid-shaped cover. It was crafted out of wood and covered with ancient symbols that had been burned into it—a pentagram, the signs of the zodiac, ancient Egyptian hieroglyphics, and other symbols I didn't recognize.

"He slid the box across the counter, and as I grasped it for the first time, my hands burned, as though they were on fire."

Mrs. Sinclair's eyes were shining and, I could swear, darkening as she spoke. I moved closer to Drew and took his hand.

"I lifted up the cover and peered into the box. It was lined with mirrors, even the lid.

"'This is beautiful,' I murmured, mesmerized by the illusion of infinity inside that box. It was as though it were a gateway to forever. Or the beyond." She shook her head. "And in a way, I suppose that it was.

"'Beautiful and deadly,' the man said to me. 'You need to be very careful with it.' He reached into the pocket of the threadbare gray cardigan he was wearing and produced a thin volume. 'Read this before you even think about using that box,' he told me. 'It's important.'"

Mrs. Sinclair sighed. "Of course, I knew better. I was a famous horror novelist." She let out a strangled laugh. "And so, I took the box, tucking the book into my purse, and left. And I brought that thing back to Havenwood, causing the ruin of us all." She fished a handkerchief out of her sleeve and dabbed at her eyes. Then she covered them with the handkerchief and let out a sob. She didn't speak again for several minutes.

"Were you thinking of using the box for inspiration for a novel?" I asked, hoping to bring her back from wherever she had gone.

She shook her head. "Not only that." She turned to her son. "Oh, Adrian," she said, her voice wavering. "How can I continue the story? How can I possibly utter the words?"

He crossed the room and perched on the ottoman in front of her chair, taking her hands. "You have begun, Mother," he said, his voice soothing. "You must continue. I'll be right here." He looked at Drew and me. "And so will we all."

"Very well," she said, taking a deep breath and shoring up her tattered nerves. "I might as well just finally say it. Admit it. We all went through it, everyone at this house, but we haven't spoken of it since, and it's time the truth was said aloud in the very room where it occurred.

"I brought the box back into this house in order to conduct a séance, just like the one that sent Seraphina running away in fear."

My eyes grew wide, that same nausea reaching out from somewhere deep within me. "But why? Why would you do such a thing? Especially because you knew what happened to Seraphina! Somebody died that night; we know that now!"

She nodded her head slowly. "Yes, of course you would have those questions. Anyone would. But not me. Because, darling, I was a famous horror novelist." She drew out the words until they were almost nonsensical. "I had been called the female Edgar Allan Poe. My books were considered classics; they were part of the curricula of students worldwide. The problem was, darling, my readers were expecting another book from me, my publisher was demanding it, and I was out of ideas."

"So, you thought a séance would give you some ideas?" I asked, not wanting to believe what I was hearing.

"Not just that, I'm afraid," she said. "Remember, I had written some of the most frightening books of our time, imagined some of the most macabre scenarios and most demonic villains. I had been down every dark and lonely road known to man. I needed something fresh. Something real. My imagination was tapped out. I knew full well that the last séance Seraphina conducted here at Havenwood went horribly wrong; I knew full well it was because of the Devil's Toy Box. I still sought it out and brought it into this house because I wanted to experience the horror of it. I needed to experience it. It's like an addict, my dear, needing more and more of her drug of choice to feel the effects."

Her words hung in the air like fog, wafting around us. I held my breath, not knowing quite what to say next.

"And so," she went on, her eyes shining with tears, "I put the box on the table." She gestured across the room to the round table behind the sofa near the windows. "That very table. And I waited for a few days, until the time was right. And then I announced to everyone that we were going to have a séance."

"Everyone?"

"Adrian and Katherine, Drew, the staff, everyone at Havenwood at that time," she said. "I didn't invite outsiders, not knowing what would happen. Also, remember, this was supposed to be inspiration for a new book, and I didn't want random people aware of that, either. So I decided it would just be family and household staff."

She took a sip of her drink and eyed her son. "Go on, Mother," he said, smiling at her. "It will be all right."

She turned her gaze to me, then, her eyes looking like those of a frightened child.

"We gathered around the table, Adrian, Marion, a few other staff members, and me. There were seven of us when we started, as I recall."

I shot Drew a look. "Not you?"

He shook his head and opened his mouth to respond, but Mrs. Sinclair cut him off. "He was the only sensible one among us," she said, smiling at him. "He knew about the power of the box and refused to participate. He tried to dissuade me from going ahead with it, but, of course, I knew better."

I could feel beads of perspiration form on my forehead. "But don't you need a psychic for something like that?" I asked, my mouth suddenly dry. "I mean, it's not like the average person can conduct a séance."

"We did have a psychic here for the séance that night, my darling Julia," Mrs. Sinclair said slowly, as though she were talking to a child. "Someone with a rare and special gift." She caught Adrian's eye, and he nodded his head, almost imperceptibly. And then she turned to me and spoke the most terrifying word I had ever heard.

"You."

FORTY

I looked from one to another of them in turn, my mouth agape, my mind scrambling in several directions at once, all gelling at the corner of "run" and "now." But I was frozen with terror, unable to move.

"That's insane," I said, my voice cracking. "You have to know what you're saying is impossible."

Adrian and his mother exchanged fearful glances.

"Darling, we know this is a shock," Mrs. Sinclair said, rising from her chair and coming to kneel in front of me. Her voice was low and soothing. "We knew this conversation was ahead of us, but we had hoped it would be later, when you had gotten to know us and you'd fallen in love with Havenwood all over again. Frankly, we hoped you'd remember, all on your own. That just the mere act of being here would jog your memory."

"But there's nothing to remember," I said, drawing out the words. "I've never been here before. I'm not who you think I am. I'm not a psychic. Why would I come to lead a séance if I wasn't a psychic?"

Mrs. Sinclair smiled. "You wouldn't."

Something about the way they were all looking at me, smiling nervous smiles, chilled me to the bone. I found my strength and pushed myself off the couch, taking a few backward steps toward the doorway.

Adrian stood up quickly, as did Drew. Both men moved to-ward me. My hands flew up before me in a warning.

"Don't come any closer," I hissed, not having the slightest idea what I'd do to back up that threat. But they stopped where they were nonetheless.

"Please don't leave," Adrian said. "You're in no danger here, Julia, even though it feels like you are."

"I don't know who you think I am, or what you think this is, or why you asked me to come here," I said, tears stinging at my eyes. "But you need to be perfectly clear on one thing: I am not the person you think I am. I have never been to Havenwood before. I have never met any of you before coming here. I have never con-ducted a séance and I don't know anything about—"

My stomach churned and seized with the same type of roiling nausea that had overtaken me that morning. I realized it had been threatening to bubble to the surface during this entire conversa-tion. The room shimmered and swayed, and I felt my eyelids get-ting terribly heavy and my body succumbing to the force of it all.

The next thing I knew, I was flat on my back and opening my eyes, with Drew, Adrian, and Mrs. Sinclair kneeling beside me.

"Does she need a cool washcloth?" Mrs. Sinclair asked. "Would that help? I'll ring for Marion."

"What happened?" I coughed out.

"It appears that you fainted," Adrian said.

I shook my head from side to side.

"Don't worry, I was here to catch you," Drew said, smiling at me and taking my hand in his.

I pulled my hand away, scrambling to my feet and backing into a corner of the room.

"Oh, darling," Mrs. Sinclair said. "Don't react like this. I know you're frightened. But the truth was coming out on its own, espe-cially with what happened last night. I wish it had stayed hidden until you were ready to hear it."

"I don't think this conversation is such a good idea anymore,"

Drew said. "She's obviously upset. We should have let her remember on her own."

"I hoped she would," Mrs. Sinclair said. "But when she didn't—the ruse of it was too much. All of us pretending we had never seen her before. One of us was going to slip, sooner than later. And then what?"

"And the incident last night—you have to agree, Andrew, that the whole issue is coming to a head now," Adrian said.

These people were obviously insane. All of them. I glanced across the room, calculating how many steps it would take to get from the east salon to the front door. I had to find a way out of here. I didn't care that it was the middle of winter and we were in the wilderness. I'd prefer my chances with the wolves and the Windigo than staying with this lot.

"I want to leave," I said. "I don't want to hear any more of this."

"Maybe she's right," Drew said. "Maybe we should continue this at another time. When she's ready."

I shook my head, backing farther into my corner. "There's not going to be another time," I said. "You all seem to believe that I was at Havenwood years ago, presiding over some event that changed all of your lives. Ruined all of your lives. I wasn't. You're mistaken. I'm not that person." My body was shaking, and tears were stinging my eyes. "You've got the wrong person. I would never take part in a séance. Never."

Drew was walking toward me, then, his palms up, his expression pleading. "Julia," Drew said, his voice low. "Please. I know this is confusing. But remember that you trust me. Nothing has changed from earlier today. Everything is exactly the same."

"How can you say that?" I asked, looking at each of them. "Nothing is the same! Nothing at all."

"No," he said. "That's not right, Julia. Believe me, nothing has changed."

"Really?" I said, a shrill tone in my voice. "An hour ago, I was living at a beautiful, albeit haunted, estate with people I was starting to love." As I said that word and thought of the afternoon I had spent with Drew, my voice splintered. "Now it feels like I'm in an insane asylum."

Mrs. Sinclair took a few steps closer to me and took my hand. "You're not at that dreadful institution, darling. Not anymore."

Her words hovered around me in the air and, try as I might to deflect them, they somehow bored inside, reverberating off the corners of my brain. *Not anymore?* What could she possibly mean by that? She was the one who was in the asylum, not me.

Still, something about what she said knocked the very stuffing out of me. I sunk down to the floor and wrapped my arms around my knees, resting my head on my arms and sighing. I closed my eyes and wished I could disappear.

It was Adrian who brought me back into the moment. I opened my eyes to see that he was kneeling in front of me. He rested his hands on my knees and had a slight smile on his face.

"Come back to us, Julia," he said. "We're here to help you. I know you're confused and suspicious and even fearful right now, but please. If you listen to the rest of the story, it will all become clear. And my original offer still stands. Do you remember my original offer? If, after hearing it all, you still want to leave Haven-wood, I will personally arrange for you to slip unnoticed into the world, with a new identity and an ample bank account to go with it. You know I can make that happen for you, don't you?"

I nodded. His voice was like a sedative.

"So, please," he said, taking my hands, "take your seat back on the sofa, let Drew freshen your drink, and let's hear the rest of the story. I promise you, if you want to leave after hearing what my mother has to say, I will personally pack your bags. Agreed?"

I didn't know what else to do, so I allowed him to lead me back to the sofa, where Drew was waiting with a glass of brandy for me. I sunk down into the soft leather and took the glass he held out to me, my hands shaking.

"But I've never been here before," I said to Drew, tears escaping my eyes. "I'm not . . ." My words trailed off into futility.

I took a sip of brandy. What had I gotten myself into? And how could I possibly get out of it? *Think, Julia. Think.* I knew I had to come up with some concrete reason to make them believe they were mistaken. Mistaken identity, that was what it was called! As simple as that. When they realized they had the wrong person, they would most certainly apologize, we'd all have a good laugh, and then I could go on my way.

What was I doing ten years earlier? I'd have been out of college and working, certainly. My first and only book had been published . . . hadn't it? My friends . . . ?

But it was no use. Every time I tried to cast my mind back to that time in my life, I hit a brick wall. My memories were a blur of images, words, and sounds, none coherent enough to translate. I remembered marrying Jeremy, and most everything that came after that. Some of it, anyway. Bits and pieces. With spaces in between. My frequent blackouts, like the ones I had when I first arrived here at Havenwood, didn't help. My medication . . . ?

Mrs. Sinclair's voice brought me back into the present. "Tell me, darling," she said. "What's on your mind?"

"That's the problem, Mrs. Sinclair." I sighed, slumping against the back of the sofa. "I have no idea."

FORTY-ONE

*S*he nodded her head and smiled a knowing smile. They were all smiling at me, their eyes expectant and wide. I didn't know why they were looking at me when it was Mrs. Sinclair who was supposed to be telling the tale.

I turned to Adrian. "You asked me to listen to the rest of the story," I said. "I'm listening. If you're so sure that I was the psychic who conducted a séance at Havenwood ten years ago, which is impossible by the way, then tell me, how did I come to be here? I didn't even know Havenwood existed until you showed up on my doorstep in Chicago."

"Bringing you to Havenwood all of those years ago was my idea," Mrs. Sinclair jumped in, putting a hand to her chest. "If you're going to blame anyone, Julia, blame me."

I furrowed my brow. "Why would I blame anybody?"

"For what came after," she said. "For what happened to you. But I'm getting ahead of myself. I needed something besides the Devil's Toy Box to re-create Seraphina's séance. I needed her descendant."

"Why?"

"Because, my dear, I wanted it to be as authentic as possible. I knew Seraphina couldn't be here to conduct the séance"—she shot a glance at Drew and chuckled—"obviously, but I had read that these types of gifts, psychic gifts if you will, tend to run in families. I wondered—were there any descendants? If so, did they inherit Seraphina's gift?

"So, while I was searching high and low for the box, Adrian was on a hunt of his own," she continued. "We would've never found you, never known you existed, if not for that letter. It gave us Seraphina's real name, her sister's name, and, from its postmark, an approximate location of where she settled after leaving the world of Spiritualism behind."

"It wasn't too terribly difficult to track you down," Adrian said, "even without the online genealogical sites of today. Goodness, if I had had any of that, I'd have found you in an afternoon. As it was, it took weeks of visiting libraries and courthouses, poring through records."

"That's how you came to know my family tree," I said, remembering seeing it in this very room. That day seemed like lifetimes ago now.

"Not only that," he said. "Your book had just been released, and it caught our attention because we knew you were Seraphina's only living descendant. The fact that you mentioned my mother in the acknowledgments cemented this rather odd proposition for us."

"When we saw the book, we knew it was meant to be that you should come to Havenwood," Mrs. Sinclair said. "Predestined, as if Seraphina herself had sent you."

Adrian went on. "I paid a call on you in your charming duplex just off Lake Calhoun in Minneapolis. Do you remember it, Julia?"

I shook my head. "No," I said. "That never happened."

"Do you remember the duplex apartment, though? At least that? Try, Julia."

My mind sputtered and skipped. Images flashed before me. A floor-to-ceiling fireplace. A deep porcelain tub. Walks around the lake on warm spring days.

"I do remember the place," I said, nodding my head slowly, trying to focus my mind into the past at the images that were fading from view. "I lived there for several years."

"We talked there," he continued, his voice low and melodious. "About Havenwood. About my mother and your book."

"No," I said, once again feeling the beads of perspiration begin to form on my forehead. My pulse seemed to race. "You were never there. The first time I laid eyes on you, it was at my house in Chicago."

Adrian turned toward his mother. "Is it time?"

"I believe it is," she said.

"Time for what?" I asked, my breath shallow.

"We've been waiting for the right time to show you something, my dear," Mrs. Sinclair said, rising from her chair and slipping onto the soft next to me to stroke my hair. "I believe it may help you remember."

Adrian stood and turned toward the door. "Give me a moment," he said, walking out of the east salon. I listened to his footsteps on the library floor, fading and then becoming louder until he appeared in the doorway once again.

He crossed the room and handed me a book, a book I recognized. My book. I took it from him with shaking hands and laid it in my lap.

"Open it to the title page, Julia," he said gently. "It will prove to you, without a shadow of a doubt, that what we're telling you is the truth."

To Amaris Sinclair,

With the greatest admiration.

> *Your devoted fan,*
> *Julia Harper*
> *Havenwood, May 14, 2003*

I don't know how long I stared at that page, my heart beating furiously in my chest. I could feel my hands becoming cold and clammy, and perspiration dripping down the back of my spine. I couldn't take a deep breath and was panting as though I had just run a marathon.

"Julia?" I heard my name, spoken softly in the distance. My vision narrowed, focusing only on those words on the page. The east salon and everyone in it fell away.

I couldn't make sense of what I was seeing. It was my book. The inscription was in my handwriting. There was no doubt I had signed a copy of my one and only novel for Amaris Sinclair years earlier. I had been to Havenwood before. Everything they were saying was true. And yet it wasn't. How could it be? I had absolutely no recollection of it, none at all.

Why couldn't I remember?

To keep my nausea at bay, I closed my eyes and rested my head, which had begun to pound, on the back of the sofa, finally able to take deep breaths. I inhaled and exhaled as I heard the fire crackling in the fireplace and felt it warming my cheeks. Its flames danced and swayed in my mind, sending up shadows behind my eyelids.

I sensed that my memories were floating somewhere in the darkness of my mind. I could see them, in the distance, coming toward me almost in the same way a bottle with a note in it would float from the sea to the shore. The bottle was there but out of reach. As long as it was beyond my grasp, I was safe. But it was drifting closer and closer. I wanted to open my eyes, or do something, anything, to keep myself away from whatever horrible truths that bottle held. But I could not. The truth finds its way into the light, no matter what you've done to contain it. There was nothing I could do but brace myself for it to overtake me.

Images—dark, strange, nightmarish scenes—flashed in my mind, one after another after another like a slide show, and little by little, they melded into one horrific whole.

At first, my memories of this long-ago séance were distant, as though I were watching them unfold on television. But then they became stronger and larger until I was so engulfed by the memories that it was as though I was reliving the moments, in terrifying detail.

I saw Adrian, Mrs. Sinclair, and a woman I knew to be Katherine, along with a few others, sitting around the table in the east salon. Candles flickered, their delicate yellow glow illuminating the room and all of us with the type of soft, magical light I usually associate with late afternoon on a sunny day. The box was sitting in the middle of the table. We clasped hands and I began calling to the spirits of the dead.

I wasn't quite sure why we were even going through the trouble of having a séance to summon them. Havenwood was filled with ghostly figures that floated through the corridors and peeked out of the paintings. All we needed was to walk down one hallway and we'd meet more spirits than Scrooge did on Christmas Eve.

But the famous author wanted her séance, so a séance we would hold. I had never conducted one, and had told Adrian as much when he made the invitation, but he was unconcerned about that. As long as I was able to communicate with the dead, that was all that mattered to him. And that had never been a problem for me. Ever since I was five years old and figured out that the grandmother who had been tucking me in each night was not exactly alive, and hadn't been for decades, I was surrounded by spirits. So I agreed to his request, not knowing what I was getting myself into.

I should have known something was wrong at the outset when I realized there were no spirits in the room with us. That was a first. When I called them, they came, hungry as they are for communication with the living and so rare is it for them to find a conduit such as myself. Usually I had a backlog. But not that night. There was no one whispering in my ear about last wishes and hidden wills, no one wanting to give the living hope that there is indeed a life everlasting, no one wanting revenge for wrongs real or imagined. The room was as silent as an empty grave.

But then I heard something, a clattering and scratching, coming from the box in the middle of the table.

"It's working," Mrs. Sinclair whispered, her eyes glowing in the candlelight. "Open the box, Julia! Open it!"

I had never heard of anything like that box sitting in the middle of the table. But what could it hurt? It was just a box. So I did as she suggested.

All at once, a great whoosh of air extinguished the candles. I could see my breath in front of me as my teeth began to chatter despite the warmth of the fire blazing in the fireplace just feet from the table. What I can only describe as a great torrent of air circulated around us, and on it, I could hear the deep, dark, low growls and snarls of something, I knew not what. But I knew a sense of evil had filled the room the likes of which I had never before experienced.

I sensed a heaviness on my chest that was pushing me backward in my chair, and before I knew it, I hit the ground and slid, chair and all, toward the opposite wall, as though something was pushing me. I knocked my head so hard on the wall that the room spun around and around, the stars blinding me.

I struggled to my feet, my head pounding.

"Get away from me!" Katherine screamed, pushing at something that was not there, or, rather, not visible. Blood oozed from scratches on her face.

Drew burst into the room, throwing the double doors open so hard they hit the walls behind. Three enormous malamutes bounded in behind him, snarling and growling.

Before Drew could say anything, I watched as he flew across the room and was pinned against the opposite wall, his eyes bulging, his face contorted, his feet not touching the ground. "Adrian, help!" I called out. I tried to run toward Drew, but the dogs kept me at bay. They didn't want me anywhere near what was happening there.

"I command you to let him go," I bellowed, not quite under-standing why I was saying the words. It was as though someone—Seraphina perhaps?—was taking over. "In the name of God the Father Almighty, I take authority over you and command you to let him go."

Drew dropped to the ground. His face was red and he was shaking, but at least he was breathing. I turned to see Mrs. Sinclair on the floor, her white dress now crimson, Adrian kneeling at her side.

I took a few steps toward her—was she hurt? It was then I no-ticed she was wiping her hands on the front of her dress.

"No matter how many times I try to wipe them, I can't get the blood off my hands," she muttered to Adrian. "It keeps coming back."

Then I caught sight of Katherine, whose expression seemed even more frightening than anything I had just witnessed. She was standing stock-still, staring at the opposite wall, her eyes wide, her face a mask of terror.

I turned in the direction she was staring and saw her daughter, little Audra, suspended high in the air. How had the child gotten into the room in the first place? She had been asleep in her bed when we began the séance. She was simply floating there, as if held aloft by unseen hands. Her arms dangled limply at her sides, and her head was back, as though she was looking into the heav-ens. But I knew heaven had nothing to do with this. The dogs were crouched beneath her, snarling and growling at whatever it was that had her in its grip.

"Adrian!" I shouted, and when he looked up, he let out a cry so horrific that I thought it would knock me to the ground. He rushed over to Audra and tried to reach her, jumping, to no avail. By this time Drew had scrambled to his feet and was pushing a chair un-der her.

And then we heard the laughter, dark and low and menacing. It was coming from Audra's angelic face.

Somehow, I found my voice. "I command you to release this child," I bellowed, loud and strong, with much more force than I possessed, or felt. "In the name of God the Father Almighty, I take authority over you and order you to release this girl."

Audra's head sprang back into position and she gazed down at me, her sweet face now distorted with unspeakable evil.

"*Mary had a little lamb,*" she said in a singsongy, feathery voice. "*Its fleece was white as snow.*"

"Release the girl! I command you!"

"*Sing a song of sixpence / A pocket full of rye . . .*"

Katherine's strangled screams pierced the air as she fell to her knees. "Do something, Adrian!"

"Give me the girl!" I demanded.

"*Jack and Jill went up the hill . . .*" The voice wasn't coming from Audra anymore, not really. It was coming from near the fireplace.

And now the back of the room. "*Old King Cole was a merry old soul . . .*"

And now just above her screaming mother. "*Four and twenty blackbirds / Baked in a pie . . .*"

That was enough. This had to stop. I had to do something. I was the only one who could. "Take me instead," I shouted. "Release the girl and take me!"

With that, Audra dropped into her father's waiting arms, and the next thing I knew, I was on the other side of the room against the wall, a great force bearing down on my chest.

The scream came from somewhere deep inside of me, radiating outward until it engulfed me.

The last thing I saw was Mrs. Sinclair standing in front of me with arms outstretched, her white dress covered in blood. "Julia," she was saying. "Julia."

And then that was all there was.

FORTY-TWO

My eyes fluttered open. I was lying in my bed at Havenwood under a nest of quilts. Rays of sunlight were peeking around the edges of the thick curtains. I lay there for a moment, trying to get my bearings. How had I gotten here? The last thing I remembered was being in the east salon talking with Drew and Mrs. Sinclair and Adrian . . . I shook that thought out of my head. I didn't want to think about the last thing I remembered.

Drew was sitting in the armchair by the fireplace, his feet on the ottoman, his head resting against the back of the chair. He was wearing light sweatpants, a T-shirt, and slippers. I rustled around in bed and his eyes popped open.

"You're awake!" he said, his voice heavy with sleep. "How do you feel?"

"I don't know," I said. "My head is fuzzy. How did I get up here?"

"Adrian gave you a sedative." He leaned forward in his chair. "Do you . . . ?" I could tell he didn't even want to say the word.

"Remember the séance? I do."

I remembered it all—Adrian's visit to my apartment on that unusually warm spring day in Minneapolis, his offer to come to Havenwood to re-create a famous séance, and much more than that. The unspeakable things that happened as a result.

"I was so terrified last night," Drew said, his voice soft and low.

I closed my eyes to try to block out the memories, but it was no use. They were with me to stay.

"I was, too. Like I said, I remember the séance, I remember being here before, but I'm still really confused about a lot of things."

"What sorts of things?" Drew asked.

"Well, like what happened after that night. It's all a big blur until Jeremy and I got married."

"I think we can shed some light on some of that," he said. "But how about we have some breakfast first?"

I pushed myself up and glanced at the clock. It was well past nine.

"We've missed it," I said, running a hand through my hair.

He smiled. "You can have breakfast any time you bloody well want it. I'll call down to Marion and order us up a feast."

So many questions remained unanswered. Not only about my life after I left Havenwood that first time, but my life since I returned. It all seemed like a muddle of confusion. As soon as I felt strong enough, I knew it was time to straighten it out.

So, that is how, several days hence, all four of us gathered again after dinner, this time in my favorite room in the house, the west salon, for a conversation that I fervently hoped would have a better conclusion than the first.

The floor-to-ceiling windows revealed the landscape outside, the moon reflecting off the snowy whiteness and casting a soft glow. A fire blazed in the fireplace, and we all were equipped with our obligatory, standard-Havenwood-issue after-dinner drinks.

"I suppose we should start where we left off, my darling," said Mrs. Sinclair, who was standing next to the fire, her long gown, covered in jewels, flickering with the flames.

I took a deep breath and nodded. And we began.

"I called an ambulance as quickly as I could get to the phone,"

Mrs. Sinclair said. "You were incoherent, Audra was . . . well, darling, she seemed to be dead. Katherine was bleeding and I was covered with blood. The others in the circle that night, household servants, were unhurt, but they left that very night and never returned."

"Wait a minute," I interrupted, my skin tingling. "Audra didn't die?"

"No, thank God," Mrs. Sinclair said, taking a sip of her Dubonnet cocktail.

I turned to Adrian. "But I thought you said she *was* your daughter. It sort of implies that she's gone."

"She is gone," Adrian said, his shoulders slumping. "She was in the hospital for weeks, not waking up from whatever it is that happened to her. When she finally did, she was in a psychiatric hospital for months after that. And when she finally came back to herself, much like you, she didn't remember anything. She didn't remember me. Or her grandmother. Or anything about this house, or the life she lived here. Katherine had divorced me by that time—she never came back to Havenwood after leaving it that horrible night with our daughter—and she convinced me that letting her go would be the best thing for her."

"Oh no," I said, looking from Adrian to his mother and back again. "That can't be. You two are so loving and wonderful! How—" But his eyes, filled with tears, stopped my words.

"Think about how it felt, just a few days ago, for you to remember that night," he said softly. "Now think about how it would feel if you were a child."

My breath caught in my throat. "But ten years have passed," I tried. "Surely . . ."

He just shook his head. "I watch out for her, in my own way," he said. "My 'business trips'? I'm looking after her, from afar. When she turns twenty-one, she will receive a check from an anonymous benefactor, who will take care of her every need for the rest of her life."

"I'd argue she needs a father more," I said.

"She has one," he said, brushing away the sadness that had escaped from his eye. "Katherine remarried. He's the only father Audra knows. A good man, all in all. Believe me, I've checked him out. No, Audra disappeared from my life that night forever. I had a daughter that meant the entire world to me, and then she vanished. In the blink of an eye."

Mrs. Sinclair muffled a sob into the handkerchief she was holding up to her mouth.

"I am so sorry," I said. We remained in silence for a while, respecting the grief they were both feeling.

But there was more of the tale to tell. And soon, Mrs. Sinclair took it up again.

"And as for me," she said. "You can see, now, why I refused to write another word. The horror of that night was too much to bear. My greediness for more and more, my insatiability for fame and all the trappings that came with it, caused me to unleash real evil in this house, not something from my imagination, but real, unspeakable evil. Coming face-to-face with that will take the horror novelist right out of you. At least, it did for me. And the aftermath. We lost Audra, the light of our lives. As soon as I realized that, I was finished with writing, with fame, with anything related to it."

That was all well and good, I thought, but what about the mental institution?

"Vanishing from the public eye completely was the only way to go," she went on, winking at me. "You must realize that by now. No questions, no reporters. You're free."

She did have a point. Still, I wondered if she was going to tell me the whole story or not. She seemed to be glossing over the part where she wound up in an asylum.

"And that all brings us back to you," Mrs. Sinclair said. "Obviously, you remember the séance. Anything else after that? Have any other memories come to you?"

I tried to cast my thoughts back, but that same brick wall stood in the way. I shook my head. "Nothing."

"Where did you meet your husband?" Mrs. Sinclair asked.

An odd question, I thought, but when I opened my mouth to answer it, I realized I had no idea. "College?" I offered. "Through friends, maybe?"

"Are you sure?" she asked.

I shook my head, my mind in a jumble. Where did I meet Jeremy?

Mrs. Sinclair crossed the room and sunk down onto the sofa next to me, taking my hands in hers. "Are you ready to hear it all?"

"I am," I said, my voice a bit louder than I intended it to be. "I want to know everything, so I can move forward."

"You left here that night on a stretcher, Julia. You were in a catatonic state for months. You were sitting up, your eyes were open, but you did not speak. You didn't answer when people talked to you. It was as though whatever happened to you that night during the séance, your body and soul simply couldn't handle it."

My mind was swimming. Not me. This couldn't possibly be about me. She was talking about herself, wasn't she? What about the phone call I had heard between Adrian and her psychiatrist?

"You shut down," she went on, patting my hand. "And who could blame you? You saved Audra's life, of that I have no doubt, and put your own in jeopardy in the process. You were willing to sacrifice yourself for her. None of us ever forgot that, Julia."

I shook my head. It couldn't be.

"You had been at Havenwood for several months before that night," she continued. "We took to you then just like we did now, darling." She winked at Drew. "All of us. Some more than others. And, of course, after that accursed séance, we felt responsible for your care."

"That's just not possible," I protested, looking from one to the other. "*You* were in a catatonic state, not me. Isn't that right? That's the reason you dropped out of sight and stopped writing. Isn't that so?"

Mrs. Sinclair took my hand and brought it to her lips, kissing it a few times before continuing to speak. "Darling," she said gently. "No."

My thoughts were muddy and vague, as though I were trying to remember a movie I had seen long ago, not something that really happened to me. And then images began to hover in the corner of my vision—flashing lights, a small white room, a lawn filled with sweet-smelling grass. Could it be . . . ?

"You were in the hospital in town, at first," Mrs. Sinclair went on, seeming to choose her words carefully. "After that, a psychiatric hospital. When you came out of the catatonic state, we were all overjoyed. But then we realized you didn't remember any of us. You had long-term memories, but not short-term ones. We visited, but . . ." Her words trailed off into a long sigh, and she dabbed at her eyes with her handkerchief.

I shook my head. Catatonic state?

"The doctors thought it would probably be better if we just let you recuperate on your own," Adrian took up where she left off. "Our visits would agitate you. We made you suspicious and afraid, and you'd retreat even further into your own world. They believed, and we came to believe, that you were associating us with that night. We were actually hindering your recovery."

"I fully intended to simply take you out of the hospital and bring you here to Havenwood, with a full-time nurse if that's what you needed," Mrs. Sinclair said. "But we couldn't. Your doctors advised against taking you back to where it happened; they were adamantly opposed to it. And as dear as you were to us, you weren't a relative. Our hands were tied. So in the end, we had to let you go."

My head was beginning to pound. "This is a lot to take in," I said, rubbing my forehead. "Why did you mention Jeremy?"

"That's where you met him, my dear," Mrs. Sinclair said. "The psychiatric hospital. He was a patient there as well."

My mind reached back to my earliest memories with him: long walks on the lawn, afternoons by the lake, our wedding day. It might have been in a hospital chapel, for all I knew. I just wasn't sure.

This caused my stomach to turn. "What was he in for?"

"We were never able to find out," Mrs. Sinclair said. "But with everything that happened later . . ."

A light went on. "The police told me he was a sociopath."

"He was released before you were. He married you and, as next of kin, took you from the hospital."

I could see it, then, in my mind. A car pulling into a circular driveway. Jeremy standing there. Me running into his arms. What they were saying started to make a sick kind of sense.

"You had total amnesia about the séance and some time before and after it, much like people who are in auto accidents lose whole days," Mrs. Sinclair went on. "Your stay in the hospital didn't do anything to improve that. In fact I gather it never improved until you came back here to Havenwood."

"But . . ." My mind was running in many directions at once. "If all of this is true, how did you find me? In Chicago, I mean."

Adrian cleared his throat. "Because we weren't family, nobody notified us that you had left the hospital. You married this man, he changed your name, and you basically disappeared into the fabric of the world. Goodness knows how he managed it. Connections with organized crime, perhaps. He was certainly a criminal, based on what came after. We had no way to track you down."

"A decade passed, Julia," Drew said. "We looked for you, but it was as though you disappeared off the face of the earth."

"Until the scandal," I said, remembering the newspaper articles and television coverage.

Adrian smiled. "I despised the man who took you from us, but I came to love him for the notoriety. When I saw you on the news, I couldn't believe it. There you were! A decade later, we had found you! If you had been living a happy life, we'd have been glad for you but stayed away. From the news reports, however, we knew you were in trouble, and even in danger. And so it was our turn to rescue you, just as you rescued Audra."

They were all smiling, but this time, unlike the other day, it warmed me. These people were looking out for my best interests. They truly were my family.

"When I arrived on your doorstep that day, I didn't quite know what to expect," Adrian went on. "When it was clear you didn't remember me, or us, or anything that had happened, I knew we'd have to tread carefully with you."

"So you concocted the story about wanting me to be Mrs. Sinclair's companion."

"We did that before I visited," Adrian said, nodding. "We knew that if you didn't remember us, you'd need a reason to come to Havenwood. It seemed like the only way to get you to leave with an absolute stranger."

"We got in touch with your psychiatrist," Mrs. Sinclair added. "He gave us further advice and monitored what was happening here."

"But why would he talk to you at all? You're not family, and he opposed you taking me back to Havenwood initially."

Adrian smiled. "Let's just say he was persuaded. The threat of a lawsuit on your behalf and all the publicity that would surround it convinced him to cooperate with us. All we wanted was for you to regain your memories. Or barring that, we hoped you'd fall in love with Havenwood all over again. Our main concern was helping you, Julia. You needed rescuing. We were not about to leave you alone to deal with the situation your husband created. You deserved much better."

I sighed and leaned back against the sofa. It all seemed to be tied up into a neat bow. Except it wasn't.

"There's something about this story I don't understand," I

began. "I don't quite know how to say this, but . . . I've seen Audra. In this house. With all the ghosts here, I assumed . . . But you told me she's alive and well."

Mrs. Sinclair and Adrian exchanged glances. "What did you see, exactly?" he asked.

"A girl, wearing a long nightgown, floating in the air. Reciting nursery rhymes." The thought of it sent a chill through me.

Drew pushed himself up and poured himself another drink at the sideboard. "This isn't good," he said, locking eyes with Adrian.

"It might simply have been flickers of her memory coming back," Adrian said. "Images from that night trying to bubble to the surface, as it were. The doctor said we should watch out for that."

"But, coupled with what she saw in the library the night of the blackout—"

"What did she see?" Mrs. Sinclair interrupted.

Drew and Adrian exchanged glances. "Well, the thing is she saw you, Mother."

"Me? I wasn't in the library that night. I'd never creep around this house during a blackout."

My hands started to feel clammy. "If it wasn't you, then who was it?"

But I knew the answer to that, before I even got the words out. It wasn't a memory. And it wasn't Mrs. Sinclair. It was Gideon.

FORTY-THREE

We need to banish that thing from this house once and for all," I said to them.

Mrs. Sinclair sighed. "Oh, darling, you're not the first to say that. Believe me, we've tried."

"And Seraphina tried," Drew piped up. "It's in the journals. Before she left Havenwood, she tried."

"But it didn't work," I said.

"No," Mrs. Sinclair said. "Not entirely."

"And Andrew and his family lived here with it?"

"It's one of the reasons for the dogs," Drew said. "They were first brought to Havenwood in Andrew's day to defend against this thing after the first séance. And their descendants continue in that role to this day."

I thought about the night of the blackout, how those three magnificent animals stood between me and what I thought was Mrs. Sinclair. And how they came to my room those nights when I was frightened.

"Remember, Julia, that first day?" Adrian said. "I told you there was nothing in here that would harm you with those dogs by your side."

I nodded. He didn't mean just wolves and bears. He meant Gideon. But then something else occurred to me. "Why does this thing have a name?" I asked.

"Andrew first coined it," Drew said, a slight smile on his lips.

"He had boarded up the east salon after that first séance, forbidding anyone to enter. His son kept asking why. Finally, he told the boy that Gideon needed to be left alone."

"And the name stuck," I said. "Havenwood's own private bogeyman."

He nodded. "I suppose."

Adrian stood and looked out the window. "We stirred it all up again by opening the room and conducting that infernal séance ten years ago." He sighed deeply. "After that night and everything that happened, we closed the room again, just as Andrew had done more than a century before. And truthfully, for years we thought it was gone. But it seemed that when you came back to Havenwood . . ."

"You have reawakened it," Mrs. Sinclair finished his thought.

"Well, it's time we put it back to sleep," I said, looking at each of them in turn. "And in order to do that, I need to know as much about this thing as possible."

Adrian furrowed his brow. "Don't you think you've had enough of this for a while?" he said. "We've got the room closed up again—it's not like we have to do anything now."

I shook my head. "No," I said. "I'm tired of waiting. It seems like that's all I've done since I got to Havenwood—you'd start this story, and then something would happen to delay it. You'd tell me it would keep until another time. The way I see it, the time is now."

$\mathcal{I}$ wished I had known about what had happened during Seraphina's séance when I first came to Havenwood all those years ago. I wouldn't have conducted a séance of my own. And I certainly wouldn't have opened the box. But what was done was done. The only thing left now was to undo it.

I began by doing some research in the old occult books in the library. I wanted to learn as much as I could about this spirit, or whatever it was, in order to know how to deal with it. I didn't want to spend much time in that room, so I hurriedly collected several volumes on the occult and took them into the west salon to study, putting as much distance as I could between me and the room where it all began.

I learned Devil's Toy Boxes trap spirits, and not benevolent ones. Something about the mirrors attracts them, or so say occultists. Maybe I could get it to go back into the box, I thought. But Mrs. Sinclair dashed that hope.

"I'm afraid Adrian destroyed the box, soon after that night," she told me. "He took a hatchet to it and cut it to smithereens."

So that was it, then. None of us wanted to bring yet another of the boxes into the house, so we were back at square one. I sat at my table in the west salon, all the books on the occult open, trying to think of the best way to proceed, when suddenly the thought hit me: a séance had summoned this thing into our lives, and a séance was the only way to banish it.

I walked from window to window, door to door, archway to archway in the library and east salon, anointing them all with olive oil, whispering prayers under my breath, carrying a stick of smoldering sage. It was an ancient technique, as old as time, that my mother and grandmother had taught me, and, presumably, Seraphina had taught her own daughter. That's how secret knowledge is passed down. I might have forgotten a whole block of time in my life, but not this.

Women with gifts such as ours, women who could see the dead, need protection from the dark side. And what was happening at Havenwood was as dark as it got, conjuring up images from the most horrific night of my life.

Mrs. Sinclair, Drew, Adrian, and I gathered around the table in the east salon after I had anointed the doors and windows with oil and smudged the entire room with sage. The table was covered with candles, alongside crucifixes and Stars of David. A smiling Buddha sat in one corner. Overkill? Maybe. But I wasn't taking any chances.

"Let's join hands," I said reaching out for Drew's and Mrs. Sinclair's. Everyone closed their eyes, and I took a deep breath. *Here we go,* I thought.

"In the name of God the Father Almighty, I command you, evil spirit, to leave this room," I said, speaking words I had learned in one of the books describing how to banish evil. "In His name I take authority over you and order you to go away from this place, never to return."

Nothing.

I repeated what I had said, louder this time. "In the name of God the Father Almighty, and in the names of all who have come before me, I command you, evil spirit, to leave this room. I take authority over you and order you to go away from this place—"

And then the rumbling started. The growling. Knocking on the windows, on the doors. A glass windowpane shattered, sending shards everywhere. And then the thudding began—loud, piercing sounds coming from the library.

Everyone's eyes shot open, nearly at the same time. We stood and hurried through the doorway to find books flying off the shelves and hurling themselves across the room, smashing into walls and through windows.

"Not the first editions shelf!" Mrs. Sinclair cried, draping herself over it and shielding her prized possessions with her body as the precious volumes slammed into her torso. "This old girl can take a few hits to save a first edition Hemingway!"

"I call you by your name, Gideon!" I bellowed, louder than I ever thought was possible. "You're not listening to me. I said: I *command* you, evil spirit, to leave this room. I take *authority* over you and *order* you to go away from this place back from whence you came."

It was in front of me, then, the demon, first a shroud of black with no face, then morphing from one disguise to another: Audra, Mrs. Sinclair, Marion, even Drew and Adrian, their faces distorted and ghoulish.

"Sing a song of sixpence," came a low growl.

"I command you in the name of God to leave this room!"

"A pocket full of rye . . ."

A pocket! I remembered what I had stashed in mine. A crucifix and a Star of David, together on a chain. It had been given to me by my mother. I held it out before me. "You are not welcome here. I order you by all that's holy to leave."

At this, the house started shaking at its foundations. Paintings flew off the walls, tables and chairs toppled, the fire in the library's fireplace raged. I felt strong hands on my chest pushing me backward until I collided with the opposite wall.

I took a deep breath and bellowed with the voice of a thousand generations: "Gideon, I banish you from this house! Leave this place and never return!"

And then silence. All was still.

FORTY-FOUR

Havenwood, early spring

Spring was flirting with the Northland. The sun was rising high in the sky and the snow was melting, the animals poking their noses out of their dens for the first time in months. And all was well in the castle in the wilderness.

Gideon hadn't returned to Havenwood. As far as we knew, I really did banish him that night. After it was over, the four of us, along with Marion and the staff, started the long process of cleaning up the library and east salon, placing the books back on the bookshelves, righting the tables, fixing the windows, and hanging the paintings back on the walls. It took weeks, but we finally got it done.

We didn't talk much about that night, not for a while. I was shaky and fragile, dealing with the onslaught of memories I had repressed for a decade. I was keeping those memories a touch removed, just a hairsbreadth from my reality. They were a lot to take in. And although Mrs. Sinclair, Adrian, and Drew offered to fill me in on everything else that they knew and I didn't, I chose to wait until I felt strong enough to hear whatever they had to tell me.

So I took some time for myself. Drew and I rode the horses every day, horses I now remembered from my first trip to Havenwood. Oftentimes, Mrs. Sinclair would join us. I was becoming a horsewoman, and while I wouldn't use "accomplished" as an adjective, I was at least average. I loved Nelly's gentle soul. She was a good antidote to the horrors that I couldn't get out of my head.

The dogs were my constant companions, sensing, I believe, that they had to shore me up. I spent many hours reading alone in my room in front of the fire, the dogs snoring softly by my side. I was growing to love the sound of their breathing, so hypnotic, so restful. I wasn't sure if these were the same dogs that had tried to help us during the séance—that horrible night had been a decade ago and I wasn't sure how old these dogs were—but they were just as protective. Malamutes had always had a strong presence at Havenwood, and likely always would.

I was staying. After all the horror I'd been through, all the sadness I'd endured, and all that I'd pieced together about the dark parts of my life, in the end, I realized these people were the closest thing to family that I had. I didn't want the new life and new identity Adrian had offered me. I wanted to remain at Havenwood, with its spirits floating through the hallways, protective dogs, and an eccentric writer. I'd be safe from the rest of the world. My ever-growing relationship with Drew cemented the decision.

I'd learned that he and I did fall in love when I was at Havenwood the first time. That explained my familiarity with him, how close I felt despite having just met him. We didn't spend a day, or night, apart. I wasn't going anywhere, not while he wanted me to stay.

The only lingering question was answered one late spring day. While the four of us were sitting on the patio soaking up the newly strong sun, we saw a car driving slowly down the road. It pulled into our driveway and stopped. A young woman emerged.

Adrian pushed himself up from his chair, but his knees buckled and he nearly fell to the ground as she walked up the patio stairs.

"I had to come and see it for myself," she said. "I remember bits and pieces."

"You're the image of your mother," he said, his words splintering into tiny shards.

"She forbade me to come," she said, her green eyes shining, so like those of her grandmother. "But I was here before, once, over the winter. I looked in the windows but was too afraid to come in."

Drew and I shared a glance. So that was who was in the window. Not a man at all.

"We're very glad you're here now," Adrian said, his eyes shining with tears. "My darling Audra. Welcome home to Havenwood."

As I watched father and daughter fall into each other's arms after so many years, with grandmother looking on with tears streaming down her face, I backed away, not wanting to intrude on the reunion I knew was the silent dream in Adrian's heart.

Drew slid his hand into mine. "Fancy a horseback ride?" I knew he wanted to give the Sinclairs some privacy as well.

I cast my eyes out into the wilderness, the pine trees bright green with a layer of new growth.

"Why not, Andrew McCullough," I said to him as we headed off toward the stable. "Why not?"

EPILOGUE

Havenwood, late autumn

*I*t was the scratching that awakened me, a sound like a dry and brittle branch hitting a windowpane. At first, it worked its way into my dreams as a gnarled finger on an even more gnarled hand tapping on the headboard of my bed, but as I slowly awakened from that rather unsettling image, drifting up from the depths of sleep, I realized it was real scratching I heard. I shook my head and opened my heavy eyelids. What greeted me, I will never forget.

I was lying in the bedroom I now shared with Drew in the main house. The full moon shone in through the window, illuminating the darkness with a soft glow. But . . . where were the curtains? Had I not drawn them before crawling into bed? No matter, I thought and rolled onto my side, reaching for Drew. He was not beside me. When my hand alit on the space where his sleeping form should have been, I sat up with a start.

It wasn't his absence that startled me so; he oftentimes wandered at night. It was the feel of the bedspread. Dusty, damp, and gritty, as though it had been dragged on the cold ground. I reached for the bedside lamp, but felt nothing but the chill night air. The lamp was gone. *What in the world . . . ?*

I looked around the room and slowly came to the realization that it was not the same room I had fallen asleep in just a few hours earlier. Not really. I noticed the wallpaper was peeling off the walls, even hanging in great strips in spots. The windows were bare, some of them cracked, their curtains lying in a heap below them. The fireplace was empty, no softly glowing embers from the fire Marion had lit earlier, no wood at all. Our headboard was covered with dust. I was trying to reconcile what I was seeing with what my mind knew to be true—*that wallpaper can't be peeling, can it? Why are the curtains on the floor?*—when I heard it again. The scratching, just behind my head. But this time, I knew it was the scuttling of tiny feet. Claws. I jumped out of bed and my feet hit the cold, bare floor—*where was the rug?*—and I was out the door and into the hallway like a shot.

"Drew!" I called into the darkness as I hurried down the hallway, my voice a high screech. "Drew! Where are you?"

I reached the grand staircase and gasped aloud as I saw the threadbare carpeting under my feet. The stairway was in complete disrepair—the stairs themselves had crumbled and splintered, and I had to be careful to find a sturdy spot on each one as I descended. This didn't make any sense. I had just seen Marion vacuuming these stairs only hours earlier!

"Mrs. Sinclair?" I shouted. "Adrian? Is anyone here?" There was no response, only a deathly silence.

I passed through the foyer to the living room. The couch was draped with a sheet, the walls were bare—their paintings nowhere that I could see. Most of the furniture was gone as well. The movement of the curtains blowing in the breeze shifted my attention to the windows, which were cracked and open like the ones in my room. A nest had been built in the fireplace, and I could see eyes, shining at me through the dark.

A chill worked its way up my spine as I hurried toward the front door. That, too, was gaping open. What had happened here? What was going on? I ran outside, intending to look for Drew in the stable, but I stopped dead when I saw it—just an old, rickety barn tilting dangerously to one side, some of its wooden slats having fallen off long ago. I stood in the moonlit night, staring at Havenwood—most of its windows broken, its facade crumbling, the whole place emanating a deep and utter darkness that I still cannot fully describe—and in that moment, I knew. Nothing was alive here, and hadn't been for a very, very long time.

The terror of that realization wrapped itself around me and began to tighten, my heart beating faster with each breath. I stepped back slowly, wanting to turn and run, to be anywhere away from this house. I turned my gaze toward the woods and shivered. Could I make it to town in my bare feet and nightdress? I considered it, but then another thought hit me. *Would town even be there when I arrived?*

I sunk down onto the cold ground, not knowing what else to do. I clutched a handful of dirt, wanting to feel something solid and real between my fingers. I might have sat there that way all night, if I hadn't heard it. Softly at first, and then louder. Bagpipes.

That did it. I sprang up and ran toward the only place I could go—the dilapidated, crumbling, empty shell of what had once been the most magnificent home I had ever seen. Just before reaching the house, I tripped and fell to the ground with a thud, my knee landing square on a rock. *I'll think about the pain later,* I thought, scrambling to my feet and hurrying up the patio steps inside. I slammed the door behind me (a lot of good that would do considering all the broken windows) and made my way through the darkness up the stairs to my room. I had no idea what had happened to Havenwood or where Drew and the Sinclairs were, but I knew one thing: I needed to get out of here. I would dress and sit inside until the sun came up. Then I'd start walking. The town might not be there, but something would. Certainly the whole world hadn't been turned into a deserted ghost town.

Once inside my room, I opened the door to my closet . . . but found it empty. Not even a hanger. Where were my clothes? Where was anything?

I wrapped my arms around me and sunk to the floor in a corner of the room. I rested my head on the back of the wall and closed my eyes.

When I opened them again, I was next to Drew in our beautiful bed, safe and warm. I looked around the room slowly, almost afraid to breathe. All was as it should be. Curtains were drawn over the windows. The lamp was on the bedside table, along with my water glass. The wallpaper was hung perfectly. I exhaled.

Drew opened his eyes and smiled. "Morning, my love."

"Hey."

"Sleep well?"

"I had a crazy dream," I said, snuggling closer. "Havenwood was deserted. Like a haunted house. It seemed so real."

Drew draped an arm around me. "What is it that Edgar Allan Poe said?" he asked. "'All that we see or seem / Is but a dream within a dream.'"

"Well, if this is a dream, I don't want to wake up from it," I said, kissing him.

It was only later, as I got in the shower before getting ready for breakfast, that I noticed it. My knee was red and swollen. The same knee I had hurt in my dream.

As the water washed over me, I let it wash away any thoughts of the night before. *Put it out of your mind*, I told myself. The day was beginning at Havenwood. The love of my life was in the next room waiting for me to go down to breakfast. And that was all I really needed to know.

ACKNOWLEDGMENTS

*W*riting this book was such a joy. I had a lot of fun coming up with all of the twists and turns. I fell deeply in love with Andrew McCullough, I wished I could live at Havenwood (even with its ghosts), and I adored Amaris Sinclair most of all. I think she's my favorite character in any of my books so far. I had a great time writing *The Vanishing*, and I hope you had a great time reading it.

That's really what it's all about for me. With my novels, I'm not trying to define a generation, right any great wrongs, or change the way you think about the world or your place in it. I just want to craft a good story that will delight you, entertain you, grab you and not let go, and send some shivers up your spine along the way. As I'm writing, I really do think of you curling up after a long day with a cup of tea or a glass of wine and one of my novels. I love nothing more than when a reader says to me: "I couldn't put your book down!" For a writer, it doesn't get much better than that.

With that in mind, I offer my sincere thanks and everlasting gratitude to:

My wonderful team at Hyperion, including editor in chief extraordinaire Elisabeth Dyssegaard, marketing guru Elizabeth Hulsebosch, and publicity maven Kristina Miller, along with everyone else who worked so hard on this book, from the eagle-eyed copy editor to the artist who designed its fabulous cover. It has been such a pleasure to work with you all.

The best agent in the business, Jennifer Weltz, and her fantastic cohorts at the Jean Naggar Literary Agency. I am so incredibly lucky to have you in my corner.

The staff at *Duluth Superior Magazine*, a monthly lifestyle magazine where, when I'm not writing and promoting novels, I am the editor in chief. Especially to founder Marti Buscaglia, publisher David Hileman, art director Matt Pawlak, sales and marketing diva Toni Piazza, and web editor Asha Long, I thank you for putting up with the hectic schedule of an author on a book tour. I couldn't juggle it all without your indulgence of my absences, and I'm proud we haven't missed a beat despite me doing readings and author events here, there, and everywhere.

The booksellers and librarians who have promoted my books, hand-sold them to readers, and recommended them to book clubs. Getting my books into the hands of readers has meant everything to me, and I am profoundly grateful. I also thank you for opening your stores and libraries to me, promoting my readings, and working with me to get people in the door. I especially appreciate the author dinners and other events you've organized around my visits—a simple reading becomes a party, and who doesn't love that?

The people who have come up to me or written to me with ghost stories. One question I always get at readings is, "Do you believe in ghosts?" My answer: "If I didn't before, I do now." That's because at every one of my readings, someone will tell me a ghost story of their own. Sometimes it's a "things that go bump in the night" story, but usually it's a personal tale of something otherworldly that happened when a loved one passed away. These are heartfelt stories and I'm honored that people share them with me. Please keep sharing—I love to hear them.

And finally, thanks to all of the readers who have attended my events, read my books, and are waiting for the next one. When I'm writing, I'm thinking of you, remembering your comments and questions, and hearing your voices whisper in my ear. Thank you so much for being my muse.

READING GROUP GUIDE

Discussion Questions
*(Please do not read these before you read the book.
They will spoil the ending!)*

1. Did you have sympathy for Julia's predicament caused by her husband? Do you think it's possible for one spouse to be ignorant of the other's illegal activities? And was the very current issue of Ponzi scheming too real-world for this gothic suspense novel?

2. Under what circumstances would you accept a live-in job offer from a stranger?

3. The character of Amaris Sinclair is complex and ever changing. Sometimes she seems very old and frail; sometimes she seems young and vibrant; sometimes she seems to have ulterior and sinister motives for inviting Julia to Havenwood. What are your impressions of her? Did you trust her? Why does she seem old and young at the same time?

4. Wendy Webb has said that, in all of her novels, the setting inspires the story. How much did Havenwood color the story for you? Could it have been set anywhere else? If so, where? Does Havenwood remind you of anyplace you have ever seen or been to?

5. Do you believe in legends like the Windigo? Had you heard of it before, and if so, what might have inspired the region's native people to create tales about such a horrible monster?

6. Animals play a big part in this story. How does the trio of Malamutes fit into the narrative? Were you comforted by

their protection of Julia against the strangeness of Haven-wood, or did you wish she was completely on her own? Has the intuitiveness and protection of animals had an impact on your own life?

7. When Julia arrives at Havenwood, she begins to see spirits and hear voices. She believes she has been hallucinating because of stopping her medication cold turkey. What would you think in the same situation? If you saw something that you really believed was a ghost, would you stay in the house?

8. Do you believe in ghosts? Have you ever seen one?

9. Do you have much knowledge about the Spiritualist Age? Do you think the majority of psychics during that time were charlatans preying on wealthy people who were desperate for word from their departed loved ones, or legitimate? How do you explain the popularity of the movement among people like Edgar Allen Poe, Arthur Conan Doyle, and Charles Dickens? Are there any psychics working today who you think are legitimate?

10. Can psychic ability be passed down within families, like musical ability?

11. Is Adrian Sinclair sinister, menacing, dangerous, a good guy just trying to help his mother, or all four?

12. Who do you think set the fire?

13. Is Drew the immortal Andrew McCullough? Is Julia the reincarnation of her great-great-grandmother? Is there anyone you would wait a lifetime, or travel through time, for?

14. After the first séance in the house, an evil spirit was called forth. Yet Andrew McCullough stayed in the house and raised a family there. Why?

15. Did you have any idea that it was Julia, not Amaris, in the mental hospital?

Desperately seeking
*"a perfect read for a dark and stormy night"?**

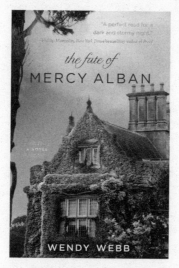

The Fate of Mercy Alban

A novel by bestselling author Wendy Webb
An IndieNext Pick | A Midwest Connections Pick

Long-buried family secrets, a packet of old love letters, and a lost manuscript plunge Grace Alban into a decades-old family mystery about a scandalous party at Alban House, when a world-famous author took his own life and Grace's aunt disappeared without a trace. The night has been shrouded in secrecy by the powerful Alban family for all these years. Grace's mother intended to tell the truth about that night to a reporter on the very day she died— could it have been murder? Or was she a victim of the supposed Alban curse? Grace soon realizes her family secrets tangle and twist as darkly as the mansion's secret passages, and she and her teenage daughter may very well be its next victims.

* Philip Margolin

A Hyperion Trade Paperback available wherever books and ebooks are sold.